The Rebel Christian Publishing

Copyright © 2022 Valicity Elaine

ISBN (eBook): 9781957290225
ISBN (Print): 9781957290232

This is a work of fiction. Any references to historical events, real people, or real places are used fictitiously. Names, characters, and places are products of the author's imagination. Inclusion of or reference to any Christian elements or themes are used in a fictitious manner and are not meant to be perceived or interpreted as an act of disrespect against such a wonderful and beautiful faith.

Cover image provided by Shutterstock
Artist: Lightfield Studios

The Rebel Christian Publishing LLC
350 Northern Blvd STE 324 – 1390
Albany, NY 12204

Visit us: http://www.therebelchristian.com/
Email us: rebel@therebelchristian.com

Series Order

Withered Rose
Clipping Thorns
Starting Over

Other Books by Valicity Elaine:

Mafia Romance
Fractured Diamond
(Coming November 2022)

I AM MAN series:
I AM MAN
I AM LOST
I AM BROKEN
I AM FREE
I AM COMPLETE

Cross Academy series:
Cross Academy
The Howler's Cry
The Nine Births of Carnage (2022)
The Testament Relics (2023)
Cross Academy: Book V (coming soon)

Others
Patches
The 'I' Word

To Jesus Christ

Starting Over

Withered Rose Book III

By Valicity Elaine

A Rebel Christian Publishing Book

A note from the author
*** <u>Warning</u> ***

If you read Book I and II in this series (*Withered Rose*) then I'm sure you don't need this note. But for those who may be reading out of order, I must give you a fair warning. This story is a work of Christian fiction, but I will not make the claim that it is a 'Clean & Wholesome' story.

There are no graphic scenes of sex, no foul language, and no graphic gore. However, the story does follow a young couple involved in the **mafia**.

Our protagonists are married, so I did not shy away from depicting their encounters. However, I am still a Christian author, and I do believe there are certain lines that should not be crossed in Christian fiction. Everyone has a limit; unfortunately, those boundaries can be different for some or others. This is why I have taken the opportunity to warn you before the story begins.

Readers may find some content to be sensitive/triggering, such as abuse, gang violence, manipulation, human trafficking, etc. This book is best enjoyed by adult Christian readers.

Please continue at your own discretion.

A rose with thorns is still a rose. A precious little thing.

—Amory Jäger

One

In the silence, I clamped my hand over my mouth to muffle my cries. Salty tears streamed down my cheeks as I heaved into my palm, snot dribbling over my raw knuckles. My sore shoulders shook with each sob, my broken ribs ached each time I drew breath. I was broken. In mind, body, and spirit. But as much pain as I had already endured, I knew there was more to come.

The stone floor was cold beneath my bare feet. I adjusted my position, trying to sit as close to the wall as possible while avoiding the puddle of urine I'd left just off to my right. There was a tooth on the floor, not far from me. I wouldn't kid myself by thinking it belonged to one of the men who'd attacked me. As I worked my jaw, swollen tongue fishing around in my bloody mouth, I found the hole in my gums where the lost tooth had once been. Oberon had probably knocked it out. He had thrown the first punch when I was dragged into the room.

My own uncle.

My sobs turned to whimpers as I heard footsteps approaching my dark little room. The quiet solitude had broken my mind—crippling every thought, filling them with fear in its silent aguish. I was stuck in a dimly lit room with no windows and only one giant, metal door with a massive crank to let me know I was locked inside. I had no idea how long I'd been in the room, but I had used the bathroom three times— once when I'd been punched so hard, I couldn't help myself— and twice because I just couldn't hold it any longer after the men had left.

Three days, I reasoned, wiping at my puffy eyes. They hadn't fed me, hadn't let me bathe, hadn't even treated any of my injuries. But they made sure to check on me every five hours. I kept track of every hour in my head, ticking them off on my bloody fingers after counting to 3600—the number of seconds in an hour. When they checked on me for the third time and still hadn't brought any food or bandages with them, I realized they weren't checking to help me recover, they were making sure I hadn't died.

The footsteps drew nearer, just outside the door now. I gasped and scooted even closer to the wall, trying to hide in the shadows. The movement sent fire through my behind, rubbing brush-burns against my naked bottom, but I kept struggling. As if I could get away.

When the door opened, the creak was loud enough to swallow the shamefully feminine squeal of fear that escaped me. I was huddled in the corner, hands up in defense of the burning light streaming in, my swollen eyes peeled open as wide as they could.

There was a man standing in the doorway. It wasn't until I heard his rumbling baritone that I realized it was my father.

My fear nearly tripled.

"Amory," he said calmly.

I choked out a sob.

Klaus, Onkel Oberon, a General named Elias and another named Adolf, a bodyguard named Otto, and a grunt called Jürgen entered the room behind my father. Screams echoed around us—it took me a moment to realize they were coming from me.

I wasn't afraid of another beating; it was the sight of Jürgen that sent a chill up my spine. He was only a grunt, but he had been the most brutal. He had been the one to strip me naked in front of all the others. He had been the one to hold me down. But he hadn't punched me. He hadn't kicked me. His hands brought gentle touches that sent talons of fear clawing down my body.

The other men had watched it happen, expecting me to fight back, but I'd been too weak after two days of brutal violence. It didn't hurt as much as it shamed me. Humiliated me. But that was the point of all this. To break my mind and body.

That day had been so normal. At fifteen, I'd ridden my bike out to Staten Island to meet up with Giovanni. There was a guy there who would sell us cigarettes to smoke while we watched pretty Russian girls toss rocks into the canal. But when I got there, I realized Gio had brought his kid sister along so we couldn't bum smokes off anyone—not in front of her at least. Gio had said his father would kill him if Rosa came home smelling like smoke. So we'd walked the docks without any cigarettes and whistled at the Russian princess when she walked by with her body guard.

Sofia Volkov. She had been pretty even as a girl. And she'd had a pretty older cousin named Dominika.

That day, Dominika had tagged along with Sofia, walking a few paces behind her cousin during their little stroll. Sofia was wearing a white dress that made her look like an angel, but Dominika...

Dominika was wearing a red blouse and a tiny little matching skirt I'm positive her Uncle Mikhail knew nothing about. Neither Gio nor I could keep our eyes off her. We followed her along the docks, whistling and shouting at her until she finally turned and gave us a seductive smile. Gio, ever the flirt, had dared her to come over and give one of us a kiss. She had shaken her head but when her cousin and her guard had turned away, she held a finger to her lips and then flashed us.

I had almost peed myself, standing there staring at Dominika with her shirt up and her pale breasts right there for me to see. It was the first time I'd seen a naked girl in person. Gio too. Neither of us had any idea how to react except to stare and stumble over ourselves as she lowered her shirt and sauntered away, giggling the entire time.

We tried to follow her, but as soon as we crossed the crowded streets, their guard started yelling and we had to take off. Three Wolves chased us all the way to the ferries—I had to carry Gio's kid sister as we tore through the crowd, laughing and howling. When we boarded one of my father's boats, Gio turned and mooned the guards who'd been chasing us, and we shouted the lyrics to a Russian song as we waved at them while the ferry pulled away.

When I was snatched out of my bed that night, my first thought was that I was being punished for what'd happened with Dominika. She wasn't a mafia princess, but she was high-ranking enough for us to be whipped for looking at her body without her father's permission. But as I stared up at my father and the six German men he'd allowed to beat me, I realized what this really was.

Uwe Jäger pulled up the legs of his pants before he squatted in front of me, looking right into my battered face as he said, "Do you want the pain to stop?"

I nodded. "*Bitte, Vater.*"

"I'm going to ask you a question," he said calmly, "if you answer correctly, I'll tell them to leave you alone."

Just to mess with me, Elias stepped forward and I realized he was holding a bat. My ribs ached at the sight. Not even a day ago he had taken that bat to my body, like I was a criminal—not the son of the Jägermeister. But I was fifteen. I wasn't some innocent kid anymore. I was a man. At least that's what this whole thing was supposed to make me into. A mafioso. A Hunter.

5

I was being initiated.

Jürgen smiled down at me from over my father's shoulder. I inched backwards, trying hard not to cry anymore. But it was hard to focus on Vater when Klaus was wrapping a chain around his fist and Otto was staring at his razorblade, inspecting it. My skin stung as I watched him, remembering each time he ran the knife over my back and chest. I would have scars for the rest of my life because of him.

"Amory," Vater's voice brought me back.

I blinked at him.

"*Ja?*"

"My question," he said slowly.

I nodded.

"You're fifteen now. Old enough to join me in the business. When you're older, you will replace me, son. You will run the entire German mafia. But first you must be initiated. You must start at the bottom of the barrel. As a grunt. And when you are ready, you will wear the crown."

I nodded again, wincing as I swallowed.

Vater leaned toward me, his dark hair falling into his face. The light from the hallway made shadows dance along the concrete walls, a pillar of darkness covered half of my father's face as he gazed at me. His stare was intense, regarding me like he was looking at a stranger. Not his own child.

I resisted the urge to shiver as I stared back. I didn't want him to know how afraid I was.

"Do you accept this position?" Vater asked softly.

My mouth opened to answer, but no words would come.

Vater sighed into the silence and pushed to his feet. Klaus took a step—I started screaming again.

"Wait—Vater, wait!"

Uwe watched as Klaus came closer, chain in hand. The sound of the links rattling together was oddly reminiscent of the sound of chattering teeth. I wanted to scream—I already was screaming. Shamelessly. Loudly. And scooting away like I was a mad, feral animal.

Oberon slapped me so hard, I thought he loosened another tooth.

"Please!" I squeaked, throwing my hands up in surrender.

Vater calmly slid his hands into his pockets. "Do you accept this position, Amory?"

The mafia was ruled by Uwe's command. I wouldn't be able to escape him or his beatings if I said yes. But I had a greater fear of what would happen if I said no.

"I—I…"

I wet myself.

I couldn't help it. I hadn't even known I'd had to pee; I only felt the sudden warmth bloom in my bladder and then it was running down my dirt-stained legs, puddling around my feet.

Elias laughed.

My father sighed again.

I scrambled back and took a deep breath. "I accept this position!" I had no idea if it was too late or not, but I was willing to agree to anything if it meant Vater would call off his men.

They all stopped moving toward me and glanced back at my father. The silence that stormed through the room left me dizzy and weak in my pee-streaked knees.

Very slowly, Uwe pulled his hands from his pockets and turned to leave. He spoke over his shoulder as he reached for the metal door. "Bring him."

They dragged me naked through the halls of the warehouse and then shoved me into the back of an SUV. I passed out during the ride; I don't know if it was because of nerves, exhaustion, or injury, but when I woke, I realized I was in a bed with my wounds finally wrapped and a bowl of soup waiting on my bedside table.

A primal sort of hunger overcame me as I spied the bowl. I ignored the screaming pain in my bones and muscles as I crawled across the bed and took the soup in my hands. I didn't bother with a spoon, just drank the salty chicken broth right from the bowl, enjoying the warmth as it trickled down my chin and neck. When I finished, I burped and wiped my mouth with the back of my hand, immediately feeling lightheaded and sluggish at the same time.

There was a water bottle on the little table, I grabbed it and twisted the cap, hands trembling as I raised the drink to my bruised lips. Half of it spilled down my chest, making me realize that I was naked from the waist up. Someone had finally given me a pair of underwear to hide my shame. But the flesh that was exposed was hidden by a different sort of cover.

Scars. Wicked carvings going through my chest and over my back. Thick, bulging scabs bubbled over recent wounds.

Every move I made left me wincing as I looked down at myself. I was ugly. Grotesque. But I didn't mind. I'd been initiated. That meant I was entering an ugly world. There was no room for beauty—only ashes.

I reached up to scratch my head and realized they'd shaved my head. That must have happened while I was passed out. Every new grunt had their hair removed, though I wasn't sure if it was out of punishment or convenience. Half of mine had been ripped out from Onkel dragging me by my hair. The rest had been matted with blood.

As I ran my hand over my smooth scalp, I wondered how the rest of me looked. My face, my back. Probably just as bad as the parts of me I could see.

The door to my room opened to let Uwe inside. He was followed by a pretty woman wearing a white dress and low heels. She looked older than me, probably late teens or early twenties. I wasn't sure.

Vater closed the door, the sound of the lock sent a tendril of fear brushing over my heart.

"Amory," he said evenly, "welcome to the German mafia."

I nodded.

"Thank you, Vater."

"You survived the initiation."

I nodded again.

"But there is one more test."

My eyes flicked to the woman who only smiled at me. I didn't know what to make of the look on her face—was she encouraging me? Comforting me? Mocking me?

Vater spoke again. "You let Jürgen turn you into a little girl." His voice was dark, like the whole thing was all my fault.

I lurched forward as the memories of Jürgen's hands on me replayed in my head. I wanted to vomit, and I'm sure I would have if I hadn't slapped a hand over my mouth. I'd just gotten my first meal in three days, and I had no idea when I'd get another. I didn't want to waste my food.

Vater straightened his shoulders, making himself look taller. "I don't have any daughters."

I swallowed, trying to control my breathing, trying to ignore the clammy feel of Jürgen's hands ghosting over my body, touching me in places that were forbidden, in ways that were sinful. The pain wasn't half as bad as the shame, the fact that my father and uncle had watched. The fact that all I'd done was scream and cry. I had brought shame to Vater. I should have fought back. But I'd been too weak.

Vater jerked his head at the woman, never taking his eyes off me. "It's time to prove to me you aren't a little girl."

The woman stepped forward and slipped down the straps of her dress. It fell to the floor at her feet; she stepped out of it and gracefully removed her heels. When she stood upright again, that odd smile was on her face—it was the only thing she was wearing.

Every hair on my body raised. I felt my muscles stiffen. I felt my mouth fall open.

"Vater," I exhaled.

He snapped at the woman. "Get on the bed."

"*Vater*," I said again.

He took one large step forward and suddenly his hand was around my throat. "You *will* take her," he hissed in my face. "Or you will never leave this room."

With a shove, he released me to fall back into the covers. I stared at him in shock, wishing for the days when he would have whipped me for looking at a girl inappropriately. Now he wanted me to lay with one right in front of him.

I had no fanciful dreams about the first time I'd have a woman. I wasn't waiting for marriage—or even thinking about it. And I wasn't interested in finding my soulmate. I wasn't even sure if I had a soul. I secretly hoped I didn't ... because I was sure Vater would have taken that from me too.

No matter what I'd imagined of my first sexual experience, I hadn't guessed it would play out like this. As some sort of twisted gang initiation.

This is the part of mafia life they never mention. In the cool movies, in the dark thriller stories, in the dirty little romance novels you read at night. They don't tell you how you're beaten and raped and then forced to sleep with someone you don't know. They don't tell you that the men who hurt you are your own relatives and friends. They don't mention that the goal is to survive initiation, but while you're being initiated all you wish for is death.

Waking up alive seems like a curse once it's all over. Because that means it was all real. It wasn't a dream, or even a nightmare. It's reality and there is no escape.

The mattress sank with the weight of the woman as she crawled over to me. I ignored her, keeping my swollen eyes locked on Uwe.

"Vater…" I tried once more.

His voice was a growl and his fingers twitched as he glared at me, aching to reach for the gun holstered at his hip. I believed he would shoot me if I disobeyed his order. So I swallowed and steeled myself for the command I knew was coming.

"Prove that you're a man, Amory. It's time."

Two

I stare down at my father's lifeless body, blinking rapidly as my memories recede to the dark pit I'd kept them locked in for so long. I can't recall the last time those thoughts surfaced in my head. I don't remember the last time I relived those three dark days.

I don't want to.

The scars on my back and chest have been enough of a reminder. I've lived with them for over fifteen years now. I've seen the horror of my flesh every time I've looked in the mirror, felt the ache of the knife splitting my skin all over again each time I stepped into the shower. Over the years, I've tried to cover them with tattoos. Hired an excellent artist who's treated me well, but even she had a hard time coming up with designs to make me look suitable whenever I undressed.

The man responsible for these scars is in a coffin now. So is his brother.

Now I'm supposed to conjure up some tears and tell the onlooking crowd that he was a good father and that I miss him so very much. I can't find the words. I can't think of *anything* to say as I stand at the podium in the church—not even a lie.

I could swallow my dark memories, smother them with a reminder that it was all just tradition. Something Vater himself went through when he was fifteen, as well as Onkel and Klaus and Elias too. Even Jürgen was initiated the same way, probably worse since he was just a Hunted grunt.

But that didn't make it alright. Not while it was happening and not afterwards, when I was given my reward for surviving.

Vengeance

Two years after those horrible three days, I was assigned my first execution. The German way is to release the man who'd been sentenced to death and hunt him down yourself.

I spent three days prowling the streets of Brooklyn, searching for the man my father had saved especially for me. Because of what he'd done to me.

I had smiled as I'd pulled the trigger and ended Jürgen's life. But there was no joy in the act. No redemption. No satisfaction. Just a raw, potent hatred that seemed to grow each time I pulled the trigger after that night.

It swells in my chest now as I stare down at Uwe's corpse. Dressed in a three-piece suit with his hair combed away from his aged face and his eyes glued shut.

I want to spit on him, but that would cause a scene.

My father was not a good father. He was an even worse husband. And he was a terrible human being in general. I have no kind words for him, not even at his own funeral … but I do miss him.

That's the sad truth that sends shivers over my scarred back. I miss my father. From the moment I saw his car go up in flames I've felt a hollow ache in my chest. Because, even though he was a crappy guy in every other area of his life, he was an excellent Jägermeister. He was a respectable mafia boss. And he was the best mentor I had in this dark life.

I need him. Now more than ever.

How am I supposed to take over the Hunting Grounds? How am I supposed to get us through this war that is rapidly spiraling out of control?

I've been an underboss for a couple years now. I've been ruling in my father's stead long enough to have the trust of the men standing guard in the cathedral. But I don't trust myself. I have no confidence in my decisions. It was my decision to ignore the warning Voice of God that got my father killed. It was my decision to cover up Wolfgang's crime that started this entire thing.

I'm thirty-one years old now, but I suddenly feel like that fifteen-year-old kid who peed himself and cried out to his father for help. Except my dad is dead now. And there is no one to call off the men who want my head. There is no one to say the word and end my suffering. Not anymore.

Someone in the crowd clears their throat and I realize I've been standing at the podium for longer than normal. I grip the sides of the wooden stand and swallow; the sound is picked up by the mic and sent echoing through the grand sanctuary. I wait until it dies down before I try to speak.

"Uwe Jäger was my father."

Christina sniffles and my eyes snap to her. She's crying, has been nonstop since she heard the news. My heart breaks for my mother. Breaks for the woman who should be weeping tears of joy because her abuser is finally dead. But Mutti has always been too kind for her own good. She loved Vater, despite all his shortcomings. Without thinking, I glance over at Rosa whose eyes are also red and weepy. I absently wonder if she loves me despite mine.

Not even an hour ago, I'd had her in my bed. It hadn't been sweet. It hadn't been loving. But Rosa hadn't complained, not until the very end. She'd laid there and taken everything I'd given. Accepted my pain for pleasure. Took my misery in exchange for ecstasy—as fleeting as it was. She didn't deserve what I'd given her. She didn't deserve *me*. But this is the hand we've been dealt. This is our cup. I vow we'll drink from it together.

I clear my throat again. "Uwe leaves a legacy behind. One that is under siege."

In the back, Hans nods his big head and Maximilian, bandages wrapped from his wrists up to his elbows, lifts a fist in support. Murmurs ripple through the men in the room. They are not crying like the women; they're silently screaming for blood.

I'm not surprised to see the difference in how they're handling this. While the men cry for vengeance, the women

16

weep for the lives that will be lost to attain it. It's a cycle of blood and death and violence. It's been this way since before I was born—since before Vater was born—and I don't think it will ever change.

"This is the mafia," my father used to say, a cigar between his lips and a finger of whiskey in his hand. "Nothing about our life is pretty or fair. If you make the mistake of thinking it ever could be, you'll only end up hurting yourself."

That was the single most significant piece of advice he'd ever given me. It never sank in until this very moment, as I glance down at his cold body.

Things will never change.

Even if we win this war. Even if we destroy the Volkovs and I get vengeance for Vater's and Onkel's deaths. The cycle will repeat itself. Mikhail will leave behind one fatherless daughter and one bloodthirsty son who will make a vow of vengeance. He will never let me live a day of peace until he repays me for the punishment I plan to deliver to his father. His отец.

Still…

I can't let this go unanswered. I've got hundreds of angry German men and grieving German women looking to me for some sort of plan. Some sort of retaliation.

Now is not the time to have a change of heart. To make room for Rosa's God in my life.

These people before me don't need a preacher. They need a leader. A Jägermeister.

17

"Dry your tears," I say sternly, looking at Christina and gazing briefly at Rosa. "This will be the last time we bury one of ours."

Conrad is at the front of the room, nodding and pressing his lips into a thin line. His father's casket is right beside Vater's. They're going to be buried together, brothers in life and death. Conny is only my cousin, but right now he feels more like a brother. As much as Wolfgang is my brother. He's my righthand man now, the only guy I trust with my life. This organization belongs to us. Neither of us is ready to take charge, but the rest of the people in the room don't need to know that.

"The Wolves took two men from us. Two brothers," I say angrily. "We will hunt them to their graves for this."

The words send a chill down my spine. I even notice the way Rosa seems to stiffen and blink up at me. Her hand goes to the silver crucifix dangling around her neck. She absently fingers it, a contemplative look taking over her features. I can see her lips moving, even from my stance at the podium. I'm not sure if she's praying for me or for herself. But the sight of her immediate worry leaves an uneasy feeling rolling over my shoulders.

I shake it away and focus on my father. Force myself to look at his lifeless frame. I can't afford to let my wife get to me right now. I can't afford to have a conscience. This life is easier without one.

"We have been granted ten days of peace to honor our dead," I say into the mic. "We still have seven days left. Use

18

them wisely. Because the fighting will begin again when the days are up, and it won't stop until one of us is dead." I lean forward, my shoulders tense and bunched together as I squeeze the sides of the podium. "When the dust settles, we will remain. That's a promise."

I turn and march away before anyone can applaud or start crying. Frankly, I don't care how they feel about my remarks. I'm the Jägermeister—I don't have to care. So, I square my shoulders as I push through the cathedral doors and descend the front steps. Douglass is waiting by my car, but I wave him off when I get closer.

"Stay behind and make sure Rosa gets home. I'm heading to The Club for a few hours."

He nods but doesn't turn to leave right away. "When will you be home?"

I know he isn't asking for me. Douglass doesn't care when I get back, but Rosa will bug him about it until his nerves are wrung. I can see the tension in his jaw as he clamps it shut, waiting for an answer.

I sigh. "Tell my wife I'll be home before midnight."

He nods once and then heads back into the church.

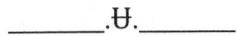

It's the middle of the afternoon when I walk into The Club but the air is thick with smoke and there's a man at every booth. I'm not surprised. With the ten days of peace, we're all a little more relaxed. Those of us who aren't mourning are celebrating and the ones who are mourning are coming out because we're tired of being depressed.

Normally, I go straight to the VIP section and wait to be served, but as I make my way through the lounge, I spot a familiar dancer at a booth in the corner. My feet change direction on instinct and I'm heading her way before I know it.

She's a slender woman, light brown skin sparkling from glitter and little jewels she's stuck to her breasts and abdomen. There are three men at her booth, their arms draped over the backs of the leather seats, none of them see me approaching but when I get closer, one of them looks up and then motions to the others.

"Jägermeister," the first man says.

His German accent is so thick I don't even bother speaking English to him. I doubt he knows it very well. "Don't get up," I say in my native tongue. "I'm here for the girl, if you don't mind."

The men exchange looks and then simultaneously glance up at the woman. She's still dancing, tiptoeing around the pile of bills at her feet as she grabs the pole and swings herself around. Her dirty blonde hair whips around her as she moves, and I catch a whiff of her vanilla scented shampoo.

"Is she yours?" the first man asks in German.

I nod and step forward, extending my hand to the woman. When she stops dancing, I can see how youthful she is up close. It sends bullets of guilt punching through me, but I remind myself that she's eighteen and getting paid well. I shouldn't feel so responsible for her, but some part of me does.

Maybe it's because she looks eerily similar to my wife. Maybe it's because I know she was kidnapped and forced into this life, never given a choice—not even when she was a child. Whatever the reason, I close myself off to the guilt and think of my father's dead body as she takes my hand and carefully steps down from her platform.

"I'll send another woman out for you," I tell the men.

They nod and stare as I walk the dancer to the backroom. She doesn't speak, just squeezes my hand until we're in the safety of the private lounge.

I turn and lock the door behind me and then close the blinds before I speak. "Amana."

She nods. "Amory."

It's been a few days since I hired her as a spy to help fish out the mole in our gang. I'm not expecting much information yet, but with her growing popularity, I was hoping for something.

"How's work been?"

"Alright." She crosses her arms to cover her bare breasts. It's at that moment that I realize she's completely naked except for the six-inch stilettos strapped to her feet and the jewels stuck to her skin. "You interrupted a pretty good gig."

"They'll probably request you again." I shrug, unbuttoning my suit jacket and passing it to her.

"Yeah, but they'll just want to know what I did with you back here."

I raise an eyebrow.

"They're all so curious about how you like your women."

21

I can't help but laugh. I've had my fair share of women in this dark life, but I've never been so open about it the way Wolfgang and Maximilian are. Even Conrad flaunts his mistresses around The Club. But I take pleasure in being discreet. I'm rarely even this open with my business, taking Amana away from her clients in broad daylight. Leaving The Club with her in front of all my men just a few nights ago. I'm sure the boys are gossiping as much as the dancers are. But that's what I wanted. To draw attention to Amana so she'll have a list of men to question and pry information from.

It's not until she blows out an exasperated sigh and flops onto the sofa that I realize the toll this must be taking on her. She's a topless dancer during the day and a private escort by night. I might have removed the collar Volkov had strapped around her neck, but I hadn't rescued her from this life. She's still a prostitute. She's still got to sleep with men she doesn't know or want—I've just given her a raise.

As some sort of apology, I nod at my jacket which she's just draped over both her shoulders. "Check the breast pocket."

Her eyes light up as she finds the envelope stuffed with money. "Another payment."

I nod. "As promised."

"Thanks." She hugs the envelope.

"Does the money make a difference?" I ask quietly. I don't like the way her eyes drop to the coffee table, so I distract myself by going to the bar and pouring myself a scotch. "Does it make all this worth it?"

22

Amana flicks her terribly dyed hair over her shoulder. "I have more clients than I did in Staten Island. But I'm getting paid more and I don't have to sleep with anyone until after five." She shrugs. "It's not what I want to do. But I won't have to do it forever. Not if we keep having these meetings."

"You have plans?"

She smiles at me, looking so much like a little girl that I have to look away. "I'm saving to go to college."

"College?"

"I want to study art history."

Before I can respond, she holds up a hand and laughs. "I know it's nerdy, but I had this client in Staten Island—he was one of my regulars—and sometimes he would talk about his work afterward."

Pillow talk. I gulp down my drink, trying not to imagine this eighteen-year-old girl having lazy chats with a middle-aged man who'd paid her for sex. I can't stop myself from wondering if he took her while she wore the collar or had the decency to remove it first. To treat her like a person. Not a slave.

"He worked at the Metropolitan. And the things he told me were mesmerizing." Amana talks like I'm not even there anymore, gazing off at nothing with stars in her eyes as she hugs the envelope of money to her chest. "The Met has over two million works in seventeen different departments. Can you imagine that?"

I can. I've been to the Met more times than I care to mention. There's a stupid charity event every year that all the mafia heads attend to show the public that gangsters have hearts too. It helps keep up a positive public image for our organizations—show everyone we're not just bloodthirsty mafioso ruling the city through violence. We are. But the charity ball helps us and everyone else pretend we aren't. Plus, we collectively donate over five-hundred million bucks to the six fortunate charities who are invited to attend. It's crazy how easily everyone jumps in line when money is thrown at them.

With the war going on, I haven't paid much attention to the news or the calendar, but it's the middle of summer now. I'm pretty sure the Met Ball is coming up soon. That means everyone will be there. Volkov, Moreno, King James, Giovanni, and all their Generals. It could turn into a bloodbath, but not with the news cameras and the charity workers there. This is a public event, one that will be broadcast live all night. Not even Volkov would risk damaging his reputation by attacking a charity gala.

This could be the perfect opportunity to gather intel.

I pour myself another drink and glance at Amana. She's still rambling about artwork with such enthusiasm, I almost feel bad for interrupting her as I say, "How would you like to go to the Met?"

She freezes. "What?"

"There's an event coming up soon. If I can get you on the staff, will you work it?"

She hesitates, clutching her envelope tighter. "What sort of work?"

"At the Met, you'll be serving drinks. Once it's over, you'll be serving men."

She sighs, making me feel like a monster. At this point, I'm no different from Volkov. I could pretend I'm better than him by giving Amana higher pay and asking her permission first. But the truth is that she doesn't have a choice and the money is something that just makes me feel better about the whole thing.

I gulp down my scotch and wipe my mouth. "I'll pay you double."

For a moment, Amana doesn't speak. She just stares at me, assessing me like she's looking over a new car—instead of deciding how badly she wants to go to art school. She never should have told me her plans or dreams. I'm not the nice guy who's here to make them come true. I'm the villain who's willing to use them against her.

I need vengeance more than she needs to protect her dignity. I need information more than she needs respect.

"Triple," I say firmly. "But that's as high as I'll go."

Amana stands and gives me a look that's dangerously close to a glare, but before I can get angry at her audacity, she disarms me with a smile. "I'll go to the event. But the only man I want to serve is you."

I give her a slow blink. "I'm a married man."

"We don't have to do anything. Just make them think we are."

She's got a point. Just having these meetings and spreading rumors that we're together has gotten her a number of interested clients. If she shows up at the Met on my arm, it will draw the attention of every General in the room. Maybe even

25

Volkov himself, especially since she's one of his former girls. He won't be able to resist the temptation to get a moment alone with her. And if she's smart, she'll use that moment to get the information I need.

But going to the Met with me could also backfire.

"You realize what you're asking, right?" I say with a warning in my voice.

Amana only nods.

"Coming out as my mistress will put a target on your back."

"I can handle myself."

I'll give her credit for surviving four years in one of Volkov's whorehouses. But this is different. It isn't bending over to please some gross Russian waving dollar bills around; it's spying on the Alpha himself. If Volkov senses something is off, he could kill Amana. Or worse—slap another collar around her neck.

I step closer to her, impressed when she doesn't shrink away. My jacket is way too big on her, leaving some of her skin exposed, even though she's buttoned it closed. I reach out and slide my hand between the folds of my coat. She still doesn't flinch away, not when I push the material aside to expose her, and not when my hand glides over her flesh. The only reaction she has is a slight wince when I peel one of the jewels from her bare breast. It's a pink gem made of cheap plastic, warm from being on her skin for so long.

I retract my hand and examine the pretty jewel, "You're still just a girl, Amana."

"I'm eighteen now. And even before then, my childhood was stolen years ago." She lifts her chin. "Don't feel sorry for me, Amory. I'm using you as much as you're using me."

I laugh. "And how is that?"

"You think your intel is the only thing I'm after?"

I raise an eyebrow.

"There are men who come here with connections. Important men. The kind who can get me into college even though I never went to high school. The sort of men with the power to get me a scholarship I'd never have a chance at getting if I didn't know them." Amana's eyes burn with passion. "I have my own agenda. I'm not doing this just because you asked."

My head bobs in a slow nod. She might be young, but she's far more experienced than I gave her credit for. Somewhere deep inside, the guilt I feel churns into pride, and I find myself smiling at her.

I reach out to tug a lock of her horrible blonde hair. "Wear your natural color for the ball."

She gives me a dangerous smile. "You gonna pay for the dye?"

"Is ten thousand not enough?"

"That money is for the meetings. Not for getting fancy."

I pull out a wad of cash and pass it to her. "Get yourself a nice dress too."

Amana grins from ear to ear as she counts the money and then stuffs it into her envelope. "This should be enough."

"I'll get you the money for the event later."

She drapes my jacket over the sofa as she turns to leave. Her last word to me sounds more like a command than a goodbye. "Triple."

This girl is draining me. I'm thankful Rosa isn't involved with our finances, otherwise she'd be left to wonder why I keep withdrawing tens of thousands of dollars. Instead, she'll be wondering why I'm going to attend the Met Charity Ball with my wife and a mistress.

The money is the least of my problems.

Three

The sound of the doorbell surprises me. Amory never rings— it's his house, he doesn't have to—so I know it isn't him when a servant enters the lounge and tells me I have guests. But since it isn't Amory, I have no idea who to expect when I get the news.

"Oh well," I mutter, closing the Bible I'd been reading. It's early afternoon, I usually have prayer and study time in the mornings or evenings but after Uwe's funeral, I feel like I need to be in prayer every second of the day.

Amory hasn't been himself. That isn't a surprise considering all that's happened. But his behavior is still shocking. Even the way he looks has changed. He's letting his beard grow in, which is handsome on his square jaw, but it's certainly out of character. Amy has always had facial hair, but he's normally meticulous about it—clean cut, closely shaved dark hair that stands out against his pale skin. Now he walks around with scruff that makes him look like he just got back from a week-long camping trip and forgot his razor. I want to say something, but I don't know how because his behavior has changed as much as his appearance.

He treats me like some caged mafia wife now. He isn't there when I wake up, I don't get a call during the day, and if he comes home before I fall asleep, he only makes time to have sex and then passes out right after. It's like clockwork. Lovemaking without any love involved.

I feel dirty. Used. Like I'm just here for him to bury the troubles of his day or help him fall asleep with a smile on his face. But I don't raise an issue about it. Because I've decided speaking to him won't help anything. It'll just lead to an argument and drive this wedge further between us.

Only God can save us now—and I don't mean the city. I mean our marriage, our sanity, the love we once had for each other. It's still there, somewhere. But it's buried beneath all the death and misery we've experienced.

Less than a year ago, I lost both of my parents. Now Amory has lost his father and his uncle and there will be more death to come. I don't know how much more we can take, but I know we can handle it if we focus on God.

If only.

If only I can get Amory to listen to me when I try to talk to him about the Lord. Lately, he's completely closed himself off to any spiritual talk. I suddenly miss the days where I thought it was a struggle just to get him to pray. Now, the more I pray the worse it gets. I have no idea what to do.

Someone clears their throat beside me, and I look up to find a servant standing behind a crowd of well-dressed women. Gisela, Petra, Viktoria, Christina, a woman I recognize as Silke and her sisters—even Olivia and my cousins are here.

The sight of them shocks me so much, I'm left speechless for a few moments. When I finally gather myself, I squeak out a greeting. "What are you all doing here?"

Christina steps forward. "I came to say goodbye to the house."

That's right. Since Amory became the Jägermeister, we've moved into the Jäger estate. He had men bring all our stuff over and rearrange the furniture Christina and Uwe left behind. The place isn't perfect, but it's livable. Amory told me I could decorate the mansion however I want, but part of me feels uncomfortable doing that. There is so much history and culture here, over 200 years of mafia life encased in this million-dollar home. When I think of it that way, the place feels more like a tomb than a house, but still.

Petra steps forward. "The rest of us came to officially welcome you as Mistress." She inclines her head and then lifts a small box. "We brought housewarming gifts."

I glance at all of them. This room is full of high-ranking women. Royalty. A queen amongst princesses, duchesses, and countesses. We are mafia, but our stature is not to be taken lightly. There isn't a soul in this city—in this state—who wouldn't recognize our faces and step aside if we passed them in the street.

I lift my chin and motion to the coffee table in the center of the room. "Thank you for your gifts, please set them aside. I'll open them in my privacy."

Petra nods and sets her gift down, so do the other women. When Christina comes closer, I take her gift and reach for her hands. "How are you?"

She shakes her head. "Do not worry about me, child."

"You're my responsibility now." It's true and she knows it.

In the Italian mafia, we have a tradition of sending former Mistresses back to Italy to live the rest of their days with the motherland gang. I've heard the women of the Spanish mafia remain as an advisor to the current Mistress or even the capo himself. But in the German mafia, the former Mistress becomes a quiet figure, hiding in the shadows, keeping her head down. Her wellbeing is placed on the shoulders of the next Mistress, meaning, I'm expected to look after Christina while Amory holds this mafia together.

Shifting power isn't easy. Amory was fortunate to have the complete trust of the German mafia, but things could have gotten bad. Someone could have challenged his rule, someone could have demanded that they pick the next Jägermeister themselves.

While he fights his battles, I'm expected to keep the peace amongst the women.

In a way, my job is more important than even Amory's. Because the men he faces every day come to him with ideas that have been planted in their heads by their seemingly meek wives.

The men call us little lambs. Quiet housewives. Obedient flowers. But we are anything but. As I glance at the ladies before me, I see no flowers or lambs. I'm staring at pit vipers and foxes. Cunning little creatures who know how to hide their fangs and fight in the quiet. Our battles are different, but they are just as deadly because, sometimes, our husbands are our own enemies.

I shiver as I think of how Uwe treated Christina and how Conrad raised his hand to Gisela when she'd upset him at the hospital. It had been shocking to me, but no one else in the room had seemed to notice. I can't help but wonder what happens when no one is looking. If Gisela faces that sort of abuse behind her white picket fence.

Christina squeezes my hand and gently pulls away from my grasp. "I'm doing fine."

"Christina—"

"If you think I didn't have a plan in place for when this happened, then you underestimate me."

I blink at her.

"Uwe's death was sudden. But I was prepared." She leans closer. "You must always be prepared for anything in this life. Even a young woman like you."

My shoulders fall as I realize what she means. Amory could die just as suddenly as his father did. I don't want to think about it, and I certainly don't want to make arrangements to take care of myself for when it does happen. But I have to face reality. I have to accept that I'm a mafia wife. Thinking any other sort of way would only be foolish.

I give my mother-in-law a firm nod and then look out at the other women. They're milling about the room, enjoying refreshments my very attentive staff brought out for their pleasure. Olivia, Adella, and Nona make their way over when I catch Della's gaze. All three of them are smiling wide.

"I know things have been tough lately," Olivia says as she hugs me. "But I'm so proud of you. You're a Mistress now."

I grin. "I guess I am."

"Grandma sends her condolences and congratulations," Adella says. She passes me a glass of lemon iced tea and brushes her bangs aside. "Papa Jamie still doesn't think it's safe for us to travel so only Nona and I came to see you."

"I appreciate it. Please tell grandma and grandpa I said hello."

Nona places a hand on her hip. "Are we going to train during the grace period? We still have a week and I'm itching to punch something before we get locked away in safehouses again."

"We should spend our free time going out," Olivia says. "Not training."

I press my lips together. "You want to go out in the middle of a war?"

"We have a grace period!" she reiterates with a giggle.

"Volkov broke the last grace period," I remind her.

I know Uwe's death hasn't impacted Olivia at all, but he was still a boss, and he was murdered during the two-day period Volkov himself had initiated. It's easy to believe he'll honor this grace period since Uwe *was* a boss—but still. I don't trust the man at all. He attacked Stonehall. Anyone bold enough to do that during a peace agreement is foul.

"The Mistress is right," Adella says. "It isn't safe to go clubbing." She gives Olivia a reprimanding look.

Like a child, Olive pokes her lip out and sinks into the sofa. I sit beside her and pat her knee. "There must be something we can do inside."

Silke and her sisters approach with their eyebrows raised. "I'm surprised you want to plan anything with all the preparations you must be busy with."

I raise one shoulder. "The movers have made everything very easy. There's hardly been any unpacking for me to do."

Edeltraud snorts, it's an odd sound coming from such a pretty face. Then again, her beauty isn't normal either. She's got smooth pale skin and wavy red hair that's unusual for a woman with strong German roots. Her face is almost ethereal, and I can't stop staring as she says, "My sister is talking about the Met Charity Ball, not moving into the estate."

My mind goes blank, partly because Edeltraud's accent is so thick I almost didn't understand what she'd said, and also because when I did realize what she'd said I had no ready response.

"The Charity Ball?" I repeat dumbly.

All the women are suddenly blinking at me like I'm stupid.

"Don't tell me you've never been?" Della says with a smirk.

I shake my head and stare down at my hands, clasped together in my lap. "Papa never let me go."

"Don Gio was very strict," Olivia explains. "I've never been to the ball either. Since our fathers were best friends, they often made joint decisions."

"So both of you grew up ridiculously sheltered?" Nona laughs at me.

I scowl at my cousin but Adella's jab to her ribs alleviates the burning desire to say something nasty to her.

"What preparations should I be making?" I ask Silke.

She puckers her lips in thought. "Well, my mother is having a dress made—"

"Wait," I interrupt, "is it wise for us to go to the Ball while we're in the middle of a war?"

"The ball is in five days," Edeltraud says. "It will still be during the grace period. And it's a public event. I don't think the Wolves would dare to bring harm to so many innocent people."

I nod. She has a point.

"I guess I need to find a dress." And talk about it with Amory. I glance at Gisela. "Has Conrad mentioned the Ball?"

"Briefly. I was hoping to discuss it with you today. And all the rest of the ladies, too."

I smile. This almost feels like high school—those last few exciting days before prom, except we're not just going to some dumb school dance. The Met Charity Ball hosts six organizations who'll receive hundreds of millions of dollars in donations from mafia bosses and their families.

It's a publicity event for us and a cash cow for them. The public gets to spend 500 bucks per ticket just to rub elbows with the notorious gangs of New York. Sometimes celebrities even show up—I heard last year there was an NFL star who came and a Victoria's Secret model whose name I can't remember. I had watched the event on television with Olivia, like we were still schoolgirls squealing over the Oscars.

The women crowd around me, waiting for me to lay out plans. Dress designs, color combinations, they'll even wear whatever shoes I tell them if I insist. I am their Mistress now— their queen—and even the likes of Christina and Viktoria must respect my authority.

But I don't plan to use my position to boss them around and tell them what sort of clothes to wear. I have been placed here for a specific purpose. It isn't to influence or brainwash these women into being obedient wives, it's to feed them.

I take a nervous breath before I clear my throat and look at the ladies. "Before we start talking about the Ball, I want to talk about something else."

Petra leans forward curiously. "What is it, Mistress?"

"How many of you believe in God?"

The question stuns them. Petra glances around to see everyone else's reaction. When no one moves or speaks, she brushes a blonde lock behind her ear and raises her hand.

"I believe in God. But I don't know if I believe everything you say about Him. Or everything in the Bible."

"That's fine," I say calmly. In time, she will learn.

I stand and move to retrieve my Bible from the table beside the couch. Everyone's eyes are on me, wondering why on earth I've just started talking about God. They say it's rude to discuss politics and religion at dinner, I say it's rude to ignore an opportunity to spread God's Word.

I'm just as uncomfortable as the women who are watching me, but I will not pass up this chance. These are the most powerful women in the mafia. Gathered right here in my home. Waiting for my command. God placed me here for a reason. If I can influence them then they can influence their husbands and this city will fall. I must speak the Truth now more than ever.

If I fail God now, what purpose will all my struggles have served?

"We are at war," I say in as strong a voice I can muster. "You don't have to believe. But I want you to at least consider the possibility of there being a God."

Silke nods, but both her sisters are making faces. They look like they're thinking of a reason to suddenly leave.

"Think of it this way," I say. "The Bible could all be wrong. It could be some made up lie to fool millions of people for thousands of years. If that's the case, then I've willingly chosen to believe this lie. I've lived a good, chaste life, and when I die nothing will happen." I swallow, clutching the Bible as I stare at the women one by one. I pause at Edeltraud. "But the opposite could also be true. The Bible could be entirely correct. And if I choose *not* to believe it ... when I die, I will wake up in the eternal flames of hell."

The room falls silent. Every unblinking eye trained on me.

"If you are going to gamble, bet on the side that wins. God wins in the end. Remember that."

After a few moments of very uncomfortable staring, Petra clears her throat. I'm shocked to see tears in her eyes. "My uncle just died. I was not sure if there was anywhere for his soul to go—I was not even sure he *had* a soul. But now …" she pauses to wipe at her eyes. "Now I think maybe it's better to believe and end up in heaven than to doubt and guarantee that I will wake up in hell."

"You can't just scare us into believing in your religion," Edeltraud speaks up.

I look right at her. My voice doesn't shake when I reply, "It *isn't* scary when you know there is an all-powerful God who will save you from eternal damnation."

She frowns but doesn't speak again.

"Ladies," I sigh. "Our husbands and brothers and uncles are dropping like flies. What have you got to lose? What harm will believing bring to your lives?"

Christina steps forward. "I just lost my husband and my brother-in-law." Her chin trembles as she glances away and takes a shuddering breath. "I won't bother asking why God allowed it to happen. It's not like Uwe was worth saving anyway." A sorrowful laugh fills the air. "But I want to believe, regardless of what happened to my husband. Who knows… maybe God would have intervened if I had been a praying woman when I was supposed to be. But even if He hadn't, I want to believe. I am choosing to believe."

I wish I could offer her comfort as she starts to cry. But I can't think of anything to say. This is the hardest thing I've ever done. Trying to convince a bunch of grieving women that there is a God who loves them, all while we're in the middle of a war. Right after burying two prominent figures in our organization. What I'm attempting is almost laughable. But God never promised I would win souls. He only told me to feed His lamb. So I will. Whether they believe is ultimately up to them. But I won't let their doubts discourage me from fulfilling my purpose.

The sigh I release is enough to fill the room. "I'm not asking you all to become Christians right this moment. But I will ask you to pray with me before we leave. How's that?"

Petra shakes her head. "I want to get saved today."

Christina steps beside her. "So do I."

I gape at them as they smile through their tears.

Christina takes my hand. "It is time, Mistress."

Four

Even though we've been granted ten days of peace, I feel absolutely on edge. It isn't because Volkov has a history of breaking treaties, it's because I don't know what to do once our ten days are up. I've been so consumed with trying to catch this rat that I haven't had time to sit down and think of what comes next—whether we catch him or not.

Today, I've decided to plan. I dig through the files we have stashed in a safe at the estate, thankful for my father's meticulous records, and I stare at the information before me.

For hours.

We have men from every part of Germany. We have men from across the United States. We have men we've Hunted from every single mafia in the city. If our rat is high-ranking and well-connected, like we assume, then we're in trouble.

Maybe this is punishment for all the men we've Hunted. Maybe this is divine judgment against one of the most ruthless gangs in New York. Maybe this is just part of mafia life.

Whatever the case, I've got to do something.

I make a web chart tracing the connections between every General I know of, but the information just raises more questions. How many men does Conrad have working in his club? What sector of Brooklyn has Klaus entrusted to his righthand man? With Oberon gone, I've given his division to Conny who split the territory with Hans. I didn't like the decision, but I promised Conrad he would have complete control over his father's former sector, so I didn't give him grief when I heard the news. Plus, I trust Hans.

I know... that's the strangest thing I've ever said, but after everything that's happened—especially the events in Staten Island—I'm not convinced that Hans would betray us. Or Conrad. Or Klaus. They are the only men in this organization that I fully trust. I don't even have to mention how much faith I have in Douglass. I'd give my life for that man without question, and I know he would do the same.

So then ... who?

"He isn't German..." I mutter, gnawing on the eraser to my pencil. The acrid taste of pencil lead is bitter on my tongue. I grimace and heave out a sigh as I start crossing out names.

I'm looking at this the wrong way. It isn't a question of which of my men would betray me, it's a question of which of the *others* would stab me in the back.

The Hunting Grounds has the most to lose right now. The Stronghold and the Garden could cut ties and cover their losses at any given moment. Whoever is selling our secrets is someone who's trying to push them in that direction. Someone who doesn't think it's worth it to be allied with us anymore.

I stare down at my chart again. Klaus has gotten close with Marco Segreto, but I know Eike used to have drinks with Aldo Romano before he was shot in Staten Island. Either one of those Italians could be stealing secrets from my men. Then again, Oberon used to work closely with Tyrese Willis before his untimely death. And Vater got along with King James.

I shake my head, but not because none of this makes sense, I'm frustrated because it seems believable. I just don't want to accept it.

Any one of those men could have gone behind my back. Men I trusted. Men I thought would stand beside me if not to honor our alliance, then at least to make sure Rosa is safe. King James is her grandfather; Tyrese is her uncle. Marco Segreto is married to her best friend. Aldo Romano is her best friend's brother. In my petty jealousy, I had wished death upon him just for flirting with Rosa. Yet ... he could be the very one bringing death to our door.

"Who?" I whisper, running my hand through my thick hair. It's gotten longer recently, and my beard is growing in. I've got stubble for days, but right now I don't care. I have to find this mole. If it means losing sleep, I'll do it. If it means looking scruffy while I work tirelessly, I'll do it. Even if it means forsaking everything ... I'll do it.

I've *done* that.

I've turned my back on the things that matter. I've set aside my morals and even my marriage to make sure I catch the people responsible for this betrayal. For the death of my father and uncle. I've paid my dues to this organization in blood, sweat, and tears, but now Rosa is paying her price. Every day I ignore her for work. Every time I stay out instead of coming home to see her. And every time I'm home just to use her body for my pleasure.

I've lost everything, but she's still giving. Still suffering. At my own hands.

"I'm a terrible husband," I mutter.

Mercifully, my phone buzzes before I can sink further into my self-pity. I sigh as I glance at the screen and accept the call. "Conny," I rasp.

He greets me in German. *"Guten Abend, Bruder."*

I pause. Conny's been calling me his brother a lot lately. Maybe because we've both lost our fathers and must protect our little brothers now. Maybe because we're the boss and underboss of the Hunting Grounds now. Either way, I don't mind his endearment.

"Bruder," I say back. "Talk to me."

"Gisela is driving me nuts."

I chuckle and lean back in my office chair. The cool leather feels good against the jagged scars carved into my back. "She's just worried about you. All the wives are on edge right now."

"No. She isn't bugging me to stay safe or be careful. She keeps going on about the stupid Charity Ball."

I groan. I'd almost forgotten about that thing. Just a few days ago I enlisted Amana as a spy for the Ball. I still haven't

44

told Rosa about the whole thing—Conny's mention of the event summons a wave of anxiety I'd just managed to bury.

"I forgot about the Ball," I mumble.

"You're still going, right?"

"I am."

"Are we planning something?"

"No. There will be civilians there."

"And Wolves."

"They're not worth the backlash of a public attack."

"Then why are we going?" he snaps.

"To gather intel."

Conrad grunts into the phone and then hisses out a string of curses in German. I don't scold him for his language or his attitude. He lost his father too. And almost lost his brother. Morgen's in hiding now because of the Wolves. No one wants revenge more than he does. Except me, of course.

"We will get them, Bruder," I say. "They will bleed for what they've done."

"I know." Conny's voice is tight. I hear him clear his throat and I know there are tears running down his cheeks. He's never been able to control his emotions very well. It's why he stays away from Gisela and spends so much time at The Club, he's afraid of losing his temper with her. There have been a few times where he *has* lost his temper. Where he's done things to her that he's regretted later. But right now, he isn't violent. He isn't angry. He's full of misery.

I sit in silence as he sobs into the phone. It cleaves my heart in two, makes me want to hang up, but I force myself to sit there and listen. I haven't cried at all over my father or uncle. Conrad is crying for the both of us—I don't want to miss a single tear.

He clears his throat again. *"Es tut mir leid."*

"Don't apologize," I tell him.

The other end is silent for a moment. "I should go."

"Get some rest. And go easy on Gisela. She's just trying to make the most of this."

"I know. I'll be good to her."

"Goodnight, Conny."

"Goodnight, Jägermeister."

I sit back in my chair and stare at my phone and then at my charts. It's late now. The growl of my stomach says it's probably close to dinner time. I don't want to leave my work, but after hearing Conny weep like a woman, I want to take my own advice and go see my wife.

My office door opens with a yawn that seems to echo throughout the estate. I grew up in this house, but I still feel awkward walking the halls without my father or mother here. Christina has a villa on the outskirts of the borough, but I heard she's been staying with Viktoria since the funeral. I'm glad they're together. I'd prefer to have them both move in with me, but I haven't discussed it with Rosa yet. She gets along with both women, but I'm not sure how she would feel about living with my mother and aunt. I make a mental note to bring it up when I see her—which happens to be right this moment.

As I round the corner to head to the dining room, Rosa and I almost collide. She lets out a squeal and jumps back in shock, then she blinks and frowns.

"Amy...?"

"Hey." I lean down and kiss her which makes her gasp against my lips. "You seem surprised to see me."

"I am surprised," she says. "I didn't hear you come in."

"I've been here all afternoon."

I expect her frown to deepen but she surprises me by dropping her shoulders and looking away. My God, she's *hurt*. Not angry.

"I was working in my office," I try to explain, but it only makes her look even sadder.

I'm the worst.

"But I'm here now. We can have dinner together."

Her eyes are wide and filled with emotion when she looks up at me. "I made plans. I wasn't expecting you."

"Oh." I cram my hands into my pockets.

I guess that's fair. I shouldn't expect Rosa to just mope around the house until I'm ready to deal with her.

"I could come along. If you don't mind," I offer.

She looks apologetic. "I'm going to see Aldo. He's going in for surgery tomorrow; we want to be there for him."

Anger bubbles in my chest. I don't care if my wife makes plans without me, but I'm not about to let Rosa prance out of this house at nine o'clock at night to go see another man. Especially not Aldo.

47

I almost curse at her, but I catch myself and decide to take a slow breath instead. *Where the heck is Douglass?* He's the one who drives her around when I'm not here. I know he didn't agree to take her to see *Aldo*. He knows how much I can't stand the guy.

Rosa touches my hand. The gesture shocks me so badly, I flinch away and immediately regret it. She's looking at me like I've just slapped her, but I close off my heart and take a step toward her.

"You're not leaving this house if it's to see Aldo."

She frowns. "You know it's not like that."

"I don't care."

"He's getting surgery tomorrow, Amy."

I honestly hadn't heard that he was getting surgery. Last time I bothered to inquire, Aldo's father told me his bullet wound had gotten infected and the doctors were doing their best to treat him. He'd gotten shot on a mission I put together, so I felt partially responsible, if not at least sympathetic. But as I gaze down at my doe-eyed wife and see the genuine concern on her face for the man she knows I hate, I can't ignore the dark urge to let her go just so she can watch me choke him in his hospital bed.

My gaze lands on her flatly. "Rosa..." I try to choose my words wisely, say this in a way my sweet wife will understand.

It isn't just that it's Aldo and that I hope he doesn't live through his surgery, it's that Rosa is the wife of the Jägermeister and she's trying to leave the house at night to pay a visit to another man's home.

I can't let that happen.

"Stay here with me," I say in a murmur.

My tone throws her off. She steps back and blinks at me in confusion and shock—I use her momentary silence to reach out and grab her by the wrist. My touch is gentle, slowly pulling her close, running my thumb over the inside of her wrist. She sways into me, dizzy from the sudden shift in the air.

I feel my chest tighten at her nearness. *God.* I'm not supposed to be turned on right now, but Rosa's a beautiful woman and I'm in love with her. I can't help it.

"Stay," I say softly.

She lifts her chin to look me in the eye. "Don't do that."

"Do what?"

"Try to seduce me."

My wife is innocent. But she's not stupid.

I take a step back and release my hold on her wrist. If I can't win her over kindly, then I'll do it through brute force.

"Rosa," my voice is stern, "you're not going out to see Aldo. Not tonight."

She glances sideways at the dark window in the hall. "In the morning then. I want to see him before his operation begins."

"No," I say quickly. "I don't want you seeing Aldo. Period."

She frowns. *Now it's sinking in.*

"Amory… we've talked about this."

We have. Multiple times. Rosa wants her freedom and equality and all that. I've said it before—I'm here for it. Just not tonight.

"And we talked about your role here."

"I'm your wife—"

"You're a *mafia* wife!" I bark.

I don't mean to snap at her, but Rosa needs to get that through her head. She needs to learn her place because right now—with Wolves lurking at every corner—staying in her place could be the difference between life or death. I can't have her running around the city whenever she wants. I can't trust her with other men, not because she isn't faithful but because I don't know who's faithful to us right now.

Anyone could betray us. Anyone could be watching, waiting for my innocent wife to be too trusting. To be too relaxed around the wrong person. They've already taken my father. I won't let them have my woman too.

Rosa steps back, clutching the crucifix around her neck. The sight of it calms me, but only for a moment. "Rosa—"

She steps back again, but I reach out and grab her, yanking her toward me so she's against my chest before she knows it.

Shockingly, she doesn't struggle. Doesn't try to pull away.

"I shouldn't have yelled," I say hoarsely.

She nods, sliding her hand up my chest. "What's going on?" she whispers.

"*So* much." I grind my teeth together. "Too much."

"Talk to me."

I wish I could. I wish I could say something, but the less Rosa knows, the better. The safer she'll be. I could take this moment to tell her about Amana. Explain what will happen at the Ball. But the truth is that Rosa can't know. I need her honest reaction. I need her anger. Otherwise, the Wolves will sniff out the truth. They'll know Amana isn't really my secret lover. They'll realize she's a spy in a heartbeat. And then everything will go up in flames.

Rosa's anger must be honest. Raw. Painful.

I shudder as I hug her even tighter. It all just hit me. How much pain I'm going to bring her. How much pain I've *already* brought her. I've mistreated her, lied to her, kept secrets from her. We never talked about it at length, but she only just forgave me over the death of her father. I wasn't sure we'd ever get over that, and then my own father died, and the sorrow of his loss brought us back together.

But I don't know about this.

I'm not sure Rosa's wounds have healed enough to handle another blow. Not one like this. *But this is what it means to be a mafia wife.* The truth carves a whole in my chest.

I'd been so obsessed with becoming the Jägermeister and taking my father's place, I'd never stopped to think that Rosa would be taking Christina's place. She would have to step up and stand beside the man who dragged her into this life. The man who lied to her. The man who broke her heart. And she would have to do it all with a smile.

She's been doing that since we got married, and she's somehow managed to remain standing. She's never stopped loving me.

I don't deserve Rosa. And she certainly doesn't deserve me.

"Amy," she says, blinking up at me.

I lean down and kiss her.

I'm so sorry. I wish I could say the words aloud, but I can't find my voice as I take her into my arms and carry her away.

This is my apology. I pray to God she accepts it.

In our room, in the comfort of our bed, my heart flutters when Rosa tangles her fingers into the knot of my tie. It's an incredible thing to feel wanted by someone you love. To be kissed, to be desired, to be undressed.

After she removes my tie, she works to unbutton my shirt. I lean back and let her, my eyes watching every movement. She isn't nervous the way she used to be when we'd first gotten married. Part of me misses her shyness, but I can't ignore the fire I feel burning between us as I catch the look of desire on her face.

There is a storm brewing around us. It threatens to overtake us, but we find our way to each other. Riding the waves of our ecstasy like we're in control. Like we can actually tame the thunder that booms around us.

We're fooling ourselves, but at least we're in it together.

I take her slowly, just the way she likes it. And when she's tired, I wrap her arms around my neck and kiss her sweetly.

"Hold on to me."

Rosa gasps as I rock her back through that storm. Her nails sink into my back, drawing a hiss from my lips. The pain is pleasure.

My wife is a woman who loves with every part of her being—even down to her soul. When she kisses me, I lose all thought. When she clings to me, I gasp. And when she pulls me close and whispers into my ear, I inch closer to the edge of the storm.

The desire burning between us pools in my chest and shoots through every part of my body. It coils until it's taut, threatening to break me. My hand punches the headboard, gripping it tightly—just to have something to hold on to. Rosa still clings to me, running her nails down my back, driving me nuts.

I pull away. "*God*—I can't—"

She silences me with a kiss. The fire burns brighter, passion twisting until it's wrung completely. When the coil snaps, Rosa screams and falls into the storm. She takes me with her.

The groan that rumbles through my chest spills from my lips like a helpless cry. I am breathless. Spent. Almost embarrassed. But Rosa is pleased. When I find the strength to push onto my elbows so I'm not crushing her with my body anymore, she smiles up at me.

"I love you," she whispers, reaching up to brush my hair from my sweaty forehead.

I laugh and kiss her hard. "You will be my downfall."

Five

Rosa steps out of the car wearing an off-shoulder dress with a plunging neckline. It's pearly white and made entirely of silk so every move she makes looks fluid and smooth. Like she's a living angel. The material flows around her, brushing against her hips, draping over her thighs which peek out between the splits running up both sides of the dress. This is the sexiest I've ever seen my wife and it takes strength I didn't know I had not to pull her back into the car and make desperate love to her like a teenager on prom night.

Get it together, I scold myself. We've just arrived at the Charity Ball, I shouldn't be surprised with how nice she looks, but these last few weeks have been tough on our marriage. Our relationship is currently held together by the threads of Rosa's prayers. Tonight, those strands of faith will be tested.

I take her hand and pause for the cameras to snap pictures of us and for the crowd to scream like we're celebrities. In a city ruled by anarchy, we *are* celebrities. Our citizens lose their heads over seeing Generals and mafia wives—not movie stars and singers.

I'm used to this sort of attention. As the Jägermeister's heir, I was raised in the spotlight, but Rosa was sheltered from all this. When I glance down at her, I realize how nervous she truly is, and I squeeze her hand to give her comfort. She offers a weak smile, but it quickly withers on her lips when I turn and extend my other hand toward the open car door.

Amana reaches out and takes it. She climbs from the back of the car to the sound of collective gasps. The only thing I can hear over the hissing is my thumping heart.

I've managed to keep the drama to a minimum by telling Rosa that Amana is someone I'm working with within the gang. But I couldn't offer more details than that. I'm thankful we spent the night making love, she was still riding the high of our passion when I broke the news that I'd be bringing along another woman. But now it looks like she's come down from her high. She's openly scowling at Amana who's taken hold of my other arm and is smiling at the cameras.

The crowd eats this up.

The new boss of the German mafia finally steps away from the business to make a debut with his foreign wife—*and* his new mistress. If Volkov doesn't kill us all tonight, this moment will be on the front page of every newspaper in NYC tomorrow morning.

Rosa's grip on my hand goes slack. I casually slide my hand over the small of her back, trying to ease her pain and still maintain my image at the same time. I need her anger to be real right now, but I don't want to humiliate her. I don't want things to be worse than they need to be.

Amana is milking this moment. She's smiling and batting her long lashes, tossing her newly dyed dark hair over her shoulder as she leans into me. I shouldn't be surprised. She's been working as a high-class escort since she was fourteen. This is her territory. This is where she shines. I just wish she wasn't so good at it.

It also doesn't help that she looks so much like my wife—which means she's absolutely gorgeous. In a little black dress with a split up the back, so high I think I see a flash of her red thong when she ascends the stairs into the Met before me. If Rosa looks like an angel, then Amana is her dark cousin. A vixen come to whisk me away from my loving wife.

I hate to admit it, but she's everything I could have hoped for tonight. If the cameras are eating her up, then I know the men inside will be tripping over themselves to know more about my mysterious new mistress. I need their curiosity. I need their interest. So, when I finally agree to share this lovely prize, she can use her time to get the information I need.

When we make it into the museum, Amana pauses and stares with her mouth open and her head tilted back. Most of the artwork has been moved to keep the gangsters from stealing it, but there are a few dozen pieces arranged along the walkway that leads into the main foyer, and even more perched high along the walls as we pass through the entrance.

That's the one and only time I see the eighteen-year-old girl I rescued from Staten Island. Once the awe settles in,

Amana remembers why she's here and who she's supposed to be and like a switch has been flipped, she becomes the vixen from the car and clings to me like glue.

Conrad and Gisela are already inside the main area when we finally make it there. Conny raises his eyebrow at me, but Glizzy actually stops walking and openly stares between the three of us. The movement is so abrupt, some of her drink spills over the rim of her glass and she gasps in surprise.

"Let me help you get a napkin," Rosa says quickly.

The two women scurry off before anyone can stop them.

"I didn't know you were bringing a prize," Conny says with a lecherous grin.

Amana gives him a devilish smirk. "He likes to keep me to himself. But I convinced him to let me out for tonight."

The way Conrad licks his lips makes me want to punch him—not because I care that he's hitting on Amana, I'm angry that he's doing it ten seconds after his own wife left his side.

I kiss the top of Amana's head. "Go get yourself a drink."

Once she's out of earshot, Conrad nudges me with his elbow. "Is she really all yours or can I …?"

"You're not sleeping with her," I grind out. "Jesus, Conny, you're *married*."

He glowers. "I know."

"Gisela is a good woman."

His frown deepens. "I *know*."

I step closer to him. Conrad is one of the few people who knows about the rat, so I know I can trust him with this

57

information. "You can't sleep with her because she's working for me."

"How?"

"Digging for intel."

We both shift to watch her flirt with the bartender who doesn't bother to card her before serving up a neon green cocktail. Before she can even take a sip, a man from the crowd moseys up to introduce himself. He has tan skin and brown wavy hair, undoubtedly someone from Moreno's gang. I'd prefer Amana to spend her time with Russians, but I'll take what I can get.

"You're using one of my girls to spy on men here tonight?" Conrad sounds angry. When I glance down at him, I realize he *is* angry. The frown on his face almost looks painful and there's a thick wrinkle right in the middle of his forehead. Just one.

"We need to find this mole," I say in German, in case anyone nearby is listening.

He curses. "And if she gets caught, they will torture her for being a rat. And then what will happen, Amory?"

I glance away.

"Then what?" he demands.

"They'll come for The Club."

He runs his hand through his hair, messing it up. "Because she works for me."

I nod slowly, and my calm demeanor sets him off even more. But we're in public, so instead of shouting at me, Conrad hisses out a string of colorful words and then glares. "The Club is my business. My *legal* source of income outside of the mafia.

It's my Plan B if things ever fall apart. How could you do this to me?"

"She won't get caught," I growl. "And she wouldn't be here in the first place if you hadn't taken in Volkov's women without asking me first." My tone makes him remember his place and he takes a step back to calm himself.

"I'm sorry," Conrad mutters.

I wave him off. "Just promise me you'll look after her if I get caught up tonight."

"Of course."

Rosa and Gisela return on cue. I relax a little when my eyes meet Rosa's and she actually manages to smile back. It's obvious she isn't happy about tonight's arrangement, but there is an odd sense of calm about her that I can't place. Like she knows there's more to Amana than what I've told her. Like she's chosen to trust me despite the situation.

I will spend the rest of my life making it up to her for the faith she's placed in me. For giving me room to do what I must in order to keep her safe and finish this war.

My smile stretches wider when she comes closer and reaches for my arm, but as I gaze out at the crowd, I catch a glimpse of Eliana Moreno and all my joy is sapped away.

This is the worst possible time to bump into my ex-lover. Especially considering the last time she was face to face with my wife, Rosa slapped the taste out her mouth.

I glance down at my little flower; she's listening to Conrad tell some story about last year's Charity Ball. With a tight smile,

I interrupt my cousin and announce, "I have something important to say."

All three of them blink at me.

"Tonight is about business—"

"You promised not to work during the grace period!" Gisela snaps at Conrad.

His lips draw back in a snarl, but I cut him off before he can lose his temper. "*Right now,* I need him working."

"Working on what?" Rosa asks.

"Nothing you need to worry about."

"Amory—"

"Just trust me!" I snap.

Rosa swallows but doesn't speak. I won't allow myself to feel guilty about yelling. Amana is putting her life on the line every time she speaks to someone tonight. Conny and I are working hard to catch this mole. I will not let our plans get derailed because our wives can't handle the mafia life they were born into.

I take a slow breath and try to ignore the slender figure I see from the corner of my eye. It's Eliana, making her way over to us. There's a lot more I want to say to the women, but I don't have time to explain.

Instead, I grunt, "Just behave tonight. I don't care what happens—remember that you are our wives and *behave*. Got it?"

Both of them nod in silence.

I avoid Rosa's gaze as a shadow darkens my view. "I wasn't sure you would show up tonight," a sultry voice says beside me.

I know Eliana is smiling before I lift my eyes to greet her, but I'm still not prepared for the seductive grin that stops my heart. There is a reason she's the only woman alive besides my own wife that I've slept with more than once. Our arrangement had been convenient—good sex for good information—but I won't lie and say it was all business. I'd enjoyed my time with Eliana. And I'm reminded of every second we spent together when she puckers her lips and arches her back the slightest bit.

Her breasts lift with her movement, and I struggle to keep my eyes locked on hers. Eliana is a seductress—a *woman*—and she knows how to work every part of her body. But Rosa is standing right here, and she knows how to work every part of *me*.

As Eliana steps forward, my wife leans closer to me, running a dainty hand up my chest to straighten my tie. She lays her head on my shoulder and folds her other arm around my waist, almost hugging me. Like a kitten, Rosa cuddles up to me and I have to fight the urge to wrap my arms around her right there in the middle of the Ball.

I've always thought of Rosa as young and naïve—even childish at times. But in this moment, with her possessively laying claim to me, I realize how much of a woman she has become. It doesn't take much to look sexy in a short dress. It doesn't take much to have a string of lust-filled nights. But it takes more than makeup and sex to set a pair of shackles over my heart the way Rosa has.

It takes a split second for Eliana to grasp what's happening. She wisely stops her forward momentum and shifts her weight from one foot to the other, catlike eyes glancing between us. "It's nice to see you and your wife."

I nod. "And you."

Conrad breaks the tension as he extends his hand. "Conrad Jäger. And my wife, Gisela Jäger."

Eliana takes his hand and then Glizzy's. She doesn't incline her head; she's Emilio Moreno's oldest daughter and she runs a sector in Queens all by herself. Although she is unmarried, she still outranks Conrad and his wife. And she reminds them of that as she glares at Gisela until the German woman inclines her own head. The tips of Conrad's ears burn red in anger, but he doesn't get the chance to lash out because Mikhail Volkov and Emilio Moreno both stroll over and stand beside Eliana.

Volkov's smile is demonic, but I'm not bothered by it. I'm too distracted by the possessive arm he slides around Eliana's waist, and the way he pulls her closer to him. My eyes dart to his hand—last I'd heard, Volkov was a married man, the presence of his wedding band is evidence that's still the case. But the absence of a ring on Eliana's finger can mean only one thing.

She's his mistress.

My heart nearly stops at the realization. I knew Emilio would go to Volkov to join forces after I dumped his daughter. I knew Volkov would likely demand one of his daughters in marriage to solidify the alliance. But I'd always guessed one of his daughters would marry Volkov's only son. I never imagined Mikhail would take Eliana for himself.

It's a dirty deal. One that turns a high-ranking mafia princess into a whore. But Emilio accepted the deal regardless. From the dejected look on his face, I assume he had no other choice. But I don't have time to figure out the details of their new arrangement. And honestly, I don't care. All that matters is the shameful look on Eliana's face as she stares at her shoes and waits for Volkov to speak.

"Jägermeister," he says, "my condolences." There is no tension in his voice, and I realize he's being sincere, if only for this moment. Volkov is a snake, but he at least respected my father as a boss. The same way he'd respected don Giovanni when he was still alive. It was his death that prompted Volkov to seek vengeance against Junior on his behalf.

Even though he is the man responsible for murdering my father, I find the strength to nod, and then I offer a nod to Emilio who still hasn't looked me in the eye. I want to kill Volkov with my bare hands. But I can't make a move on him here any more than he can make a move on me. Still … I thought it would be easier to face him. I thought I'd be strong enough to look him in the eye and handle business the way a Jägermeister should. The way my father would have.

I feel Rosa lean into me and the warmth of her nearness calms me. I hadn't realized my hands were balled into fists. I hadn't noticed how tightly my jaw was clenched. Just to keep myself from sucker punching Volkov in his mouth, I wrap an arm around my wife's waist and lean down to smell her hair. I don't care that I look like a punk in front of two mafia bosses. Right now, this is all I can do to keep myself from killing two men in a crowd of innocent people.

When I lift my gaze, I find Volkov's eyes on me, watching the exchange I'm having with my wife. He smiles and plants his grey eyes on Rosa. I know he's thinking of the crude tapes he had of us together in bed. The fact that he's seen my wife naked makes my hand twitch—I want to reach for the gun I have tucked into my waistband. But I just hold Rosa closer and exhale slowly. Trying to keep calm.

"You're here without your wife," I say to Volkov.

He opens his mouth to reply, but his words never leave his throat. The next second, Amana pushes through the crowd and takes her place beside me. The timing couldn't be any worse— or better.

Rosa goes rigid but Mikhail steps back and stares at the beautiful woman. His eyes remain on her longer than I'm comfortable with. I see the moment recognition sets in; his eyes narrow on her neck, where her collar used to be, and he sucks in a little gasp. When he speaks again, his voice is little more than a growl.

"You are here with your wife, Jäger." He smirks. "And a special guest."

Amana extends a hand. "Nice to see you again."

He takes her hand and kisses it; his words are a murmur against her skin. "I knew you looked familiar, my little kitten."

Amana boldly holds his gaze as he straightens. "I'm not your kitten anymore."

"No. You're not."

For a moment, I fear my plans may backfire. Amana isn't being the vixen she was at the bar, flirting with Spaniards and seducing secrets from unsuspecting men. Her face is hard, and her shoulders are squared.

Her words ring in my ears. *I have my own agenda.*

She could have rejoined me at any given moment, but she'd waited until Volkov showed up. She wanted to see him. Wanted to look him in the eye and let him know he doesn't own her anymore. I understand her desire, I really do, but she's putting everything at risk right now. She's placing her agenda above my own and it makes me burn with anger. *If she blows her cover, I will wring her neck*, I promise myself.

Volkov glances over at me, a sly smile tugging at his lips. "Mighty bold of you to take my own whore for yourself and bring her to this party."

Amana stiffens but doesn't speak. Her hand is still clutched in his paw, but she doesn't try to pull away. In fact, when he nods his head at the bar and leans into her, she offers him a flirtatious smile.

"Why don't we catch up?" Volkov suggests. "Let me get you a drink."

Eliana glares at both of them as they leave. She's been dumped for a prostitute. The embarrassment can't get any worse.

As if to remove himself from the situation, Emilio steps to the side and motions toward the bar. He leaves without a goodbye, too ashamed to even look us in the eye. The silence left behind is heavy and awkward, but I don't bother to fill it. I'm enjoying watching Eliana squirm far too much.

Conrad pats my shoulder. "Gisela and I are going to find our seats. They should be serving dinner soon."

I nod, and then lean down to kiss Rosa's cheek. "Go with them."

She eyes me a moment but complies with a nod before she steps away.

When she's gone, Eliana glares at me. "She's pretty."

"I know."

"So is your mistress."

"I know."

"I don't understand."

"It isn't your place to."

She huffs. "I remember when you used to tell me everything."

I laugh. "I never told you everything, Eliana."

"You told me what I needed."

"And nothing more."

"Are you really sleeping with that young girl?"

"She's eighteen."

"You didn't answer my question."

"I'm not going to."

Eliana takes a step closer. "Aren't you going to ask about me and the Wolf?"

66

"I don't care about Wolves."

She smirks and reaches out to tug on my tie. I let her pull me closer, leaning into her personal space so she can whisper against the line of my jaw, "No. You only care about rats."

My heart skips a beat, and I slowly tilt my head down to look her in the eye. "What do you know about rats?"

Her grin is sinful. "More than you think."

"Eliana—"

"There are perks to being Volkov's plaything."

My eyes fill with hatred—for her or Volkov, I'm not sure. "Are the perks worth the shame?"

She hesitates and I see a matching flicker of hatred in her own eyes. "If you want to kill your rat, meet me at the spot where you first kissed me."

It could be a trap. It could be bait just to get me alone to kill or kidnap me. But as I watch Eliana walk away and I remember the hatred she exuded; I don't make room in my heart for doubt. Eliana is a lot of things, but she's never been a liar. She spilled secrets about her own mafia during pillow talk, but she was never dishonest with me. None of the information she gave me ever backfired or misled me. I'd trusted Eliana throughout our entire relationship.

I still trust her now. I'm just not sure the trust I have is enough for me to take her up on her offer. I want to catch this rat, but am I willing to place my life in the hands of my scorned lover?

Six

When Amory sends me off with Conrad and Gisela, I excuse myself and run to the bathroom. I don't have to use it; I just need a moment alone.

My hand grips the sink as I take deep breaths, trying to calm my racing heart. I don't know if I'm angry, upset, or humiliated—maybe all three. I've tried to be stronger, to understand that this is the mafia. That neither my life, and especially not my marriage, would ever be normal or ordinary. But I hadn't expected to ever encounter anything like this. To have to endure the shame of standing beside my husband while some nameless woman clutches his arm—and then shake hands with his ex-lover.

It's almost too much.

"What is going on?" I ask myself as I straighten and stare into the mirror.

My makeup is still perfect, my lashes are dark and long, my hair is braided into an elaborate bun that leaves tendrils loose to brush against my bare shoulders. My white dress looks creamy against my brown skin, and my silver crucifix shines in the fluorescent lighting. I am beautiful, but I know that isn't the reason anyone's been staring at me this evening.

They've been staring because I'm the wife of the Jägermeister, and he's arrived with a second woman on his arm.

This goes beyond my expectations. This pushes the boundaries of even Christina's sound advice. *Be the wife he needs you to be...*

What about the husband I need him to be?

Am I expected to stand here and say nothing while my marriage falls apart? Should I have greeted Eliana with a smile? Should I pretend there's nothing going on with Amory and the beautiful young woman he's brought here tonight?

I am tired of setting aside my morals and dignity for his sake. I need my husband to start making sacrifices for *me*.

She's only working with him, I remind myself. That's the excuse Amory gave me when he explained that another woman would be joining us at the Ball. I had raised my eyebrow and given him a look that let him know I knew there was more to it than what he was telling me, but that was as far as our conversation had gone.

If I had known the woman he was 'working' with was sexy and gorgeous and would stick by his side like his lover, I would have spoken up. If I had known her 'work' would involve strutting around the Ball on my husband's arm, I would have stood up for myself. And if I had known I'd have to endure all this with Eliana Moreno thrown into the mix, I certainly wouldn't have held my tongue. But it's too late now. As much as I want to pull Amory aside and spew curses at him, I know that will hurt more than help.

It isn't an easy decision to make, but I grind my teeth together and tell myself to calm down. Behave for now, handle business later.

I clutch the Cross dangling around my neck. *Jesus, I need Your strength. Amory needs Your strength to do the right thing—by You and by me.*

When I gather myself enough to leave the bathroom, I am pulled to a sudden halt as I round the corner of the lavatory lounge and find Eliana Moreno standing in the walkway. My first instinct is to shove her aside, but I don't want to make a scene. Instead, I offer her a tight smile and try to walk past.

She steps right in front of me and places a hand on her hip. "Rosa De Luca."

"It's Rosa *Jäger*," I correct her sharply. "And Mr. Jäger is waiting for me. So step aside."

She gives me a simpering grin. "Let him wait. He's got that beautiful prostitute to keep him company."

I squint at her. *Prostitute?* Volkov had called her his *kitten* and had even used another vulgar name to describe her. But neither the woman nor Amory had reacted to the word, I'd assumed he was just being cruel. Then again, Amory did recently rescue a few dozen women who'd been working in Russian brothels over in Staten Island.

But still...

"She isn't a prostitute," I tell Eliana.

This only makes her grin stretch further as she openly laughs at me. "Why do you think she's here on your husband's arm if she isn't an escort?"

I stare at the floor, clutching my small purse so tightly my hands begin to shake. A warmth on my shoulder startles me, and I look up to find Eliana with an incredulous expression on her face.

"You cannot be this naïve."

"She's working for him," I say pathetically.

"Yes, the same way she worked for Volkov." Eliana sighs. "The way I see it, it's a plus. Now you don't have to deal with your lying husband, and I don't have to deal with that creepy old man. They'll both be busy with her."

I don't speak. I can't get my mouth to form any words because I don't want Eliana to hear my voice wobble. When I swallow, my throat feels like sandpaper, my tongue nothing more than a Brillo pad in my mouth.

She's lying, I tell myself.

She has to be. Because Amory and I have finally gotten back on good terms. We've finally started to get over the last bump in our marriage. Neither of us had been sure if we would ever recover from the secret he kept about my father's death. We had avoided each other and maintained the bare minimum of communication—a text message here, a call there. Staying in the safehouse made the distance bearable, but it didn't numb the pain. Not until I stood beside Amy in that hospital room and realized just how badly he was hurting. It was enough for me to set aside my own suffering if it meant I could help him get through his.

Even after he'd used my body without any care. Even after he'd ghosted me again. I had remained with a thread of hope in my heart that things would somehow work itself out. That God would stitch our marriage back together.

And suddenly, inexplicably, I was in his arms again. We had made love like it was our wedding night all over again. It had been so overwhelming, I thought I'd lost my very soul to his hypnotic gaze.

We were on the path to repair. We were starting over. And now this...

I shake my head.

Eliana tsks me. "You really do believe every word he says, don't you?"

"You're just jealous."

"Do you have any idea how many women he's had? How many he's used just like me?"

I take a step back, but she comes closer. I can smell her expensive perfume. It's creamy and rich, like vanilla and wildflower.

"I'm from the Spanish mafia," she says in her sultry accent, "imagine how many German women he left brokenhearted before he got bored and came to Queens."

"I'm not entertaining this," I snap, trying to step around her again, but her hand whips out and she blocks the entryway with her slender arm.

"Amory's cousin—the dead one."

Morgen? I don't say his name aloud, but Eliana sees the confusion on my face and explains, "He left a fiancé behind. Silke Bieker."

"Amory has never touched her."

She's still just a teenager, for God's sake. I *know* he would never try anything with her.

Eliana smiles. "She has two beautiful sisters."

I think of Edeltraud with her fiery red hair and Aloisia with her gentle eyes and adorable dimples. I won't let myself wonder which one of them Amory slept with. I refuse to let the thoughts into my head, but Eliana tells me without me even asking.

"He had them both."

My jaw drops open, but I quickly snap it shut. None of this even matters. Eliana just wants to hurt me. I don't believe a word she's said, but even if she is telling the truth, I will never give her the satisfaction of knowing how much her words have affected me. How much her very presence makes me want to scream.

"I don't care about Amory's past."

Eliana's eyes narrow. "What about his present?"

"He isn't sleeping with that woman."

She starts to laugh, but my words cut her off.

"And even if he is—I know for a fact he *isn't* sleeping with you. And he never will be again."

Her laughter becomes a snarl. "Careful—"

"I'm not afraid of you, Eliana." I straighten my back. "So if you're not going to do something, then step aside, because I'm done talking."

She takes a long look at me, her jaw clenching and unclenching as she glares. But just when I expect her to lash out or start screaming like a child, she gives me a nod and steps aside.

"Enjoy your dinner, Mistress."

I only nod in return.

Amory is waiting by the bar when I exit the bathroom, I make a beeline over to him but almost trip over my own feet when I realize he's standing with Volkov and that woman. I want to change direction and head to the table where Gisela and Conrad are waiting, but just as the thought blooms in my head, Amy looks up and our eyes meet.

Maybe it's because he suddenly looks away and shifts closer to that woman, or maybe it's because I can see Volkov smirking from the corner of my eye, but all of my anxiety melts away in an instant. It's replaced by a slow-burning anger that threatens to boil inside me as I approach the bar.

Eliana is a liar, I tell myself, *but Amory has given her fuel.* Bringing this woman here to shame and embarrass me. Relaxing with her at the bar like they're a couple, while I'm supposed to just go have dinner and mind my business. My husband *is* my business.

"Rosa," Amory steps forward and gives me a quick hug. He shifts me in his arms so I'm facing the dining room. "I thought I told you to go with Gisela and Conrad?"

"I'd like to be with you," I say sweetly.

His gaze seems to harden, but Volkov is speaking before any words can leave his mouth. "How could you send such a pretty woman away?" He chuckles, casting a very lewd glance at the escort. "Then again, you do have another woman waiting for you. And she's just as beautiful as your wife."

I hadn't noticed the similarities, but Volkov is right. Amory's *special guest* looks like me, as if she is my distant cousin. Where my hair is dark and curly, hers is loose and wavy, where my skin is the color of brown sugar, hers is golden and radiant. And instead of wearing a crucifix around her neck, I see the fading bruise of what I can only guess had been a collar like the ones worn by the other women Amory rescued.

I tear my eyes away from the woman as Volkov teases, "I was convinced you loved the Rose of Manhattan enough to be faithful."

Before I know it, I step forward and get right into Volkov's face. "You know *nothing* about our marriage."

Amory grabs me by the elbow and yanks me back. "My wife is tired—"

"No, I'm *not*." I twist away and give him a hard glare.

By the stony look on his face, I know Amory is about to snap, but I'm beyond caring right now. From this nameless woman to Eliana to Volkov—my marriage has been mocked by a string of people tonight. I can't take it anymore.

"The only thing I'm *tired* of is secrets," I tell Amory.

Volkov raises an eyebrow. "Perhaps you are in the wrong business, my love. The mafia is built on secrets."

My eyes are blazing when I turn to him. "And *honor*. Something you seem to know nothing about."

Very slowly, Volkov stands and steps toward me. This close, I realize how tall he is. But he's also thin and reedy and sprouting grey hairs wherever possible.

I'm not afraid, I tell myself, though my hands tremble as I grip my purse.

"Careful, little flower. You're cute when you're angry, but you're getting close to pissing me off."

I spit on the floor. "How's that for pissing you off?"

The gesture is the ultimate sign of disrespect. I've seen men spit at my father's feet and have their tongues removed. But I'm a mafia princess—a queen now—and we're on safe territory tonight.

Still …

My actions are so bold, I actually steel myself to be slapped down.

Instead, Volkov slowly peels his eyes from the glob of saliva on the carpet to stare at Amory. "The Rose has thorns."

Amory places himself between me and the Wolf. "I take responsibility for her actions."

"I have every right to demand her tongue."

"She's still my *wife*." Amory's voice is dark and threatening.

Volkov matches his glare, meeting him in this silent storm of rage. All I can do is stand there like an idiot, praying to God that I didn't just ignite a fire my husband can't put out.

Volkov looks like he wants to shoot both of us, but instead of exploding in anger, he tucks his hands into his pockets and jerks his head at my lookalike. "I will take her as payment for the insult." He smiles. "Her tongue will be far more useful than The Rose's anyway."

A muscle spasms in Amory's jaw, but he concedes with a single nod, offering no words as the woman stares at him in horror. The fearful look lasts only a moment, wiped away as Volkov snakes his arm around her waist and leads her away.

"Enjoy these last few days of our grace period, Jäger. Things will never be this peaceful again."

Without another word, the Wolf stalks off and doesn't look back. Amory stares into the crowd in the stiff silence that's left behind. I glance up at him, frightened by the tension on his face. He's still holding my elbow, his grip surprisingly gentle. I expect him to haul me away and start yelling about knowing my place, but he doesn't do that at all. He drops his hand from my arm and walks away, leaving me standing there in shock.

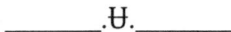

Amory and I don't speak throughout dinner. He makes great conversation with everyone else—even some nameless woman from one of the charities the Jäger Foundation has donated to. But he doesn't even make eye contact with me.

He doesn't have to.

I can feel the heat of his glare even when his eyes aren't on me. I can feel the burn of his anger even when he steps away to sign another check to some other charity. And I can sense how stressed he is when he finally touches me again, a hand on the small of my back, guiding me toward the exits after dessert, it's tense and rigid—like a plank of wood leading me around.

We smile for the cameras that wait for us outside the doors of the Met, but as soon as we're in the safety of the car, Amory's coldness returns. He slides to the other side of the backseats and pulls out his phone, scrolling messages while I stare in anxious silence.

I reach for him, just trying to get his attention, but before my hand can touch his sleeve, he snaps his head up and hisses, "Don't you *dare.*"

"Amy—"

"I don't want to hear it."

I retract my hand. "I didn't mean to—"

"I told you to behave. What part of that did you not understand?"

I get angry. "Volkov took your father and your uncle. And Morgen is dead because of him. How can you be angry that I insulted him?"

He puts his phone away. "Volkov killed my family, Rosa. But he might not have come for you—because you're a woman and you're innocent in all this." He shakes his head. "But now you've put a target on your back. He'll come for you for that insult. Just to make an example of you."

I swallow, not surprised to find my throat painfully dry. "I—B-But he took that woman as payment."

A dark laugh fills the car. "You think he'll let go of what you've done because I gave him some hooker for a night?"

"I'm sorry," I whisper.

"When will you learn your place?"

"Where *is* my place, Amory? One moment it's by your side, the next its locked in some safehouse. Then it's in your bed like I'm just some prostitute for you to use."

He glares at me. "Don't say that about yourself."

"It's how you make me feel."

Amory looks away. "I just need you to trust me."

"Give me a reason to." I sigh. "You don't have to tell me everything, but you need to tell me the truth."

The car is quiet for an uncomfortable amount of time. I settle into the seat and stare out the window.

"I'm not sleeping with Amana," Amory says softly. "We're just working together."

"Working how?"

He stares at me for a long moment. "I needed her to go home with Volkov tonight. But I can't tell you any more than that. For now."

"If that's what you needed, then I helped you. Right?"

"Volkov took her as payment. That's different. I don't know what to expect tonight..." He sighs and buries his face in his hands. "I don't know."

I could feel sorry for the obvious stress he's under, but I've shut myself off from sympathy for tonight. All I want right now is answers.

"What about Edeltraud and Aloisia?"

Amory's body visibly stiffens as he lifts his eyes to stare at me, a wrinkle of confusion forms on his forehead and then he sighs and slowly closes his eyes. "Eliana…"

"Did you sleep with them?"

When he doesn't answer, I lean away and wipe at my eyes. "Is there anyone else I should know about? Anyone that I'll have to see every day and know that she's slept with my husband?"

He grunts, but his voice comes out oddly calm. "I told you before, I stuck with hired women or ladies I picked up at bars. High-born mafia women were off the table unless I needed something from them."

Eliana's words ring in my ears. *Do you have any idea how many women he's had? How many he's used just like me?*

He isn't using me, I tell myself. He didn't even want to be in this marriage, not any more than I did. He's protecting me. Maybe not in the way I'd prefer, maybe not even in a good way at all, but he's doing what he thinks is best.

I shock myself by scooting closer to him—but he shocks *me* by grabbing me and pulling me into his lap. He hugs me, completely enveloping me in his strong arms. I can smell his masculine cologne as I inhale against him, it leaves me lightheaded and flustered.

"I just need you to trust me, Rosa. Even when it doesn't make sense." He lets out a shuddering breath. "And I need you to love me. Even though you have no reason to anymore."

I pull back and look up at him. "I'll always love you. No matter how many times you hurt me."

"Don't say that," he whispers. "I need you to love me. But I want you to be strong enough to hate me."

"Why?"

"Because loving men like me is dangerous."

"This is the mafia, I'm in danger with or without you."

He gazes at me, his grey eyes partially hidden by his thick lashes. The moonlight cast in from the window dances over his face as we ride, it shimmies and flickers with the buildings whipping by, distorting the darkness as it lights him up. I stare at Amory, finding my husband in the shadows.

He closes his eyes. "I'm so tired, Rosa."

"I know."

"This war … It's cost more than I wanted to give. More than I thought I'd have to give."

Uwe and Oberon and Morgen.

"It won't last forever."

"But it's lasted long enough." He opens his eyes and stares at me, lifting a hand to cup my chin. "I just need you to hold on a little longer. Trust me a little longer."

"Okay," I whisper against his lips.

When he kisses me, the exchange is slow; he gives me tentative, delicate pecks, like he isn't sure if it's okay to offer anything more. Then I deepen the exchange, and he groans, gripping me by the waist and moving us so I'm lying on the backseats.

His mouth is heavenly as it melts over mine, like his lips were made for the very purpose of kissing me. But just as I begin to drown in his desire, he pulls away. His face is unsure, the closest I've ever seen him to being shy.

"It's okay if you don't want to—right here, like this. But…" his voice trails off as he swallows. "I need this, Rosa. I can't wait until we get home."

I glance at the partition, which makes him chuckle. "Douglass knows his place," he murmurs against my neck. "He won't say anything."

"But—"

He covers my mouth with his own. I don't fight him. Honestly, I don't want to. I'm not afraid of Douglass looking back here to see us together as much as I'm afraid of him keeping his gaze forward and *hearing* us together. But Amory seems unconcerned and his raw confidence and burning need distracts me from my nerves.

I feel something tear, and I realize he's ripped my underwear. He doesn't even bother undressing either one of us—just unzips his pants and leans over me. I am pressed into the leather seats in the back of his car. I was right before; this really does feel like high school prom.

Petty drama at the dance. Raunchy sex in the backseat of a limo.

It doesn't have to be raunchy, I tell myself. We can burn away the lust and turn it into passion. We can make this more than just sex—we can make *love*.

I wrap my arms around Amory's neck and pull him close. "I love you, Amy."

He doesn't say it back, but I don't need him to. His love is spoken through his kisses, through his gentle caress, through the way he holds me like I'm the very thing keeping him together. His hand is pressed into the window, leaving a sweaty palmprint against the glass. His forehead is already dewy, evidence of his passion—how powerfully it burns between us. As the flames intensify, he sucks in a gasp and groans into my ear. It sounds more like a whimper, and I suddenly realize just how badly he needs this. Just how much he needs *me*.

Amory still doesn't understand love the way I do. He buries his passion in our lust and takes his pleasure in our desire. Our marriage is built on desperate emotions and burning need. I am his stress-reliever as much as I am his support and his voice of reason. For me, that Person is God.

Christ is my foundation, He is my joy and pleasure, He is the One who guides me with His Voice of reason that is the Holy Ghost. He is the One I can bury my troubles in, the One who can take my stress away.

But for someone like my husband, someone who doesn't know God … I am all he has. I am the only one who can give him endless love—even though he doesn't deserve it. I am the only one who can take his pain and offer some semblance of pleasure, if not at least a distraction. I am the one he goes to when he is stressed and when he seeks relief.

One day, I hope that rock will be God. I hope he can lean on Jesus to take his pain away. I hope he can find pleasure—pure joy—in his time spent with the Lord, not in his fleeting encounters with me. My words and emotions will only go so far.

I can reassure my husband. I can support my husband. I can make love to my husband. But I can't change his Spirit. Only God can touch his soul. Only the Lord can truly change his heart. But for now… This is all we've got. This is all I can give. But I will give it to the fullest.

I pray to God it makes a difference.

Seven

Rosa's late. I'm not too worried since she's on birth control, but no matter what the results are, this is a stark reminder that I need to be careful. I haven't used protection since she started on the pill. I don't want to use it with her—she's my wife, I hate the thought of something between us, preventing me from feeling every part of her. But I'm not ready to bring a child into this world. Not with a war going on. Not with Volkov determined to send my very soul to hell.

I wait with my arms folded over my chest as she takes the test. She wanted to do it alone, but I promised her I'd be right here when she finished. If she's pregnant, I wonder what night it happened. An immature part of me hopes it was the evening in the back of the car, but that was only two days ago. Rosa says she's a week late and she isn't sure if last month was just spotting or a light flow.

An exasperated sigh blows from my lips as I dig my nails into my arm. I have no idea what I'm doing. I can't be a father.

I wasn't even a very good son and so far, I'm screwing up being a good husband.

The bathroom door opens, and Rosa stands there in one of my t-shirts. She's holding a little pink test in a wad of tissue, her hands are trembling but her lips are pulled into a smile. I'm not sure what to make of her expression.

Excitement because she's going to be a mother? Or relief because she isn't?

"What does it say?" I ask in a surprisingly shaky voice.

She presses her lips together. "It's negative."

I know it's rude, but I crack a smile and whisper, "Thank God." I extend my hand. "Let me see it. I want to make sure."

"I followed the instructions. But I'll take another one if you want me to."

"No. I believe you. I'm just..."

She touches my arm. "I know."

"We have to be careful," I say softly. "Now is not the time to start a family."

Rosa looks away. We promised not to have children until we're both ready, but I feel like a small part of her is disappointed in the results. I wait for her to confess this, but she just bites her lip and takes the test back to toss it in the trash.

"You're the one who'll have to make a change."

I groan. "I hate condoms."

"What are you, fifteen?"

"Rosa," I glower, "this is something you'll never understand."

"And pregnancy is something you'll never understand."

Touché.

As she walks down the hall toward our bedroom, I hug her from behind and kiss her neck. "So, what's the deal? Why are you so late?"

She stops walking and cranes her neck to look up at me. The expression on her face makes me pause—her brows are flat, and her mouth is downturned, but she doesn't look angry. She looks sad.

"Probably stress."

I sigh and unwrap my arms from her small figure. "I'm sorry."

"Please don't apologize," she whispers. My heart skips at the tremble in her voice. "I'm the one who's been causing all the stress lately. Especially at the Ball."

I can't pretend she's wrong. Rosa spat at the feet of Mikhail Volkov, in a crowded room, during a grace period. Part of me had been proud of the balls she'd grown, but the other part had withered and died of shame and outrage. If I were any other man, I would have taken the strap to her rear in the backseat of that car. Instead, I'd buried my frustrations in a much healthier way—a way that'd been a benefit to us both.

I have no idea what to do anymore. Rosa is my stress and my relief. My problem and solution. I miss the days where my only issue was getting her to accept me as her husband. Now, she loves me without shame—and it is that overwhelming love that has brought me this trouble. Maybe bringing Amana along had been too much for her to handle, combined with Eliana's presence and Volkov's taunting.

No matter the case, the damage is done.

"Don't worry about what happened at the Ball anymore," I say in a serious voice. "I'll deal with it."

"What about that woman? The one Volkov took with him?"

The Wolf decided to take my escort home with him as payment for Rosa's disrespect. It had seemed like a nightmare on the surface, but that'd been the plan all along. I'd been hoping Amana could flirt her way into his arms and my hopes had begun to dwindle when I realized he'd arrived with Eliana. And then Rosa had her outburst and set things back on track.

It sucks that she's got a target on her back now, but that's nothing new. Volkov had already decided he wouldn't hold back after I killed Yuri right in front of him. Rosa might have made him more determined to get to her, but there had always been a target on her head.

I sigh. "Amana will be fine."

"How do you know?"

"I saw her last night."

I'd sent a team of men to pick her up from Volkov's house the morning after the Ball. She stumbled into The Club wearing nothing but a man's button-down shirt and a cheap blonde wig. My anger had boiled at the sight of her, but she'd insisted she was fine and that there was nothing to worry about. After Conny's doctor examined her and determined that she was, in fact, perfectly fine—if not just a little sore—I calmed down a little.

"She's doing okay," I say to Rosa.

Actually, she's more than okay. Her time with Volkov had been exhausting but productive. He didn't give her a name, but after a few drinks, he'd bragged about having a mole in our ranks and had promised to tell her all about him if she agreed to stay by his side.

"The Hunters are the prey now," he'd told her. "They *will* fall when the grace period ends. Get out while you can."

Amana told him she would think about it. I wish she would have stayed just to get the name, but she wouldn't have had a way to get the information back to me. And I can't blame her for scurrying away at the first possible opportunity. Volkov had held her captive for four years before Conrad took her in, I'm surprised she was brave enough to leave the Met with him in the first place.

I was prepared to ask Amana to return to Volkov—I know that makes me a monster, but I need that name and I'm willing to sell out a hooker to do it. Mercifully, she had other plans in mind. Volkov had taken her for the night, but when he'd gotten tired of her, he'd passed her off to his companions. She's only eighteen. She doesn't want to have anything to do with prostitution or mafia life anymore. But she's good at what she does.

Amana made quick friends with the men Volkov introduced her to. They liked her so much, she set up a private session with them for this evening.

I don't like it at all. One woman with four men is not going to be enjoyable for her in the least bit, especially when the men are Russian Wolves who only want her because she got away. But I don't allow myself to think of the repercussions. My mind only has room for the goal—the name. If I focus on anything else, I'll lose myself in the guilt and grief.

Rosa hugs me to get my attention. I blink down at her and pet her head, which makes her frown.

"I'm not a dog."

"You're a rose."

"You don't pet roses."

I smile and scoop her into my arms. "What do you do with roses?"

Rosa laughs as I kiss her. "Put me down!" she says, but I know she doesn't mean it, so I carry her to our room and close the door behind me. I'll put her down, but it'll be on our bed, and I'll be right there with her the entire time.

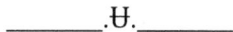

My phone rings in the middle of the night, I almost fall out of bed trying to grab it from the bedside table. Rosa groans beside me so I slip out the door and take the call in the hallway.

It's Conrad, and he only says one thing before he quickly hangs up. "Get to The Club."

I don't waste any time. It's the second day after our grace period ended, I'm honestly surprised something didn't go up in flames at sunrise on the first day. Well ... something did go up in flames, but it wasn't in Brooklyn.

When I sent a team into Staten Island to retrieve Amana, I gave them a second task. Plant explosives along the docks. The ferries are useless to us since we aren't travelling between boroughs very much anymore. But the Island uses their boats to send and retrieve all their shipments—boatloads of the Moreno's cocaine and hundreds of kidnapped women from outside the city.

It was a dirty trick. Planting bombs during the grace period, but Volkov had played dirty first. He'd killed my father during the treaty he'd initiated. He couldn't possibly believe I'd keep my word after that. Allowing him to have Amana for a night only worked in our favor, not only was she able to gather intel and set up another meeting, but we were given an excuse to be on the Island without raising any eyebrows.

Now, the Wolves have retaliated.

I hear the sirens before I see the smoke, and I see the smoke before I find The Club. Well, what's left of it. Most of the building is nothing more than charred bricks, but the parts that remain standing are recognizable enough for me to make out the lounge and a couple leather booths still intact, though partially melted. The front wall has been totally destroyed, but I'm not sure if it's because of an explosion or just a very intense fire. I suppose it doesn't matter.

There's a group of men out front; cops, firefighters, and soldiers from the Stronghold, the Garden, and the Hunting

Grounds. Niccolò Romano greets me when I step from my car, his face is grim, but he tries to smile.

"Jägermeister…"

"Where's Conrad?" I ask quickly.

He nods toward the west side of the building, and I spot him standing in the rubble. "Get rid of the cops and round everyone up. Tell them to meet at warehouse fifty-five."

Niccolò turns away and starts yelling at the men nearby. He's the underboss of the Italian mafia, he could be the mole, but right now I trust him to at least get the men together. I don't really have a choice, anyway.

Conrad doesn't look up when I approach. His face is vacant, his eyes are two holes in his head, his mouth is just a hard-pressed line buried in his beard.

"Conny," I say gently.

He stirs, but still doesn't look up from the debris. When I step closer, I realize he's staring down at a body covered by a bloody sheet.

"They left her on the sidewalk. So she wouldn't be lost in the explosion." Conrad finally looks up and I see remorse and anger both fighting for dominance of his features. "They wanted us to find her body."

"Whose?" I already know the answer, but I'm not ready to accept it yet. I need another minute—another second—to process what's happened. "Whose body?" I whisper, staring at the stained covering.

Conrad kneels and pulls the sheet aside.

Amana's face is bloody, but most of it is gathered around her mouth and neck. I don't have to look twice to know how she died.

"They slit her throat and cut out her tongue," Conrad says in a surprisingly calm tone. "A snitch's death."

For a moment, I just stare at her. At her dead eyes, rolled to the back of her head, at her mouth ripped open and the bloody gap inside, at her throat with blood crusted around the laceration that took her life. I had known the risks when I'd asked her to work for me. But looking down at her dead body is an entirely different experience.

It's almost surreal. And I wish I could somehow rewind time and change my mind. But it's too late. Amana is gone. Because of me. She died for me. For a mole who's name I still don't know. But now the Wolves know I've been looking and Conrad's the one paying the price.

"How did her cover get blown?" Conny asks through gritted teeth.

I finally look away from her body. "I don't know. Anything could have happened. They could have suspected her from the start and invited her back just to torture and kill her."

He curses in German. "They keep killing our people."

"We've hurt them too—"

"But not like this!" Conrad covers her up again and then stands to look me in the eye. "We've taken buildings and boats. We've rescued some hookers. But when will we draw blood, Amory? You promised they would *bleed.*"

I shove him back a step. "*Think*, Conny. Those brothels were the heart of their borough, their ferries were their veins. They have lost every source of income they had. Just because we haven't taken someone important doesn't mean they aren't bleeding."

"It doesn't feel like they're bleeding," he mutters, glancing away in shame. He knows I'm right but he's too stubborn to admit it right now.

"They have taken people from us. They have made us grieve. But we have cut them at their roots. We're *winning* the war, Conrad. Don't be blinded by your emotions."

He stares at the debris piled around us. I don't bother filling the silence; I need the quiet. I need to think. Because I understand where Conny is coming from. The death of my father and uncle were only two people, but they were very important people. Losing them almost broke me, in my mind and my heart. But I turned my searing pain into burning rage and used that to strike them where I knew it would hurt just as badly.

I will never get my father back, but they won't recover from their wounds anytime soon either. Still ... with all the pain they've caused, I have to wonder if maybe their methods are more effective than I'm willing to give them credit for. Conrad is unraveling. The men were spooked from hearing about Stonehall's explosion. And now there is distrust spreading with The Club going down.

The men aren't ready to hear about the Wolves losing boats and strip clubs. They want to hear about vengeance.

They want to see the streets run red with Russian blood. I have to fight this battle differently, but I can't fight with a rat running loose. It was hard enough to get the explosions to the ferries. But I made sure I sent in only German men—and even then, I told them about the mission right before they left. They had no idea I'd been planning another attack until I pulled them aside five minutes before they drove off. But I can't plan every mission that way. I can't depend on spur-of-the-moment tactics.

I look over at Conrad. "Take your vengeance," I say firmly.

He blinks at me. "What do you mean?"

"You want blood? Go get it. I'm placing you in charge of the offensive teams for Staten Island."

His eyes go wide. "Jägermeister..."

"While you're fighting the Wolves, I'm going to focus on the rat."

Understanding calms his features and he gives me a slow nod. "How are we playing this?"

"I need to know the names of every client Amana ever saw."

"My computers were all destroyed in the fire, I have a backup drive at home, but they won't include the men she was seeing tonight."

"That's fine. Can you get the list to me tonight?"

"I can have Morgen send it over. He's out of town, but it's all online. He'll be able to gather the information and send it over."

Morgen's been in hiding since I staged his death a little while ago. It's supposed to keep him safe, but I feel like his presence might be needed right now. Not because we need his skills as our resident hacker, but to boost the morale of the men. They need encouragement as much as they need blood. Seeing Morgen alive may be enough to placate them while I work on drawing out the rat.

"Tell him to deliver the list in person," I order.

Conrad gasps. "You're bringing him back in? The Wolves will come after him as soon as word gets out that he's alive."

"They're already coming for us all. Might as well rub it in their faces that they failed at least once."

He strokes his dark beard. "I'll contact him right away."

"How soon can he get back to New York?"

"A few hours. By morning at the latest."

"Tell him to pick up Wolfgang along the way."

Conrad coughs like he's choking on his spit. I understand his shock. Wolf has been in hiding for what seems like ever. He was holed up at Stonehall until the mole betrayed us and had the gates blown off. Since our father's death, he's been in his own safehouse receiving treatment for his injuries. He spent a few days in a coma, but he's better now. Sore and suffering nightmares and covered in burns, but he's better.

"You want to bring Wolf into this?" Conrad asks incredulously. "He's the reason all this is happening."

"Exactly. It's time he takes responsibility for his screwups. Let him fight. We need his brutality anyway."

Conrad can't disagree with me. If there is anyone he can trust to shut off his emotions right now, it's my little brother. He's still recovering from the explosion, but right now, it isn't important if he holds a gun. He just needs to be present. He needs to see what he's done and show his face to the men who've been fighting because of him.

More than anything, I need to make Volkov angry. Having Wolf on the streets again will piss him off. And pissed off men make mistakes. He won't pass up an opportunity to come for my brother, and I'll be waiting when he does.

Eight

When I see my brother, he takes one look at me and drops his gaze to my hand. His eyes focus on the signet ring weighing down my right middle finger. It's ugly. Gaudy. Pure silver with a massive amethyst stone set in the center. Our father had worn it with pride—he actually thought it looked pretty. I hate the thing, but I can't pretend it's insignificant. I can't pretend it holds no power.

"*Bruder*," I say softly.

We're in a warehouse on the outskirts of Brooklyn, it's just before sunrise but it feels more like midnight. I never went back to sleep the night before. Conrad and I spent the next few hours planning and prepping the next phase of our war with the Russians. I want everything to be ready. I want all our angles covered.

In the dim morning light, Wolf looks young and boyish—like the brother I remember as a kid. Six years younger than me with dirt-stained cheeks and long lashes that fluttered when he blinked. I remember his hair before he shaved it, wild and red—rare for a German—which got him picked on quite a bit. All the teasing stopped when he was old enough to jam his fist into the faces of his bullies. One time, he hit Eike so hard he broke his nose and shattered his jawbone.

He'd been ten years old at the time. I was sixteen and more than impressed.

"Someone needs to teach that kid how to fight," Conny had laughed.

I'd flicked my cigarette to the ground and nodded, blowing smoke between my lips as I said, "I'll teach him."

Wolf's been fighting ever since.

"I need you," I tell him as I step closer.

Wolfgang watches me almost cautiously. He's always been an excellent fighter, but in all his years in the mafia, I've been the only one to ever beat him.

I was part of his initiation. Snatched him out the bed when he was fifteen and tried to kill him the same way my own uncle had tried to kill me.

I can see fear flickering in his eyes, like he isn't sure if I'm serious. Like he doesn't trust me. He shouldn't. I will die before I let Volkov touch my brother, but I have no problem putting a bullet in his head myself. He's a weed. A scar. But he's my brother, and right now he's all I have.

"You are reckless," I tell him in German. It's his uncontrollable anger that's got us here now. He takes pride in his antics, earning himself a reputation for being wild. He isn't

99

a wolf at all, he's a mad dog. And right now, I'm holding his leash.

"I need your recklessness," I say.

A smirk dances across his face. "It's yours, brother." He takes my hand and kisses the ring. "*Jägermeister.*"

"Get him cleaned up," I tell Conrad.

My cousin laughs and yanks the water hose from the stand on the wall. Wolfgang gasps before he's sprayed down. I ignore his cries as Conny deals with him; he is not gentle, wrestling him out of his clothes and kicking him when he's down. Conrad is just as crazy as Wolf, but that's what we need right now. Morgen is here too, watching with a grin as Wolf gets beaten like a child. He hasn't done anything wrong; Conny just wants to remind him who's in charge.

When he's finished, he shaves Wolf's scruffy head and cleans up his facial hair. His eyebrows are the only evidence of his fiery red locks. His lip is busted and there's a cut going through one of his eyebrows—it matches the scar going through my own. Morgen doesn't look much better; he wears a patch over his missing eye now. He lost it after I shot him in the face, shaving the sides of his head so he wears a mohawk to show off the wicked scar going across his face and head. The trail of the bullet. His ear is split, and he lost 30 percent of his hearing in it, but he's alive. That's all that matters.

"Are we ready?" I ask my brother and cousins.

They nod, watching me closely. Waiting for instructions. When I open my mouth to speak, movement by the door cuts me off. I turn to find Douglass waiting for me, his hands folded into his pockets.

I wave him over.

Conrad doesn't like it, but I don't care. The men in this room are the only ones I trust right now. I won't treat Douglass like a grunt—he is far from that now.

"We are all we have right now," I say solemnly.

Morgen lights a cigarette, blows the smoke at his brother. Wolf grins at Douglass, they slap each other up.

"Trust no one outside this room. Understand?"

They nod.

"Conrad will handle the Wolves. Wolf, you're working with him."

My brother smiles and fist bumps his older cousin.

"Douglass and I will focus on the mole. Morgen, you'll be in charge of intel for both teams. Got it?"

"Yes, sir."

"They burned The Club. They blew up a salon. They destroyed a law firm. They killed my father. They took Oberon."

Conrad and Morgen stare at the concrete as I speak, I can see Conny's jaw clenching. Losing Onkel impacted him the most.

"We will have our vengeance. But we must be careful. From now on, keep comms to a minimum unless we're in person. And keep your wives out of this."

Wolf snorts—he's unmarried—but Conrad looks guilty and Morgen just stiffens. I already know Conny tells Gisela everything, but that's got to change for now. The less she knows, the safer she'll be. Besides, with Conny's attitude lately, I doubt they've been talking much anyway. He's always been rough around the edges; I've noticed Gisela's bruises every now and then, but with the war, and losing Onkel, and now The Club, he's been stressed. It's not an excuse. It is what it is.

"You can see Silke this evening, Morgen."

He looks at me with shock written all over his face. I can't help but grin.

"She misses you. You'll have the evening to spend with her."

Conrad smacks the back of his head. "You won't be touching her."

He groans. "Can we move up the wedding?"

"Don't want to die a virgin?" Wolf teases.

Morgen glowers. "I promised her she'd be my first."

I raise my eyebrows, truly shocked. I had no idea Morgen was really a virgin. It's a rare thing for a man his age—especially in this organization. He's too kind for his own good.

"We'll have a ceremony tonight," I say, and before anyone can argue, I raise my hand and tell them, "Notify her family and tell them it's an order. They have my blessing as the Jägermeister, but Conrad will attend on my behalf."

"Why me?" he asks.

"I don't want all of us in one place anymore. Since you'll be her brother-in-law, it's better for you to go."

And I've also got plans tonight.

"Can I attend?" Wolf asks.

I nod. "As long as Maximilian goes with you."

"I don't need a babysitter anymore."

I roll my eyes as I walk away. "Yes, you do."

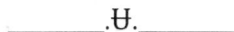

I wasn't lying when I said I have plans tonight. With my little cousin and my little brother both out of hiding now, I have the men I need to boost the morale of our gang and to deal with the Russians while I catch the mole. Part of catching the mole means digging through the intel Amana left behind.

It took me hours, but I finally started making connections through her list of clients. She was working her way through more men than I thought was possible. I won't question if she was actually sleeping with them, or just getting them drunk enough to talk. I don't want to know. But she was working hard, and it was paying off. Right up until the end.

The men on her client list goes through almost every mafia in New York, the only gang she never saw was the Morenos. There were plenty of Hunters, Stronghold soldiers, Gardeners, and even a few Wolves. From grunts to underbosses ... Amana was busy. But not all of her clients were dirty. She took notes on the ones she suspected, some of the names stood out when I'd first glanced at the info.

She was suspicious of Eike, Tyrese Willis, and Maximilian who visited her six times—four of them were in a row. I had no idea he'd ever had the time for hookers while he was on Wolf's security detail, but he'd found a way. If he hadn't ended up in the hospital, I would have immediately suspected him, but he'd almost died in that accident. I doubt he was willing to get himself killed just to get Wolfgang out of the way.

Conrad's name is on her client list. I grind my teeth together as I stare at the notes. I'm in my car with Douglass driving me to my next meeting, a printed copy of Amana's list is crumpled in my hand.

She didn't suspect him of being the mole, but he enjoyed her more than a few times a week. Why didn't she tell me? Why didn't he?

Until the Met Ball, Conny hadn't known she was working for me. He'd been having his fill right up until her death. That's probably one of the reasons he's been so angry at her death. He really liked Amana.

I wish she hadn't died, and I vow I'll get revenge for her. But for Gisela's sake, I'm glad she isn't here anymore. I'm glad Conrad can't use her anymore. And I'm glad she's finally found peace.

My hand slides into my pocket, it's a subconscious gesture but I gasp when my fingers brush against a small piece of plastic. When I pull it out, my eyes begin to burn with unshed tears.

It's the little pink gem Amana had stuck to her boob the last time I saw her working at The Club. She'd been bejeweled from head to toe, wearing nothing but a cluster of little gems gathered on her groin area and on her breasts to cover her most intimate parts. That was the day she'd told me about her dreams of going to college and studying art history. I'd recruited her to work the Met Ball, totally unaware of the fact that it would be the last work she ever did for me.

I clutch the gem in my hand, squeezing my fist so tightly that it cuts into my palm. They had stripped her naked, cut out her tongue, and slit her throat. Then they'd left her on the side of the road like she was nothing but trash.

Amana was a human being. An eighteen-year-old girl who'd had plans and dreams. I never even learned her last name, but I'd gotten to know part of her heart. Her blood is on my hands. I'd dragged her into this mess, and she'd paid for it with her life. The only thing I can offer now is the truth.

I'm going to do everything I can to learn the secret she died to find out. The name of the mole is on this list, I know it is. I just can't pinpoint which one. But I know someone who can.

Douglass pulls over to the side of the road. There's nothing here but highway and grass. He leans back in his chair and sighs. "I'll be here when you're done."

If you walk a mile heading east, you'll find an abandoned shop. Twenty years ago, it used to sell fresh fruit from the wilted strawberry bushes out back. The area around the shack has overgrown with grass and lilies that somehow survived the greyness of the dilapidated area. It isn't a place you go to for long strolls or Sunday picnics, but it's the place I first kissed Eliana Moreno.

We had been flirting for months before I got her to sneak off with me. She'd been shy at first, unsure of my intentions, unsure of how much of herself she could trust me with. I

105

respected her reservations; I was the German underboss and she was the Spanish princess. What we were doing was dangerous. But neither of us cared.

I made love to her in a field of lilies. There's still an old orange tree not far from the abandoned fruit shack; when the wind blows, you can pick up its citrusy fragrance. The air had smelled sweet that day, and the grass beneath us had been soft. She'd been a twenty-six-year-old virgin, and I'd stolen that from her.

When I close my eyes, I can remember every detail of that day as intimately as I remember the first night I spent with Rosa. She had been timid and beautiful and had given me more than I'd ever expected. I hadn't just taken Eliana's virginity that afternoon, I'd taken her heart too.

In my defense, I hadn't asked for it.

Eliana is leaning against the slanted shack when I step into the clearing. She's wearing a pale pink dress that hangs off her shoulders, her hair is loosely curled and falls to her waist in a curtain of chocolate. She smiles when she sees me, but the expression is full of relief, not joy. Like she hadn't expected me to come.

"Where does your father think you're at right now?" I ask her.

"With Volkov."

"And where does Volkov think you're at?"

"With you."

My eyebrows lower, but she speaks before I can formulate a question.

"He told me to meet you."

"Does he know about us?"

Eliana looks away. "I didn't have a choice."

"Do you know what he could do with that information?"

"Volkov is not a man I can keep secrets from." She steels herself. "I would have taken our secret to the grave, you know that. But things are different now."

"Different how?" I try not to let my anger surface. I know Eliana is telling the truth. She's never lied to me before. Never betrayed my trust. If she told Volkov about our past, it must have been because she felt she had no other choice.

"I cannot afford to have any doubt between us. I need Volkov to trust me."

"If you want him to trust you, why are you here now?"

Her eyes flash with hate. "Because I am his mistress. He has my life in his hands, and when my little sister marries his son, he will hold her life as well. Unless someone gets rid of him."

"But he knows you're here. He told you to meet with me."

Eliana nods. "Volkov told me to see you today, but he has no idea I'd already asked you to show up."

"I don't follow."

She pushes from the shack and walks over to me, that's when I notice the bundle of lilies in her hand. She lifts one to her nose as she says, "My information comes at a price, Amory."

"Of course it does." I'm not stupid. I knew Eliana had her reasons when she offered to give me the name at the Met Ball.

Normally, I wouldn't have entertained her little deal, but I'm out of options.

"Volkov told me to meet you today because he wants me to convince you to make your wife apologize to him," she says.

Anger crackles through me, but Eliana quickly calms the rising storm.

"He could demand her tongue for what she did. Saying sorry shouldn't be too difficult."

"I'm not doing it."

"If you want the name of the mole, then you will."

I glare at her. "That's your price. My wife apologizes and you'll tell me the name."

"He wants it to happen at your home. Over dinner."

"Why?"

"To guarantee his safety."

I almost laugh. Volkov is spooked since the docks were blown to pieces. In the mafia, there's a superstition that killing a guest during dinner will leave you cursed. He thinks having him over for a meal will be enough to keep him alive. If he's that afraid, he shouldn't demand an apology, but I know Volkov. His pride's been wounded. Forcing Rosa to say sorry will give him the same joy as killing Wolfgang. And it'll boost the morale of his gang despite the blow I delivered with the ferries.

"Fine. I'll have her apologize." I pull out the list from my pocket and shove it at her. "Now, point out the mole."

Eliana takes the paper and glances at it. A smile curves over her full lips as she reads.

Eike Brandt

Giovanni Jr.

Maximilian Gehris

Niccolò Romano

Tyrese Willis

I had believed the mole wouldn't be German, but after looking at the list, I realize there's no one I trust in this city. Now, I'm about to know for certain.

"His name is on here."

"Which one?"

Eliana's smile widens. "I haven't finished naming my price."

"You asked for an apology—"

"That was for Volkov." Her features crinkle. "You think I would waste this opportunity on him?"

"Seems like you care about his agenda."

She clutches the lilies in her hand. "If I don't get you to apologize, he'll punish me."

"Has he been hurting you?"

"I have one more price," she says, ignoring my question. I don't push it because I don't want to know. Eliana isn't my ally or my friend. What we're doing is strictly business. If I allow myself to care about her, I will stir up an entirely new storm that we don't need.

"What's your price?"

She places the list on the grass and gently sets the lilies on top. Then she straightens and slides her dress from her shoulders, over her arms, and down to her ankles. She's wearing nothing underneath.

I swallow hard.

"Eliana—"

"He turned me into his mistress," she says bitterly. "I was supposed to marry his son, but when they had their doctor examine me, they realized I wasn't a virgin anymore. The marriage was called off and my sister was given to Volkov's son instead. But he kept me for himself, in exchange for his silence."

Now I get it. With her virtue lost, no high-ranking man would ever agree to marry Eliana, especially not during a war when alliances and contracts matter more than diamonds and cocaine. But Volkov will protect the Moreno mafia, even marry the second princess to his son to seal their alliance, as long as he gets to use Eliana the same way he'd used Amana.

"I'm a married man," I say calmly. "I love my wife—"

"If you don't do this, you will never learn the name of your mole."

"Why?" I grate out. "Why can't you ask for something else?"

"Because this is your fault." She's glaring at me now. "I am nothing now. And part of that is because of you. Because of what you took from me in this very field not long ago."

"I didn't rape you."

She laughs. "But it's your fault all the same. You could have made things right and married me, but you left me yet again."

She steps forward, kicking her dress aside. "Now, you're happily married and I'm Volkov's whore."

"Eliana—"

"Lay with me, Amory. And let your wife choke on her tears."

My hands are around her throat before I realize it. "I *hate* you," I seethe, tightening my grip. I hate everything about Eliana right now. She holds all the power, and she knows it. I have a list of men and I know one of them is the mole, but I can't point them out and I don't have time to sift through every name.

She will tell me his name. But the cost is too great. I haven't been the best husband to Rosa, but I have been faithful. Since our engagement, I've never taken another woman to bed. Even though I had opportunities. Even though there were women willing and ready. I didn't touch them because I love my wife.

But now I have no choice.

If I walk away, I will preserve Rosa's love and my marriage. But I will lose everything else—I could even lose Rosa in this war.

I can't let that happen. I'd rather have her alive and hating me than dead and loving me from the grave.

Eliana lets out a wheezing noise as I increase the pressure around her throat. There's a vein in her forehead, swollen and straining against her skin. She lifts both her hands in the air in mock surrender, letting me know she isn't going to fight me.

"I hate you..." I want to scream the words, but I can't produce anything more than a breathy whimper.

"I hate you too," she whispers back.

I shove her to the ground, a mean glare ruining my face as I unbuckle my belt. "You will not enjoy this."

Not because I plan to take her roughly. It's the exact opposite, actually. I handle Eliana with the same tenderness I'd shown her the first afternoon we spent in this field. It surprises her and leaves her clinging to me like the virgin she used to be. I look her in the eye as I take her, I whisper in her ear as she runs her nails down my back, and when she arches off the grass, I confess that she's a woman worth loving. A woman I could have loved if things had been different. If we weren't in rival gangs and our relationship hadn't been built on sex.

When it's over, there are tears streaming down her cheeks. She almost can't stop the sobs that escape her. I watch her roll onto her side as she draws her knees to her chest and covers her mouth with her hand. I don't feel anything. I just want to get dressed and leave.

"The name," I say hoarsely.

She hiccups and wipes at her nose. "Why?"

"You promised."

"Why did you do that?"

I look away, yanking up my pants. There are grass stains at the knees.

"Why did you make love to me?" she nearly screams.

She had expected me to hurt her. To treat her the way Volkov does. And part of me had wanted to do just that, to make her feel the red-hot anger that I felt, the gut-wrenching pain that I feel now as I think of what I'll say to my wife when

112

I get home. But I didn't do that. I showed her kindness instead. Gentleness. Tenderness. Love.

"I wanted you to understand what it was like, so you can go to sleep every night knowing what you will never have again."

The pain of rough sex would have only lasted until I was finished. But the pain of her broken heart will be with her for years. She will never forget this day. She will never know what it's like to be loved—and even if she does find a man who will treat her as I have, she will always remember that I had her first.

"You're a cruel man," she whispers, a single tear trailing her cheek.

I shrug on my shirt and start to button it. "The name."

"That's all you care about."

"It's what I came for."

She wipes at her tears and looks me in the eye, I don't miss the hint of a smile tugging at the corner of her lips. "I'll tell you at dinner."

"I want to know now."

She shakes her head. "If I tell you now, nothing will stop you from backing out of the dinner."

I want to grab her by the throat again, but I keep my hands to myself. "*Eliana*," I growl.

She laughs. "Don't worry, you'll get your name. Have I ever lied to you?"

No. She hasn't.

"If I don't get that name—"

"You'll what?" she challenges. "There is nothing you can do to me that Volkov hasn't done already."

If I gave a crap about her, I would have felt some sort of emotion at her words, but all I feel is empty. And slightly irritated.

With a huff, I turn toward the highway. "Dinner is in two days. Seven o'clock. You'd better have that name."

Nine

I was born into the mafia. I married into the mafia. I have never expected my life to be easy or charming, but I never thought it would be this challenging, either. Amory wants me to apologize to Volkov for the incident at the Met Ball. And he wants me to do it face to face, in our own home. The very thought of it makes me burn with anger, but I've already allowed my temper to get the best of me once. I'm determined to do everything I can to keep myself in check this time around. Not because Volkov deserves an apology, but because I don't want my husband to suffer this shame anymore.

Amory is cleaning up my mess. The Jägermeister of the German mafia is inviting another Boss into his home to say 'Sorry' in person. This is an insult to his name as much as it is to mine. But he's suffering the slight because of me. The least I can do is grin and bear it. But no matter how peaceably I agree to be around the Wolf, I can't make any promises with Eliana.

"Will she be coming too?" I ask my husband as I unravel the last braid in my hair. I grab my hair pick from the vanity and start fluffing my roots. In the mirror, I can see Amory securing his cufflinks. His reaction is subtle, eyebrows scrunching together ever so slightly.

When he opens his mouth, his voice comes out in a calm tone. "Is who coming?"

"Eliana Moreno."

He glances up and our eyes meet, grey pearls crashing into a hazel storm. "Why are you asking about Eliana?"

"Because she's clearly got something going on with Volkov."

"So?"

"So I want to know if I'm going to have to sit at the dinner table with a woman you've slept with."

A muscle in his jaw tics as he reaches for his tie but, to my shock, Amory doesn't react any more than that. Normally, he bites back like a pit viper whenever I bring up his past, but right now he is perfectly calm, as if he didn't even hear me.

He walks up behind me and leans down to kiss the top of my head. "Don't worry about Eliana tonight."

"But—"

"No matter what happens, just remember that I love you, Rosa. Everything I've done so far is because I love you."

I blink at him, stunned not just by his words but by the serious edge in his voice. He gazes at my reflection in the mirror, his grey eyes full of an emotion I can't put into words. The way he looks at me is intense enough for me to shyly look away. Only when I feel the warmth of his hand on my bare shoulder do I dare to lift my gaze again.

"I love you, Rosa," he says in a whisper.

I turn on the little stool to face him, and in one swift motion, he lifts me to my feet and covers my mouth with his own. I gasp into the kiss, but before it deepens, he pulls away and holds me at arm's length. His breath comes out in pants, his eyes are serious but I can see the desire flashing through his gaze every time he blinks.

"Remember how much I love you," he says, and then he turns and walks to the door without looking back.

I stare at the closed door in silence, wondering what the heck is going on. He was like this yesterday too, when he came home and kissed me until I was breathless, murmuring apologies for what he had to ask of me. I had been so overwhelmed by the romance, the anger at his request didn't kick in until I was lying in bed watching him get dressed in the aftermath of our passion.

Even then, I didn't have it in me to lash out at him, to scold him for using his body as a distraction. In truth, I was just happy that we were getting along again. We had finally gotten over yet another bump in the road. I just wanted to enjoy the moment of peace, no matter how brief it was. It seems like we're at each other's throats every other day. Sometimes I'm just too tired to hold on to my anger.

Sometimes Amory gets tired too.

I know he doesn't want to go through this dinner any more than I do, but I can't help but feel his sudden emotion has nothing to do with my apology and everything to do with Eliana. It feels like Amory is hiding something. My mind immediately summons thoughts of the last time he kept a secret from me. It nearly ruined us—it *did* ruin us. Only the sudden death of his father brought us back together and even that reunion had its ups and downs. If there is another secret, another lie burning between us … I'm not sure I can survive it.

But I don't have a choice.

I'm the Huntress of New York now. I don't get to sit back and whine about my husband's hidden truths. I have to deal with it and move on. So I'm not going to throw a fuss right now. I won't storm out the room and demand that Amory tell me everything. I'm going to fluff my hair, spray on some perfume, and go have dinner.

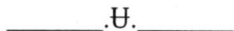

Volkov's voice drifts into the hall before I reach the dining room. I can hear him laughing in response to something Amory has said. Amy's voice is deep and smooth, his buttery German accent makes my stomach tighten—I take a deep breath to calm my nerves before I push the door open.

Everything stills as the doors part to reveal the crowd at the table. I'm not surprised by the silence or by the people present; only the seating arrangement gives me pause.

Volkov is here with Eliana, instead of his wife, but they aren't sitting beside each other. Eliana is sitting next to Amory

118

and the seat beside Volkov is empty. I won't dignify the slight with any sort of reaction. I make sure I keep a smile dancing through my eyes and a joyful tune in my voice as I lift my long dress and march over to the table.

I'm wearing a silver gown that sweeps the floor behind me as I walk, my six-inch heels clack against the tile so loudly it feels like thunder clapping through the room. I welcome the noise, it's better than listening to whatever Eliana is saying to my husband right now. She leans over as she speaks, whispering to him like I'm not even here. Amory nods and then says something back, it's not until I'm at the table that he even acknowledges my presence. His grey eyes slide across the dinner setting to rest on me so casually, for a moment, I'm not even sure if he's looking at me or simply gazing across the table in my general direction. As if I'm blocking his view of the wall behind me. It's such a detached look, it almost makes me shrivel in my chair, but I steel myself and clear my throat.

"Evening, everyone." My voice is little more than a whisper.

Eliana smirks. "Nice to see you again."

Volkov stands and pulls out my chair. "I hope you don't mind sitting next to me tonight." He smiles. "I thought it would be nice to switch things up."

I understand now.

This arrangement wasn't Eliana's idea—it was Volkov's. He's still trying to hurt Amory for my disrespect at the Ball. Placing his former lover by his side, right in front of me. Forcing us both to sit through this humiliation.

We don't have to do this. Amory could give the signal and Douglass—or even one of his servants—would put a bullet in the Wolf's head before he could even blink. But as I look at my husband, I realize that isn't what he wants. Not after losing his father and uncle. Not after almost losing his ancestral home. Amory is playing it safe.

I don't entirely blame him. Volkov would've had to gain access to our ranks to be able to plant explosives at Stonehall. He'd have to be getting intel from inside.

A mole.

If that's really the case, the rat could be somewhere in this very home. They could alert Volkov if Amory tried anything, and then we'd go from putting a bullet in his head to probably having one lodged in our own skulls.

Amy's caution is for my sake. He said as much in our room. *Everything I've done so far is because I love you.* But is there more to it than that? Is there something else going on that I don't know about?

Volkov's cold hand slides across my lower back, making me jump slightly. I gasp and glance over at him, greeted by his wolfish grin.

"Have a seat, darling."

I nod absently and follow his order. Amory is stiff in his chair, gripping his butter knife like he wants to stab Volkov for touching me. It's the only sign that he's still my Amy—not this detached man who'd barely glanced at me earlier.

Eliana's gaze narrows as she notices his death grip on the knife. "I believe we're here on business, aren't we?" she asks.

Everyone's eyes shift to me.

I swallow. "Volkov, I disrespected you earlier. At the Met Charity Ball."

He turns in his chair to face me, sliding his hand across the table to rest over mine. From the corner of my eye, I see Amory set down his butter knife. He glares at our hands but doesn't speak. Eliana touches his shoulder, and I can tell it's an effort for him not to flinch away from her. His hand slowly curls into a fist, his jaw clenches, a vein in his head pulses at his temple. I've never seen him this outraged before. It's such a deadly form of calm, I'm momentarily left speechless—until Volkov squeezes my fingers and I pull my eyes from my husband to stare at the Russian Alpha beside me.

"I'm sorry for spitting at your feet. I was out of line. Even as a mafia queen."

Volkov studies me a moment, like he's going over every word I've just said. Then he gives a thoughtful nod and pats my hand. "I accept your apology, flower."

Just then, the staff enters the dining room to serve our food. Volkov cuts into his steak without missing a beat, Amory stabs at his like he's trying to kill the cow all over again. Neither Eliana nor I touch our plates.

"This is delicious," Volkov says causally. "I hope dessert is just as good."

"There won't be any dessert," Amory growls.

Eliana touches his shoulder again. This time, I grip my own knife.

"Why not? You know I've got a sweet tooth."

"She does." Volkov sips his wine and then sucks the deep red liquid from his teeth. "But you already know that, don't you?"

Amory glares at him. "That's enough."

"Is it?"

"You brought her into my home—"

"Nothing you haven't done before."

Amory jerks to his feet and splays his hand on the table, talking very slowly. "You've had your apology, now get out."

"That isn't a way to treat a guest, is it?" Volkov leans back in his chair like he hasn't got a single worry. The smile he wears is lethal, like a razor blade splitting his face to reveal sharp little teeth.

"Calm down," Eliana says lazily. "No need for anyone to die tonight."

"Amory," I say softly. The sound of my voice immediately gets his attention. His eyes snap to me and remain there until I speak again. "Let's finish our meal."

If I can get through Volkov's slimy hands on me, then so can Amory. If I can stomach issuing an apology, then Amory can handle hearing it. If I can keep it together with Eliana touching my husband every five minutes, then Amory can remain calm with Volkov throwing insults. Neither of us likes this, but we're in it together. We've made it through the hard part, I won't let Amy's temper ruin things now.

Amory slowly sits back down, his eyes never leaving mine. When I reach for my steak knife, he gives me a subtle nod and grabs his utensils again. "My apologies," he mutters.

Eliana smiles at me. "You have such an understanding husband."

"I do," I tell her.

"Are you as understanding as he is?"

I blink at her, trying to see where this is going. "I try to be."

"You *must* be understanding to allow his former lover into your home again," Volkov says with a chuckle.

Amory exhales slowly but says nothing.

"I guess it's a trait we share," I say quietly.

Volkov laughs. "Do you enjoy sharing, little Huntress?"

"Of course she does," Eliana says sweetly—too sweetly. Her eyes meet mine and I can't ignore the sparkle of mischief flashing in them. "You shared your husband with me—and who knows how many other women."

"That was before he became my husband," I correct.

"Was it?" She raises an eyebrow.

"I'm not bothered by your taunting, Eliana."

"What if I'm not taunting you?" She leans forward, dropping her voice to a purr. "What if I'm telling the truth? That I had your husband two days ago."

My mouth goes dry, and my eyes go wide, but I force myself to remain calm. As I glance around the table, I catch the smile dancing across Volkov's face, and I see the monstrous glare taking over Amory's.

She's telling the truth, I realize, with a drop of my shoulders.

Amory's words flow through my head again. *Everything I've done so far is because I love you.* But how could any of this equate to love?

I calmly set down my steak knife and fork, dab at the corners of my mouth with my napkin. Then I meet Eliana's teasing smirk head on. "You slept with my husband again."

Her smile seems to fade.

"Did you think I hadn't known?"

Volkov glances between us.

"Maybe I'm more understanding than you gave me credit for." I shrug one shoulder and smile like I'm not bothered. "I know my husband better than you think—better than you ever did or ever will, Eliana. So if you think whatever happened between the two of you was special in any sort of way, please understand that it was only special to you."

I stand and drop my napkin over my untouched plate. "If you don't mind, I've lost my appetite."

Before anyone can say anything more, I turn and walk out of the dining room. No one speaks. No one tries to stop me.

I'm grateful, because then they would have seen the fake smile on my face crack and wither as I break down into tears. No one has to know that Eliana's confession shook me to my core. No one has to know that I can't breathe as I clutch at my chest. No one has to know that I make it to my room on my hands and knees, eyes blurred with tears, my legs too wobbly to walk.

I kept my promise. I made sure I behaved. I made sure I apologized.

I suffered through the dinner for as long as I could. But I can't stand to endure this for a second longer. I had put on a brave face at the table, if only to make sure Eliana didn't get the satisfaction of seeing me cry. But in the privacy of my bedroom, I can't stop the sobs that escape me. I tremble as I clutch one of our throw pillows to my chest, screaming into the cushion as my body is wracked with sorrow, anger, and despair.

I knew I'd have to be strong to stand by Amory's side. I knew that loving him wouldn't be easy. But I never thought it would be this hard. Or this heartbreaking.

How understanding should I be?

How much am I expected to overlook?

When do I say enough?

Ten

The room remains quiet until the doors close behind Rosa. The sound of her retreating footsteps is all I hear for the next few moments. I focus on the sound, catching every footfall and imagining it in my head; the look on Rosa's face as she marches away, storming through our home. The way her brows crinkle when she's angry, and how they bunch when she cries.

She's stronger than that, I tell myself. She delivered her apology without an issue. And she kept her composure even in the face of my infidelity. She didn't storm out in an emotional fit of tears, Rosa held her head high as she excused herself and left the way I'd expect a mafia queen would. But now she's all alone, left with the knowledge of my betrayal, and I'm stuck here with a Wolf and a scorned lover.

I sigh. "That was uncalled for."

Volkov nods and lets out a low chuckle. "Perhaps."

"She apologized like you asked. You didn't have to hurt her."

There's a stretch of silence that I want to fill with Volkov's screams, but I stay put. I just need a name. Then I can end everything. I'll kill the mole and everyone he's been working with. Then I'll come for Volkov. But I'll start with his family first. I'll make him feel everything I've felt these last few months.

Hiding my brother. Worrying over Rosa's safety. Almost losing Morgen. Losing my father. Losing my uncle. Losing Amana. And now this.

There was never a doubt that I could survive whatever the mafia threw at me. Bullets, loss, grief. Even if she made it through at a snail's pace, I even had hope that Rosa could make it in the mafia too. But whether my marriage would be able to stand is another question entirely.

The connection I have with my wife isn't ink on paper anymore. This is no longer about fulfilling a contract—I'm not sure it ever has been. I love Rosa. I would die for her. And I know she'd do the same for me. We can't separate from each other, even if we wanted to. Divorce doesn't happen in the mafia any more than it does in the Church. But we could lose our love.

We could fall apart.

Volkov knew what he was doing when he asked for an apology. He didn't come to hear Rosa say she was sorry; he came to *make* her sorry. And to make me watch.

This is my very own punishment.

It's worse than the shame of the lewd video he kept of us in bed. It's worse than the very act of sleeping with Eliana again. This is personal. It's vengeful. It makes me burn with hatred.

With strength I didn't know I had, I lift my gaze to meet the Wolf's icy stare and I try my best to keep my voice level as I say, "I'm going to kill you, Mikhail. I'm going to look you in the eye when I do it. And I'm going to enjoy sending you to hell."

The smile he's wearing slowly fades away. "I took your father, your uncle, and your cousin is dead because of me—"

"Morgen is alive," I tell him with a smile.

He blinks. "I watched him die in my own home."

"You watched me shoot him. But he didn't die."

"You held a funeral."

"So you'd believe he was dead."

Volkov shakes his head. "I don't believe you."

I laugh. "Yes, you do."

His features shrivel into rage as he leans across the table, but before he can say anything more, his phone rings and he pauses to glance at the screen. He frowns. "I must take this. Eliana, meet me in the car."

Volkov stalks out with his phone pressed to his ear, leaving me alone with my former lover. She doesn't waste a second, turning in her chair to stare at the side of my face. I refuse to look at her for fear of strangling her where she sits.

"How could you?" I whisper.

She ignores me. "We don't have much time."

"Telling Rosa was not part of the deal."

"If it were up to me, I wouldn't have said anything. Volkov wanted to spill the news."

"You think I believe that?" My hand twitches as I fight the urge to grab my knife again.

Eliana touches my shoulder. It's a surprisingly gentle gesture that stuns me enough to distract me from jerking away. Instead, I hold my breath and close my eyes, wishing I was somewhere else, dealing with something else, talking to someone else.

I open my eyes and stare at my cold dinner. "She will never forgive me."

"She will. She loves you."

I look at her. "Who arranged the phone call?"

"My little sister. I asked her to try to escape from Volkov's mansion today, cause enough of a stir to warrant a phone call during dinner to give us a moment alone."

"The name." She pauses long enough for me to grip her by her shoulders and give her a shake. "The *name*," I hiss. After everything that's happened, I'm willing to beat it out of her. I don't care if it makes me look like Wolfgang—I'll call him up so he can join me if that's what it'll take.

Eliana looks me in the eye and then she says the name like it's a song on her lips. Before I can react, the dining room doors open and one of Volkov's men walks inside. Eliana and I jerk apart before he sees us and gets suspicious. When he's close enough, he stops and respectfully inclines his head toward me, then he looks at Eliana.

"Volkov is waiting for you, ma'am."

She nods and stands. There are no last words. Not even a second glance between us as she leaves the room. I don't know if I'm happy, relieved, or upset right now. There is no time to process how I feel. I've got too much to deal with to throw my own feelings into the mix. So instead of sitting there and sobbing into my plate, I run my hand through my hair and push to my feet. I've got to go see my wife.

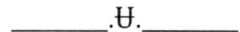

I don't hear any screams, shrieks, or sobs coming from the room as I approach. The realization allows a smidge of hope to swell in my heart, but no more than that. Rosa isn't the weak little flower I first met months ago, but she's not like her cousins—she isn't even like Eliana.

A rose with thorns is still a rose. A precious little thing.

When I push my bedroom door open, I find Rosa sitting on the edge of the bed, wiping at her eyes. The room around her is a mess. Clothes strewn about, drawers left open, her makeup all over the floor, as if she shoved everything off her vanity. She's still in her dress, silver and clinging to her body in all the right places, but I don't get the chance to appreciate her curves as she sniffles and glares at me.

"How could you?" Her voice is shaking so badly it takes me an extra moment to understand what she said.

I close the door behind me. "It's not what you think."

"You slept with her."

"I know."

"You broke your wedding vows."

"I know."

"How could it be any different from what I think?" She grips a fistful of the blankets and breathes heavily, trying hard not to shed any more tears but her emotions get the better of her. Her eyes leak like faucets, pain running down her cheeks in two streaks of raw agony.

I look away.

"You kept the truth of my father's death a secret. You flaunted some hooker through the Met Ball. And now you've cheated on me." She wipes at her face with the back of her hand, smearing her mascara down her cheek. "How much more am I supposed to overlook?"

"I didn't do it because I wanted to. You have to understand that."

She starts shaking her head.

"Remember what I told you before dinner? How much I love you. That everything I do is for you."

"So you buried yourself in another woman for *me*?" she hisses. "You broke your wedding vows because you *love me*?"

I know she doesn't want to hear it, but I tell her the truth anyway. "Yes."

The look she gives me nearly stops my heart—it's a dark mixture of hatred and dread.

"There's a lot going on right now, Rosa. Someone in the Hunting Grounds is a traitor."

Her eyes widen slightly. "A mole," she whispers.

131

I nod. "Eliana Moreno knows who the mole is. She gave me the name in exchange..." my voice trails off. I don't want to say the rest, but I won't hide from what I've done. "In exchange for me."

Rosa audibly swallows, still scrubbing at her stained cheeks. "That still doesn't make this okay. It doesn't make *us* okay."

I stare at the floor. My voice is barely a whisper. "I know."

Rosa stands and I gasp as I spot the duffle bag sitting on the bed beside her. All at once, everything clicks. The room isn't a mess because she destroyed it in a hysterical fit of anger. Everything's out of place because Rosa emptied her drawers in search of clothes.

She's packing up to leave.

I take a step forward. "What are you doing?"

She ignores me, grabbing clothes and makeup from the floor around her to toss into her bag.

I walk over and grab her by the wrist. "Rosa, what are you doing?"

"I'm leaving!" she screams.

"No, you're **not**." My voice is a snarl. "Who do you think you are?"

She twists in my grasp, but I don't let her go, blinded by my anger, shock, and a sudden sadness I feel unfolding inside of me. Rosa and I just got back on the right track. She'd finally forgiven me for keeping her father's death a secret. She'd just gotten over all the drama of having Amana at the Ball. And now this. Now I've pushed her to her limits—*beyond* her limits.

But that doesn't mean she gets to leave me for it.

132

I tug on her wrist, and she falls against my chest. Of course, she struggles to get away, shoving me back a step as she lets out a cry of anger. I trip backwards, but I take her with me, falling against the door.

"Rosa," I say hoarsely.

She gasps, crying into my chest, soaking my shirt with her tears. When she lifts her head to look at me, I surprise her with a kiss. It's sloppy and unromantic in every way, but it doesn't stop Rosa from gasping and sagging against me. I loosen my grip on her arms as she relaxes, but as quickly as she calms, she finds her way back to anger again.

It's like she suddenly comes to her senses, her eyes snapping open as she rears back and glares at me. I cup her face and pull her back for another kiss, but the exchange is cut short when I feel a sharp pain slice through my mouth.

I jerk away, catching a glimpse of the blur that flashes toward me just in time. I see the slap before it connects, but I don't try to dodge it. My head whips to the side and I stumble backwards as Rosa shoves me away yet again.

This time, I let her have her way. We stare at each other in silence. Our heavy breathing is the only sound in the room until I reach up to touch my bottom lip. When I pull my hand away, there's blood on the tip of my finger.

"You bit me."

Her nostrils flare. "You kissed me."

"I just wanted you to calm down."

"You think I decided to leave you in a fit of anger? You think I haven't thought this through?"

"You're not leaving me, Rosa."

"What are you going to do?" she challenges. "Lock me up here? Beat me into submission?"

I stare at her, anger threating to rise inside me. She's talking about my father and how he locked up my mother whenever she didn't behave. Made her a prisoner in her own home. And she's talking about Wolfgang. How he has a history of abusing women.

I cram my hands into my pockets. I could turn into my father or my brother at any given moment. There have been plenty of moments where I *wanted* to behave like them. Believe me. But I made a promise to Rosa, and I love her enough to keep it.

Still… that was a low blow.

I try to keep calm. "I've told you before, I'm not my brother or my father. I won't lock you up or hold you here against your will."

She walks over to the bed and grabs her duffle bag. "Then get out of my way."

"Rosa—"

"Was it worth it?" she snaps, gripping the bag tightly. "Tell me you broke my heart for a good reason."

"It will never be worth it," I say solemnly. "But I did get the information I needed."

She meets my gaze. "And?"

I can't tell her. Not now. Not while she's clutching a bag packed with clothes. Not when she's ready to walk out that door. But I know there's no way I can keep this from her. She will never forgive me. Not after the way I handled the secret of her father's death. Or after what I will have to do to handle this mole.

"The rat," I say slowly. Then I sigh and run my hand through my hair. "Rosa..."

Her eyes begin to fill with tears, and I know she already knows who it is. Already knows what this means.

"Please don't say his name," she begs, covering her mouth with her hand.

"I'm so sorry."

She starts shaking her head. "How? Why would he do this?"

"I don't know." Truly, I don't. I can't think of a reason Giovanni De Luca would work with the man who wants his own sister dead. Then again, we are talking about a failed mafia don who's been reduced to fifty soldiers and a bunch of abandoned buildings. He killed his own father, sold his sister to a rival mafia, and then left me with all his debts. I suppose when it became clear that the Hunting Grounds wouldn't be winning this war by a landslide, he panicked and started selling secrets to save his own hide. Not caring a lick about what happened to his own sister and his childhood friend in the aftermath.

Rosa blinks at me, swaying on her feet. "What will you do to my brother?"

"You know what I'm going to do."

She drops the duffle bag as her knees buckle, but I'm right beside her in a moment, crossing the room in just two large strides. Rosa doesn't fight me as I hold her but when she's done shedding her tears, she gently pulls away and stares at her bag.

"I can't be here," she whispers.

"I'm not letting you go, Rosa."

"I can't be here when you kill my brother." Her voice holds a tremble, but I know there's no convincing her to stay. Still … I can't just let her go. Even though I know it's cruel to ask her to stay and turn the other cheek as I put a bullet in her brother's head. Even though I know she's safer outside of NYC. Even though I know putting some distance between us right now will likely save our marriage—while staying together will only drive the wedge deeper between us.

"I have to go," she whispers.

"Go where?"

"Back to Norman. To the only family I'll have left when this is over."

Norman, New Jersey. So close and so far at the same time. That's where she was holed up when her brother dragged her back to marry me. With her little church family and her fake church boyfriend.

Arthur Hart.

I want Rosa to be safe. I want to save her from the pain of losing her brother. But I don't want her running off to take comfort in the arms of the man she used to love. Then again, who am I to be upset about that? After I rolled around with Eliana. After I flaunted Amana around like a secret lover.

Still… I clench my hands into fists as I watch Rosa pack the last of her things. I can't just stand here and let her walk out. I won't hurt Rosa or hold her hostage. My words are all I've got now. They're absolutely worthless, but I try one last desperate attempt anyway.

"You can't leave…"

She barely glances up at me as she zips the bag shut and then pushes from the bed. Not long ago, we were tangled up in that bed, in those sheets, beneath those blankets.

"I just got you back, Rosie."

She pauses, chewing on her lip as she looks back at the bed. I know she's thinking the same thing I'm thinking, but she doesn't let it get to her.

"Please don't leave me," I whisper.

Rosa slowly closes her eyes. Takes a deep breath. Then she walks past me to the door. "I'm sorry, Amy."

Eleven

Douglass doesn't speak during the entire drive to Norman. Amory sent him with me when I left, said he wouldn't stop me from going back to Jersey, but he wouldn't let me go without knowing I was completely safe. I understand his worries. Norman is a world away from New York, but it isn't far enough to avoid the gripping hands of the mafia.

Melissa, Minnie, and Arthur Hart were my only family in Norman. They'd made me feel safe. Made me believe I had truly escaped from my cursed family. But Arthur proved me wrong. Not only did he betray me, but he told me the mafia had its claws sank into every part of the country. I don't know why I was so surprised. NYC news was always making headlines back then and still does today. Photos from my wedding day were featured in magazines across the nation, there were even cameras set up outside the reception. Amory had refused to allow them inside to give us privacy. Ever since the defunding, reporters and journalists can't get enough. New York City is the new Hollywood and the mafia its celebrities.

Minnie grew up idolizing gang bosses the way I used to lose my head over popstars. She'd even known my father's name and had swooned over the Volkov family. If she knew half the things I know, she would run with her tail tucked. But Minnie couldn't run—Giovanni had his men hit her with a car when he found me. They didn't kill her, just broke her leg, but the message was clear. My brother was willing to do anything to get me back. With all that debt to pay off, he didn't hesitate to sell his own sister or kill his own father. The saddest part is that in the end, he still ran the Garden into the ground.

I should have seen this coming. I saw all the signs, if only a little too late. Conrad had mentioned failed businesses. Even Aldo had spoken up about it at Olivia's wedding. But I never knew how bad things truly were until it was beyond helping.

That's why he betrayed us. I know it is.

I can't think of any other reason my older brother—my only living family—would sell secrets to the Wolves. He must have known that I could have ended up dead thanks to his treachery, that Amory could have died. That Uwe and Oberon *did* die.

And all that time, he'd been working with Arthur. It was because of Arthur that Gio tracked me down in the first place. And it's because of Arthur that Amy insisted on Douglass travelling with me. We don't know if they're still working together. We don't know if I'm riding into a trap. If maybe

Volkov told me about Amory's infidelity to get me to leave New York so Arthur could snatch me up.

But I don't think that's the case.

If Volkov wanted to get his hands on me, he could have done it any time during the eight-hour drive from Brooklyn to Norman. For now, I'm safe. My only worries revolve around what Melissa will think when she sees me again.

Douglass pulls into her driveway and shuts the car off. I feel a wave of anxious nostalgia wash over me. I haven't been here in what feels like forever. It hasn't even been a year since I left, but so much has happened. I got married. Almost got divorced. Lost my virginity. Nearly lost my marriage. Lost my father-in-law. Lived in a safehouse. And so much more.

All because of the mafia.

When will it end? I ask God in my heart. *You said you wanted to use Amory to take back the City.* It seems like everything has gotten worse over time. But as sorrow tries to burrow into my heart, I remember one of my favorite passages from the Bible.

Weeping may endure for a night, but joy cometh in the morning.

"Psalms chapter thirty, verse five."

Douglass's deep voice startles me. It's almost a low grumble that fills the entire car, the slightest hint of a German accent hanging at the edge of each word. I stare at the side of his face as he unlocks his seatbelt and glances over at me.

"What'd you say?" I whisper.

"Weeping may endure for a night, but joy cometh in the morning. That's Psalms chapter thirty, verse five." He smiles and it's probably the most pleasant thing I've seen in a long time. He isn't handsome in a conventional sense; his face is spotted with scars and his dark skin tells a story with bruises and cuts I've never noticed until now. But his eyes are full of kindness and his voice is soothing as he says, "You were thinking out loud."

I hadn't realized I'd said the scripture out loud. Blush taints my cheeks as I stare at my hands. "I'm sorry."

"What for?"

"I..." I look up at him. "I don't know."

"We live in a messed-up world, Mistress. We see things. We experience things. Things that no one should have to go through. I would never judge you for the way you cope."

"Sounds like you cope the same way."

"Before I left the Stronghold, my grandmother made sure I went to Sunday School every week." He chuckles, big shoulders shaking up and down. "She would make sure I paid attention, asking me questions about what I learned when it was over. Even had me stand up and sing one Sunday during children's testimony service."

I watch him as he stares straight ahead, reliving the memories. This is the first time Douglass has ever mentioned his past. Even though we're both from the Willis Stronghold, even though we grew up in the same neighborhoods, we've never spoken about it. Douglass was kidnapped and forced to join the Hunting Grounds; I didn't think it would be appropriate for me to bring up his past.

He lets out a long sigh and settles into his seat. "My grandmother made sure I knew the Bible. That's all I have left from that life."

"Do you miss it?" I ask cautiously. "The Stronghold."

He adjusts in his chair. "I miss my grandmother."

"Maybe you could see her again when this is all over."

"Maybe."

I glance at Melissa's front door; it's the same as I remember. Potted plants on the porch, a little swing with only enough space for two small people—mostly, Melissa sat on it herself, singing hymns as she rocked slowly. Sometimes I'd catch Minnie out there alone, kicking her bare feet as she absently scrolled through her phone. And every now and then, I'd sit there with Arthur and watch the sunset. Lean my head against his shoulder as he told me about his day.

Those were simpler times. Maybe I'd been fooling myself into thinking I could ever live in peace for long, but I *had* found peace. And as I gaze at Melissa's home, I feel a sudden jolt of hope that maybe I can find it again.

"Let's go inside," I say, unbuckling my seatbelt.

Douglass glances over at me. "Will she be happy to see you?"

"I think so. But I won't be staying long."

He raises an eyebrow, but I ignore him and open my door. Douglass is beside me by the time I ring the doorbell. Melissa answers after a few moments, her jaw going slack at the sight of me. When she finally gathers herself, she lets out a shout of joy and crushes me in a hug.

"My Lord! My Lord! My Lord!"

I laugh and hug her back. "I'm all right, Melissa."

"I have prayed for you every day since you were taken." Tears fill her eyes as she cups both my cheeks. She pinches them like I'm her child and then hugs me again. "Thank you, Jesus." She repeats that over and over, sobbing and sniffling until someone appears behind her.

"Mama?"

Both of us stiffen. I haven't heard that voice in months. Haven't seen the adorable smile that comes with it. Haven't felt her loving embrace.

Minnie steps beside her mother with a confused look on her face. She's wearing a big t-shirt and her feet are bare—little toes painted sherbet orange. When she sees me, her face crinkles and then smooths into a frozen gaze of shock.

"Rose?"

Gosh, they still call me that even after learning the truth. Unless Arthur never told them.

The thought dawns on me for the first time as Minnie runs over and hugs me. The last time I saw Arthur, we had a very telling conversation; he revealed his true colors and intentions as he spewed hatred toward me. But he never once mentioned or even hinted at telling everything to Melissa and Minnie. Probably because he would also have to incriminate himself and confess to working with gangsters for the last few months.

I take a deep breath and swipe away the tears that run down my cheeks as I look at my family. Melissa who taught me the Word of God and showed me the love of the mother I'd lost right before meeting her. Minnie who became the sister I never had. Neither of them hates me or blames me for the chaos I brought into their lives that day. It's obvious from how they drag me inside and offer Douglass and me a seat.

Melissa puts on tea and Minnie asks if we're hungry. We drove straight through the night, eight hours, so it's early morning now. I decline the food, but Douglass accepts a mug of coffee and tells me he's going to smoke a cigarette outside.

Melissa watches him go in silence; I know she's biting back her urge to tell him not to smoke near her daffodils, but she doesn't need to worry. Douglass doesn't smoke. That's just his excuse to get outside and monitor the perimeter while we chat. It's also his way of giving me some privacy.

"Who is he?" Minnie asks, playing with the hem of her t-shirt. It's then that I realize the shirt is one of Arthur's. My throat tightens as I stare at it, thinking of how Arthur used to look in it; tall and strong with broad shoulders and twenty extra pounds of muscle. Arthur was a big man, dark skinned with a neat beard. I loved how he seemed to dwarf everyone around him, even Melissa, who's tall for a woman. But as I think of his great size now, I can only imagine him using all his brawn to drag women from their homes the same way I'd been months ago. He'd been working with Gio and Volkov. He'd been helping them collect women to sell as sex slaves. And I'd never known.

I exhale the memories. "His name is Douglass, he's a distant relative."

"So, he isn't...?" Minnie doesn't finish the thought.

I shake my head. "No, it's not like that."

"Arthur's been worried for you."

I swallow. "I'm sure he has."

"He was so distraught when you went missing," Melissa says. "No one knew what happened. We thought you'd died until you called us."

I remember that phone call, the one moment of kindness Gio showed me after dragging me back to New York. Arthur had gotten on the phone, ready to storm through Manhattan to find me if he had to. If only I'd known it was all an act.

"I guess you've been alright," Melissa says quietly.

When I look up, I realize her gaze is locked on my left hand—at the ring Amory bought me. I fiddle with it as I say, "Things have been very complicated, Mel. More than you can imagine."

She glances at the clock on the wall. "I don't have to be at the church until noon."

I laugh, not at all surprised that she expects me to explain myself. I owe them both that much. So I take a deep breath and tell them the truth. That I'm the daughter of a dead mafia boss, that my own brother kidnapped me, that he sold me to my husband—that I ended up falling in love with that man. And that he ended up cheating on me.

"That's why I'm here," I say slowly.

Melissa stares at me for a long moment. She didn't speak at all while I told my story, just sat there with a shocked look on her face. When I went into the details about marrying Amory, she sent Minnie into the kitchen to make herself boiled eggs for breakfast. And when Douglass came inside for another mug of coffee, she waved him toward the dining room to eat with Minnie.

She's obviously stunned by my story, but I don't see any judgment in her eyes, just a deep sense of curiosity.

"Are you leaving your husband?" she asks.

I pause, taken aback by the question. As much as Amory's infidelity broke my heart, I never once thought about divorcing him.

"I just wanted to get away. Put some distance between us for a while," I say.

She shakes her head. "Distance doesn't fix things. Talking about it—confronting it—that's what fixes things."

"I know—"

"Then what are you doing here?"

"It's more complicated than that," I say.

She raises her eyebrows.

"I need to clear my head. But I also need to find a way to clear Amy's."

"I don't understand."

"God wants to use Amory to break the mafia's hold on New York. But there's a war going on right now that threatens to tear the city apart. In the end, this war could be the fall of the mafia, but it could also be the fall of all of New York. I have to help him, Melissa. I have to get Amory out of the mafia before it destroys him."

She blinks at me, nervously sanding her hands together. I know she's trying to think of something to say, trying to make

146

this whole situation make sense. I'm just as confused as she is, but I know what needs to be done. I know this is all part of God's plan.

Maybe God never intended for Amory to hurt me or break his wedding vows, but it's obvious now that He can use my husband's mistakes. He can make good of this horrible situation.

"It's time," I whisper, though I'm speaking more to myself than to Melissa. "It's time for Amory to change. If he doesn't, he'll fall with the mafia. He'll tear himself apart trying to save the very thing God wants to end."

Just look at everything he's done so far... He's lied to me. He's kept secrets from me. He's cheated on me. He's lost his father and uncle. He nearly lost his brother. He's suffered at the hands of a mole. And now he's going to kill my own brother. Amory is unraveling and I don't know how much time he has left before he reaches the end of his rope.

Melissa takes a breath. "What can we do to help?"

I don't want Mel involved in the destruction of the mafia. She's already been through enough because of me.

"Pray for me," I say with a smile. "Please, Mel."

She presses her lips together. "Always, Rose."

Minnie enters the living room, wearing a sweater and a pair of leggings. Douglass follows her inside and tells me he's going to take some phone calls on the porch. I know it's his way of holding down security, so I just nod and watch him go.

Minnie sits beside me on the sofa. "You sure you aren't hungry?"

Just then, my stomach growls. "Well…"

Minnie laughs. "I can make scrambled eggs. But boiled is easier."

"Boiled it is, then."

She grins and trots off to the kitchen. I don't notice a limp in her step; some of the guilt in my heart ebbs away at the realization.

"I'm happy she recovered," I say softly.

Melissa sighs heavily. "It was rough, but God healed her right up. Her leg is perfectly fine now, better than it was before the accident."

"Melissa, I'm so sorry—"

She reaches out and takes my hand. "Don't you dare apologize."

"But I've caused so much pain and trouble."

"And you also brought us so much joy."

I blink at her.

"You lived with us for months, Rose. You became a member of this family. When you went missing, we mourned you. Arthur worried himself sick over you."

I gulp down my emotions at the mention of that man. I didn't tell Melissa how he'd picked me up in New York and told me the truth about who he really was. I didn't want to overwhelm her, and I didn't want to be the one to tell her. She should hear it from her son.

Obviously, if Arthur hasn't told her the truth by now then he likely never will, but I'm not leaving here until I know Melissa isn't in the dark anymore.

I lean forward, squeezing Mel's hand. "Where is Arthur?"

"He should be here soon, actually."

That wasn't the answer I was expecting, but I'm not bothered by it. The faster I see him, the quicker I can get this over with. Plus, Arthur might be my ticket to saving Amory. Even though he stabbed me in the back and turned out to be a dirty cop, he's still part of law enforcement. He'll have connections with officers outside of NYC—that doesn't mean they're beyond the influence of the mafia, but it does mean they're likely not under Volkov's complete control.

The front door opens, snatching me from my thoughts. Douglass enters with an odd look on his face; it isn't a look that says there's trouble anywhere, but he certainly looks uncomfortable. When Arthur walks in behind him, I realize why he's got that expression on his face.

I stand when Arthur notices me on the sofa. At first, his eyes are focused on Melissa as he smiles to greet her, but then he sees me and stops mid-stride. His face doesn't contort in anger, it shifts into fear as his eyes dart between me and his mother.

"She's back," Mel says breathily. Her innocent joy almost makes me cry. I don't deserve to call this woman my family.

Arthur nods slowly. "I can't believe it."

"It's nice to see you again," I say as kindly as I can.

"I'm glad you're alright."

Minnie darts out of the kitchen and runs right into Arthur's arms. For a moment, he is the man I remember. The man who gave warm hugs and sweet words and gentle caresses. He is the man I fell for so easily. So carelessly.

The sight of him with his little sister makes me want to scream. They have no idea who he truly is.

Arthur pulls away from Minnie with a smile. "Did you eat yet? We can stop for breakfast on the way."

Minnie nods. "I made boiled eggs."

He wrinkles his nose. "We've got to teach you to cook something else."

"I made enough for you and Rose."

I can see the way he stiffens, though he doesn't show any other signs of discomfort. He glances over at me. "Why don't we go eat, Rose?"

Melissa stands. "Minnie, come help me pick out something to wear for the church raffle."

I thank God for Mel and her ability to steer clear when she needs to.

Arthur follows me into the kitchen as Minnie whines about her mother's sense of fashion. When their voices fade behind us, I turn on him.

"You haven't told them anything."

"Of course not," he says with a snarl. "Do you want me to put them in even more danger?"

"You were connected to the mafia before I showed up in Norman. Melissa and Minnie were never safe with you."

He puts his hands on his hips. "I know you didn't come back here just to argue with me."

"I came back because I need help," I admit.

Arthur stands there a moment, lost for words or angry—I can't tell—but I take the brief silence to gather myself and say, "Do you still have connections with the mafia?"

"My dealings are none of your business."

I step toward him, angry and fed up. I'm tired of secrets and lies. I'm tired of backstabbing and betrayal. I'm tired of the mafia. It's ruined so many lives. Changed so many people. Even me.

I am not the woman I was before I got married. I am not the woman I was three days ago. This life changes you, bit by bit. If you don't get out. If you don't find your way to the light, the darkness will slowly consume you.

Look at Amory. Look at Christina. Even Gisela who's been hanging on by a thread, suffering Conrad's emotional outbursts. None of us can take much more.

"Mikhail Volkov is busy fighting a war with Amory Jäger, boss of the German mafia. Giovanni De Luca has just been discovered as a mole working for Volkov against my husband. He's going to die soon." I try not to get emotional at that realization. I knew it would happen the moment I learned of Gio's betrayal, but saying it aloud is another thing entirely.

Gio and I were only close as kids, before our father took him under his wing. Since then, he's become cold and callous and hateful. But he's still my brother. Still the boy I remember from ten years ago who would sneak me candy and kiss my cheek at night. The boy who was best friends with Amory. The one he betrayed. The one who's going to pull the trigger when he finally meets his end.

I don't know if its justice. But I can't say it's undeserved. Still...

I blink away my musings and try to focus on Arthur again. I don't have time to worry over a man who dug his own grave. I lost my chance to beg for his life when I packed up and ran back to Norman. The only thing I could give my brother was a proper goodbye, something I sent through a long text message I typed during the drive. I have no idea if he read it, but no one can ever say I didn't try.

Arthur is staring at me with a frightened look on his face.

"You had no idea," I say slowly. That much is obvious from the expression he's wearing. He's been out of the loop probably since he left New York after his ride with me months ago. It makes sense, considering how much everything's changed since then. And also considering how expendable Arthur was to my brother and Volkov.

When things got tough, they cut him out.

I glance around the kitchen, peeking outside the window above the sink to look at the driveway. Only my car and Arthur's is out there. Not Melissa's.

"Why are you picking up Mel and Minnie?"

He looks away.

"Where's their car?"

They'd had one before I left.

Arthur takes a slow gulp. "They sold it."

"Why?"

His eyes drill daggers into me. "To make ends meet."

He'd complained about making very little money before. That was the reason he'd gone rogue and started working for Volkov and Gio in the first place. I suppose since he's been cut off, things have been tough. Tough enough for Melissa to sell her car just to keep the lights on.

That breaks my heart, but it also makes things easier for me. If money is Arthur's motivation, then convincing him to help me won't be too difficult.

Without a word, I turn around and march back through the house toward the front door. I can hear Melissa and Minnie chatting upstairs, talking about Mel's attire for the raffle. Douglass is standing at the end of the driveway when I walk out the door, I ignore him and fling the car door open so I can grab my duffel bag.

When I dig it out and set it on the roof of the car, Arthur is right beside me, peering over my shoulder. I unzip it and turn to him, catching his reaction when he sees all the cash inside.

His eyes go wide.

I'd taken this money with the intentions of giving it to Melissa for her and Minnie to get away and start over if the war got out of hand and poured into Norman. Or at least to put the money into Melissa's ministry since the funding will likely suffer once the mafia goes up in flames. It'll be hard for Arthur to wash cash through the shelters without Gio there to give him any.

"It's yours." I shove the bag toward Arthur.

It sucks to hand it over, but I need to buy Arthur's help more than I need to keep Melissa's shelters afloat. I'll help her out with *honest* funding when all this is over.

Arthur licks his lips, staring at the cash. Almost ten thousand in total.

"What's the catch?"

"You get me a meeting with a cop. One that isn't dirty."

He stares at me. "What's this about, Rosa?"

Hearing my real name on Arthur's lips stirs up emotions I thought I'd forgotten. All at once, I can't help but think of Amory and his cheating and how easy it would be to even the scales right here, right now, with Arthur.

There had once been a time when Amy would have killed Arthur just because I'd mentioned him. I wonder what he would do if he could see me now.

I pull my eyes away from the tall man beside me and pretend to count the cash. "I want to get rid of the mafia."

"You know that's impossible."

I shake my head. "It was before, but not anymore. There's a war going on, one boss is dead, and another is about to follow. The gangs of New York are falling apart. They only need a little push, Arthur."

"What can Norman police possibly do to help? New York City is out of our jurisdiction."

I meet his questioning eyes. "But not outside the FBI's."

"They have their own jurisdiction too." His voice sounds tired, almost like he's talking to a child who won't listen. "There's an FBI headquarter in New York."

"And it's on the mafia's payroll."

"If they're bought and Norman FBI is beyond their territory, then there's nothing you can do."

"Yes, there is," I say.

He glares at me.

I glare right back.

"I need the help of *real* police. Cops and detectives who aren't dirty. People who will *do* something about the situation in New York. If I could just get someone to open a case—it might be enough to stir up the trouble we need. Trouble that will cause the mafia to collapse for good."

Arthur raps his knuckles on the hood of the car. "The FBI here can't do anything about the crimes happening over there, Rosa."

"Yes, they can," I insist. "They can open a joint investigation across state lines if there have been related crimes committed between their jurisdictions."

"Crimes like what?"

I smile. "Like kidnapping and human trafficking."

A long moment of silence passes between us. This is the opportunity I've been waiting for. The opening I need. It wouldn't have worked before. The mafia was too strong and too many cops were on their payroll. But now things are falling apart. Dirty cops are being cut loose; the mafia is crumbling before our eyes. This investigation could be the final straw that sends everyone scrambling.

I watch Arthur closely as he chews on all this. He's got a concentrated look on his face, lightly brushing his fingers over the cash in the duffel bag. I know what he's thinking; that this investigation will be built on my kidnapping. How I was captured here in Jersey and dragged across state lines back to New York. How dozens of women have been in that same situation. Because of Mikhail Volkov and his whorehouses. Because of Giovanni De Luca and his greed. Because of Arthur Hart and his lies.

"Rosa," Arthur says slowly.

"I won't incriminate you," I tell him. Technically, I have no idea who kidnapped me. I never saw the guy's face and I didn't see who was driving the car that hit Minnie. It wouldn't be a lie to say I'm not sure if he was directly involved.

I push the money closer to him. "That's all yours, plus anonymity, if you help me."

He starts shaking his head, but I speak before he gets the chance. "I just need a meeting. Can you set that up?"

Arthur stares at the money and then sighs. Shakes his head like he's disappointed. "I can do it."

I snatch the bag away before he can take it. "One more thing."

He frowns.

"Tell Melissa the truth about who you really are and everything you've been doing behind her back."

Arthur glares at me but the nasty look on his face doesn't last long. After a few moments, his fiery gaze slides over to the cash and he reaches for it again. I feel sick by how easy it is to sway him, but I've got what I need. I won't complain.

Arthur tugs the bag from my grasp. "Fine. I'll do it."

Twelve

It's cold out. We're crawling into a balmy autumn, but at night the air feels frigid—to the point of discomfort. I don't let it bother me as I stare at the house across the street. I need the cold to chill the red-hot anger I feel inside.

I'm on the sidewalk, hidden in the shadows as I observe the home of Niccolò Romano, underboss of the Italian mafia. It's just after midnight, but all the lights are on inside, and the driveway has an extra vehicle parked in it. I wonder why that is.

"Traitors having a meeting," Conrad grumbles beside me. He's stiff from head to toe, like a wild animal with its fur raised. He's been waiting for this day for a long time, probably more eager than I am to go in there and spill blood, but we've got to move carefully.

Giovanni De Luca is the rat we've been searching for, but I'm not entirely convinced he was working alone. For one, he's been holed up in his penthouse since before Rosa and I consummated the marriage. I thought he was paranoid about the war spiraling out of control, but now I'm thinking he was paranoid about us learning the truth and coming after him.

Either way, with him locked up in his apartment complex, he didn't have a way to get any intel to sell to Volkov. Which is why I'm here at Niccolò's home.

Niccolò has been working in Junior's place all this time. He's been at all of our meetings. He's known about all of our plans. And he took that information and gave it to Gio, who gave it to the Wolf.

The only reason I haven't decided to just blow up his entire house is because I've gotten to know Niccolò over these last few weeks. He doesn't strike me as a snitch or a mole. Maybe I just don't know him well, or maybe Rosa's got me going soft, but part of me believes Niccolò may be innocent in this. That he wasn't taking our secrets to the enemy, but instead he'd simply been doing his job as an underboss; delivering updates and reports to Gio the same way Conrad would report to me if he acted in my absence.

Gio could have taken the info to Volkov all on his own without Niccolò even knowing.

It's a gamble. But that's why I'm here now—to find out the truth.

"At least four bodies," Morgen's voice sounds in my earpiece. He's in a van parked half a mile away, typing away on his computers as he hacks and shuts down Niccolò's security system. We're waiting for his cue to move in, so they won't have the chance to call for help.

Wolfgang tilts his head back and blows cigarette smoke straight up into the air. I watch the bitter heat rise and dissipate. "You ready?"

He glances at me and winks. "Just give me the word, Bruder."

I like this version of Wolf. The one who isn't stirring up trouble and making a mess of everything behind my back. This is the brother I remember as a kid, the one who'd followed me around, eagerly waiting for orders so he could prove himself to our father and the rest of his men. It wasn't until it really sank in that he's the second born and would never truly have our father's respect or approval that he changed. Stopped caring about impressing Vater and simply lived for the thrill of mafia life.

That was when my brother went from a wolf to a mad dog.

I could say he changed for the worst, but the truth is that his brutality is the best thing that's happened to the Hunting Grounds in a while. Wolfgang is an idiot. He's an uncontrollable dog who needs anger management. But as long as you're holding his leash, he isn't bad. And as long as the job involves shedding blood, he's going to get it done.

Conrad has always said he's our best hitman. He wasn't lying about that.

Morgen speaks into the earpiece again. "Done. All security systems shut down. All phone signals blocked. You have approximately twenty-two seconds before anyone notices."

I glance at my brother. "Go."

Wolf flicks his cigarette away and stalks across the street. Conrad and I watch quietly, counting off the seconds as he moves. He is quiet as a cat, padding around the side of the house and disappearing into the shadows. I get nervous as I watch, staring at the windows. The blinds are only partially drawn, so I catch flashes of the residents inside as they walk back and forth.

I see the moment when they realize something's wrong. The internet is down, their phones aren't working, they can't get a signal. Someone walks to the window and peers out— blood spatters on the glass as a bullet goes through their head from behind.

Shrieks erupt inside, along with gunfire and hoarse, German cursing. Wolf is going nuts in there. I can see his dark figure running past the windows as they're sprayed with blood—the flashes of gunfire lighting up his form against the darkness outside. I told him he could do whatever he wanted, just leave Niccolò and his immediate family alive, in case we are wrong, and he isn't knowingly selling secrets to Gio. I don't want to shed innocent blood for no reason.

After a few moments of horrible screaming, the house falls silent.

I press my finger to my earpiece. "Moving in."

"Us too?" Morgen asks—Eike and Klaus are with him, standing guard.

"No. Stay put. Move in if we don't make contact within the next ten minutes."

"Rodger."

As Conrad and I cross the street, the front door flies open, and a bloody Italian man sprints out. Wolfgang flies out the house right behind him and tackles the man to the ground. He pummels him as we pass by, letting out a howl of bloodthirsty anger with each hit.

"That's enough, Wolfy," I say, passing into the home.

When I glance around the house, I don't feel bad at all. The only dead bodies are Italian grunts—security guards who died trying to protect the Romanos. Meanwhile, Niccolò is on his knees, blood smeared on the side of his head, wetting his dark, wavy hair. His wife is kneeling beside him, the front of her nightdress covered in blood spatter. She wipes her hands along the front of her dress as she sobs incoherently.

The last person on their knees is Olivia Segreto. Tears streak her face as she gasps for breath, screaming sobs and a string of words I can't understand because she's speaking Italian. But I don't need to know what she's saying to get the gist of things. She's holding the hand of Marco Segreto—her husband—who looks like he's been shot in the leg. Probably tried to play tough guy and protect his wife and in-laws. Idiot.

"Jägermeister." Niccolò's voice is raspy and tired, but I can hear the shock in his words. "What is the meaning of this?"

"Search the house," I tell Conrad. He leaves without another word, exchanging places with Wolfgang who walks back inside dragging the body of the poor grunt who'd tried to run away. He leaves him halfway in the doorway and halfway on the porch before he marches over to me and pulls out his handgun.

162

"Which one dies?"

I gently place my hand on the gun and lower it. "We're about to find out."

"What is the meaning of this!?" Niccolò shouts.

Olivia sobs. "Rosa is my friend—my *best* friend!"

"I know," I tell her plainly.

"Then why would you shoot my husband!"

I squat in front of her, never once glancing at Marco who lies clutching his leg with one hand and squeezing hers with the other. "I will shoot anyone I need to if it means keeping her safe. That includes you, princess."

Her face curdles in anger. "I would never hurt her!"

"But he might." I nod at her father, who's staring at me with wide, perfectly circular, eyes.

"Jägermeister, I—I would never..."

"Giovanni De Luca is a traitor," I say. "He's been selling intel to Volkov and screwing us over. It's because of him that my father and uncle are dead." I rise and nod at Wolf who aims his gun at Niccolò again. "Did you know about this?"

Niccolò stutters," I—I—no! Of course not!"

"Don't lie to me," I growl.

Niccolò literally puffs his chest, sucking in an indignant gasp and staring daggers at me. He's trying hard to seem fierce and fearless even though he's a sixty-year-old man on his knees.

I almost laugh, but Conrad stumbles back inside, dragging a man with him. All eyes shift to the two of them and I feel a sudden shock of anger storm through me.

It's Aldo Romano.

But he hardly looks like himself. He's thin and gangly, not at all the tall, strong man I remember grinding against my wife on the dance floor. He looks like a pale shadow of that man with a scraggly beard and limbs that look thin from loss of muscle. Like he's been wasting away in here.

"What's going on?" I ask.

Niccolò's chest deflates. "I knew that Gio was dirty, but I never knew he was selling secrets to the Wolves. I swear."

"What do you mean, you knew he was dirty?"

He clenches his jaw. "Aldo found financial records that indicated Gio owed money to someone—a lot of it—and he'd been stealing from the businesses to pay it back. Aldo had been digging into the records on his own, but then he was injured. Doing a job for you."

I don't miss the way he pauses to glare at me.

"He was shot in the arm. It was just a flesh wound, but it got infected and required surgery."

I glance back at Aldo and my stomach clenches. Rosa had mentioned him getting surgery before, but I thought she meant he was undergoing something simple. Not having his arm amputated.

There is a stump where his right arm used to be, forcing Conrad to wrap an arm around his waist to hold him up. As I stare at the bandages on his shoulder, everything clicks into place. Why he looks so sick and frail. Why the family is gathered at the home—he just had surgery, they're all here taking care of him. Probably staying up around the clock to look after him.

Still, I won't let that blind me to other possibilities.

"That doesn't tell me if you were selling secrets or not," I say to Niccolò.

He grunts. "Aldo got shot working for you. But his arm was amputated because of Gio."

I tilt my head to the side.

"He came to visit him in the hospital. Stayed in the room with my boy for fifteen minutes."

"Doing what?" I ask.

"I don't know. But since that day, Aldo's health has gone downhill." Niccolò wheezes and falls over to the side. He's old and tired from all the excitement of the night, I don't make him straighten up.

"I have no proof that Junior did anything. But I know it in my heart. I know it as a father who loves his son. A man who visited his boy every day, every chance he could. And now…" His voice trails off as he looks over my shoulder at Aldo, his eyes focusing on the missing limb.

Aldo is a cripple now. I can't imagine the fury Niccolò must feel over it, knowing Gio had something to do with the whole situation.

"Junior tried to kill Aldo because he found out he'd been looking into the finances. Finding things he wasn't supposed to."

"Things that could cause a coup," I mutter, thinking of the fear I'd seen in Gio's eyes when I'd gone to confront him about sending the aid he'd promised as our ally in the war.

Maybe that's why he's holed up in his penthouse. Not because he had initially feared Volkov. Or had later feared me. He'd realized Aldo had been digging, and he knew his days were numbered.

"When Aldo was hospitalized," Niccolò goes on, "I took over the duties he left behind. I found all the research he'd been doing, and I started digging too. I wanted to finish what that little snot tried to end. I wanted to complete the job my son lost his arm to protect."

"And what job is that?" I ask slowly.

Niccolò puffs his chest again, looking fiercer than the first time. "To overthrow Giovanni as don of the Italian mafia."

The room falls silent, even Olivia has stopped her sobbing, staring at her father with a shocked look on her face. I glance down at Marco for the first time, not at all surprised by his stoic expression. Aside from the fact that he's in pain from being shot, he's not panicking—because he's known all of this. They were probably in here meeting about what to do next, using Aldo's health as an excuse to be in the same room without drawing suspicion to any spies Gio may have.

It's a very convincing story. But I'm not sold just yet.

"Do you have any proof of this?" I ask. I already know Gio was in severe debt. I know he killed his father to take over the Garden and try to pay those debts. At least part of Niccolò's story is true, but I need to know that he was truly investigating him. That he has no loyalty to the man who tried to silence his son.

To my shock, Marco Segreto is the one who answers. He sucks in a painful breath and then winces as he rolls to the side and fishes out a flash drive from his pocket. With bloody fingers, he holds it up to me.

I snatch it from him and then pull the drive reader from my own pocket (Morgen insisted I take it with me—having a hacker on the team sometimes comes in handy) and plug them both into my phone. Then I tap my earpiece.

"Morgen, talk to me."

Exactly four seconds tick by before he breathes into the comms. "Holy…"

"What is it?"

"Records, documents—hundreds of them. It'll take me days to read them all, but just from the look of things, they're legit. Bank statements, fraudulent checks, loans taken out in Gio Senior's name with his signature forged. Junior was stealing millions."

"From his own organization," I whisper.

"To pay Volkov." Niccolò takes a slow breath. "I did not know who his mystery lender was for a long time. But now it makes sense. He betrayed the Garden to pay back Volkov. Then he betrayed my son to keep that a secret."

"And now he's betraying the Hunting Grounds," I finish his thoughts for him.

I can't exactly pinpoint any reason for Gio turning on us. I get that he panicked and tried to cover his financial failure by killing his father. And when that secret almost came out, he tried to kill Aldo to keep everything buried. But what reason did he have to betray our alliance? What spooked him enough to start selling secrets to the Wolves?

I suppose the only way to find out is to ask him.

I sigh and nod at Wolf. "Lower the gun."

He hesitates but follows orders.

"I believe you, Niccolò," I say calmly.

His eyes fill with relief.

"I will spare your family tonight. But I won't promise any such thing for Gio. He will die for his treachery."

"If I could pull the trigger myself, I would."

"When I kill Gio, I will look to you to fill his shoes."

"As his underboss, it is my responsibility to do so," Niccolò says firmly.

I nod. "I expect you to honor the alliance he broke." The Garden still doesn't offer much, but I want all the help I can get until the war is truly over. At the very least, it'll help to know the Italians will be under leadership I trust.

Niccolò grunts. "Of course."

I cram my hands into my pockets and give him a lazy smile. "All right, then. I think we're done here."

Thirteen

Everything is in place. We dealt with Niccolò—made sure he wasn't a snitch like his Boss—and set up a new don to take over once Gio is out. Now, all we've got to do is actually take Gio out.

We've surrounded the building, calling in every man we could spare in case things got out of hand. They're waiting some distance away, so we don't draw attention to ourselves. Things have to be done with the utmost caution right now. Giovanni was already on high alert well before all this went down. After failing to kill Aldo, he's known his days were numbered. I'm not stupid enough to underestimate him and believe we'll catch him unawares, but I will take solace in the fact that we have the numbers. And my men know what they're doing.

There are only four guards downstairs. My snipers take care of them in silence, and my front men move in to catch their bodies before they hit the ground. Niccolò was kind

169

enough to share the security codes to the entrance and the elevator. It seems Gio still trusted him somewhat, despite trying to murder his son. Then again, it's not like he had much of a choice. How else could you steal intel from your underboss if you never let him in for a visit?

My men move in quickly and quietly, guns drawn. They clear the halls and rooms floor by floor, finding only six more guards. I'm not surprised by the low numbers, the Garden was broken long before Gio locked himself away. He'd only been able to offer me fifty men for the war, I doubt there's more than twenty guys in the building.

I realize my estimation is right when I get the all-clear for my team to move in. Hans's voice comes over the comms as a deep rumble in my ear. "We're outside his apartment, Jägermeister. It's safe to move in."

I would have gone in with the front men, but Hans had insisted I stay behind and wait for clearance. He didn't want to take any chances. I appreciate his caution. It gave me the time to calm myself, to approach this as business, not as a personal act of vengeance and hatred. Even though that's exactly what it is.

But I won't be able to sleep at night if I think of it that way. It's got to be business. It's got to be another hit; another traitor being taken care of. If I see this for what it truly is, I will have to acknowledge the darker part of this truth—that I'm murdering my wife's brother.

Granted, he tried to murder me first, if only by extension, but still. He killed my father and my uncle. Morgen was taken and tortured because of him. Volkov has copies of sex tapes between my wife and I because of him. And who knows how many other tapes from the security footage. Giovanni might be Rosa's older brother, but he isn't an angel.

I grind my teeth together as I exit the elevator to his floor. *This is just business*, I remind myself, and even if it isn't. Giovanni deserves this. He must die.

If I let him live after learning of everything he's done, my men will think I'm weak and I'll be facing a different sort of betrayal. *He's got to die*, I tell myself, gripping my handgun tightly. But does it have to be me? Do I have to pull the trigger myself?

I wonder if that will make a difference to Rosa. If she'll still cry when I deliver the news, or if it'll give her some sort of comfort knowing that I didn't do it myself. I betrayed her once by keeping her father's death a secret, I don't want to hurt her again by taking her brother's life.

Whatever happens, I'm out of time for planning.

The door to Gio's penthouse is right in front of me. Hans and Klaus are waiting with a battering ram, ready for my cue. Wolf and Conrad have their guns out—even Maximilian is here, checking his weapon as he waits.

Eike is standing guard over Morgen who's in his tech van again. By now, he's hacked the security system, playing the same footage on loop so anyone watching the cams doesn't see us standing outside the don's door.

I take a short breath and stand there like I'm waiting for something to happen. In the back of my head, I *am* waiting.

I'm listening for that Voice. The one that warned me about Stonehall, and I didn't listen. The one that told me He loved me, and I didn't listen.

I'm listening now. But the Voice never comes—that's a message in itself.

The choice is mine.

But no matter what I do, someone will die. How is that all right? How is any of this okay? There is another choice, to walk away entirely. But God knows I can't do that.

"Jägermeister?" Maximilian is looking at me with a stern expression.

I nod and signal to Hans. "Do it."

When the battering ram hits, the door flies open without any trouble, like it was never locked. That should be our first clue, but we're all riding the high of our mission, adrenaline pumping through our veins, a thirst for blood and vengeance driving us forward.

Inside, I can see that the lights are completely out—clue number two—but Max rushes in before I can stop him. He's gunned down the next second, heavy body hitting the floor like a rock. When Wolf steps forward, I grab him by the collar and yank hard. I can *feel* the air split around me as a bullet whizzes past. My cheek suddenly feels like it's on fire and I realize I've been shot; it's just a flesh wound, like a cat running its claw over my face, but it still hurts, and it distracts me from the onslaught of gunfire that pops off the next second.

Like a madman, Klaus shoves both my brother and I to the floor as he steps in front of us and takes a shower of bullets to

the chest. Conrad is crouched, taking cover beside the wall—
Morgen is screaming in my earpiece, even Eike is shouting for
us to be okay.

This is hell. I am living in hell right now, and there is no
escape.

Beneath the gunfire, I can make out Morgen's words—he's
not screaming for us to escape, he's screaming in pain. "Under
fire!" he cries, and then the line goes static.

What is happening?

How is everything going so wrong?

The spray of bullets stops, and the hall goes silent. All I can
hear is the ringing in my ears and Klaus's wheezing as he tries
to suck breath through his damaged lungs. Just looking at him,
I know he's dying. I can count the bullet wounds from here.
At least six.

Wolfgang is beside me, for the first time he seems like a
little boy instead of the ruthless mafioso I know he can be. He's
curled up against me, hands covering his head as he cowers.
This isn't the first time either of us has faced gunfire or death,
but it's the first time we've been surrounded by the enemy and
overtaken by surprise.

I can hear the pounding footsteps of men rushing toward
us. I can hear guns locking as soldiers ready their weapons.
We're going to die in this hallway. Wolf knows that, and all he
can do is tremble in my arms as we wait for death to come.

"Wolfy," I whisper, shaking his shoulder.

He uncurls to look up at me; fear is all I see in his eyes.
"Alles wird gut."

He knows what it means, and he knows it's a lie.

"Everything will be fine," I say again, this time in English.

"Big words for a dead man." The voice comes from inside the dark penthouse—but the statement itself isn't what turns my bowels watery. It's the man the voice belongs to.

Mikhail Volkov.

He steps forward into the light of the hallway so I can see him clearly, just in time for his Russian troops to join us. They pour from the stairwells, guns aimed, faces mottled in anger.

Mikhail smiles and it's a devilish little grin that ignites a fire inside me. "You little—"

Someone over my shoulder cocks their gun, one of the little wolves. The sound silences me immediately, but it doesn't wipe the glare off my face.

"How?" I ask.

Mikhail only scoffs and turns to walk back into the luxury apartment. "Bring them," he orders.

The grunts grab us roughly by the arms and shoulders, stepping over Max and leaving Klaus to die in the hallway. I can't look at their bodies as we're shoved inside. I don't want to think about how many I've gotten killed today.

"My brother," Conrad sobs, snot dribbling down his beard. "Morgen…"

"Probably dead," Volkov says darkly. His sharp eyes stab into me as he shifts focus. "Like he should have been weeks ago."

The men shove us to our knees and the lights switch on. I blink away the stars in my eyes to find Giovanni sitting on his living room sofa, two Russian guards on either side of him, and Eliana standing off to the side. I want to scream at her, to call her a lying whore, but the look on her face tells me she had no part in this.

First of all … she's wearing a collar. Exactly like the one Amana had on when I first met her. This one is black and made of leather, studded with diamonds, like she's his pretty little pet. Mikhail is parading her around now, taking her everywhere he goes to shame her and use her and show the world how much power he has over the Morenos. To reduce the firstborn princess to his personal toy like this… It's disgusting, even for Volkov.

But right now, none of that matters. I'm here on my knees in front of the man who killed my family and my men, and all I can do is wait for him to deliver judgment. It burns a hole of anger into my blackened heart. This is not how things were supposed to go down. Mikhail Volkov isn't supposed to be holding a gun to my head right now. Giovanni De Luca isn't supposed to be smirking down at me right now. But there he is. And here I am.

And this is all so screwed up.

Volkov cocks his gun. "Any last words?"

"How?" I grind out. "How did you know?"

To my surprise, he lowers the gun and takes a step back. "Giovanni came to me. Said he did not believe in the Hunters of New York anymore. Said he wanted to work together. Wanted to side with the winning team."

Of course. Why am I not surprised the only reason everything fell apart was because Giovanni De Luca lost his balls? Couldn't stick it out. Couldn't handle the stresses and frustrations of war. This betrayal is coming from the same man who killed his father and sold his sister, then tried to murder his childhood friend while he was in the hospital. I am not surprised in the least.

Volkov scratches his grey head with his gun. "Of course, I did not believe him when he first showed up in Staten Island. But he proved his loyalty to me when he told me the truth."

I look over at Gio for the first time, knowing exactly what Volkov means.

"You sold us out," I say, voice like acid. "You went back on everything we agreed on. You spineless little snot."

Gio swallows nervously. "I want to live, Amory."

"Even if it means betraying everyone close to you!?" I shout.

He just looks away.

Volkov steps forward and jams the gun into Wolfgang's forehead. "You took my daughter from me. Murdered her like she was some common harlot."

Wolf looks Volkov right in the eye. "I loved her."

Everyone pauses—even me, *especially* me. I have never heard my little brother speak of any woman with love or affection in his voice, but the emotion is there. I can see it in the way his eyes water. I can see it in the way his spine straightens and how he doesn't back down from the Wolf, not even with a pistol pressed against his skull. He means every word he's saying.

"I loved Sofia," he says again, more strongly this time.

"You *killed* her," Volkov hisses.

"I didn't mean to…" He drops his head as a strangled sob breaks through. Maybe it's because he's so scared. Maybe it's because he knows his life is about to end. Maybe it's because this is the truth.

Is it possible to kill someone you love?

I have no idea, but I'm not about to waste my last few moments alive trying to figure it out. I could think about all my regrets, about every mistake I've made leading up to this point, or I could think of Rosa and how distraught she'll be when she gets news of my death. Instead, I close my eyes and think of the person I've never seen. The One who seems to know me so well yet feels so far away.

God, I whisper inside—but Volkov's voice cuts off whatever prayer I had ready.

"I have been waiting for this day for almost five years," he says. "And now you are finally here." He smiles. "Are you ready?"

No one answers, and he responds by turning and shooting Giovanni. Right in the chest.

The Italian don gasps as he clutches at his heart. He is just as shocked as I am—I don't even register the cry that tears from my lips as I watch him fall over onto the sofa. His perfectly crisp white suit blooms a splotch of red on his breast pocket as he bleeds out, the light and life fading from his eyes.

He has no last words. Offers no apologies or hissing curses of anger. He just dies.

Volkov sighs, gazing at Gio's body with a bored expression on his face. "He truly believed I would let him live if he sold you out."

Gio was an idiot. And he died like an idiot. Never saw it coming.

"I knew you would eventually learn the truth and come for Gio," Volkov says to me. "All I had to do was wait."

So that was his plan all along. Draw me out by using a mole to get my attention.

I glance up at Eliana, which makes Volkov smile. "She did wonderful, did she not? Pretending to betray me. Putting on that little sex kitten act—" he snorts out a laugh. "In a field of lilies! Really, Jäger? I never took you for a romantic."

He had known all along. Had probably instructed Eliana to plant seeds into my head, tell me that she was his little toy. That he was abusing her. That she wanted to get away. All to make it seem like she was acting against him. All to get me and Wolf here today—because it wasn't enough to simply take me out. Volkov truly wanted my brother. He's had more than a few chances to kill me before now, but he waited. Planted seeds and lies to draw us both out. Even used Eliana in all this.

Everything I knew was a lie.

But only the parts about working behind Volkov's back. That's what Mikhail doesn't understand. He has no idea that Eliana *does* truly hate him. He has no idea that she wasn't just playing me—she was using us both.

178

He learns this fact a little too late.

In one swift motion, Eliana leans over the sofa, grabs the gun holstered at Gio's hip, and fires into the back of Volkov's head. He dies with a gasp, his blood spraying Wolfgang in a burst of red. Just like Junior—he never saw it coming.

And neither did his men.

The grunts standing around hesitate for half a second, giving Eliana time to put a bullet into the head of the one closest to her. Gunfire explodes in the room before his body even hits the floor. Conrad dives away, dragging Wolf with him as they take cover together behind a coffee table. I launch forward and grab the gun from Volkov's dead hands, pulling the trigger in time to stop the Russian who's aimed his rifle at me. I shoot him in the throat—my aim is slightly off, but it stops him, nonetheless.

His body seizes as he dies, squeezing the trigger of his assault rifle and wildly spraying bullets through the room. He shoots two of his own men as he goes down; I take down the last one as I shift and fire. This time, my aim is perfect—a bullet between the eyes.

When the gun smoke clears and the toll of death is paid, I drop the gun and crawl over to my brother and cousin. Conrad is holding Wolfgang almost like a child. Both of them blink up at me when I get closer.

"It's over," I whisper breathily. I can't believe I'm saying the words. "Volkov is dead."

Wolf crumples and falls into my arms. He's such a kid right now, it's almost painful. All I can do is crush him in a hug as Conrad pats my shoulder and stands to look around.

"You're okay," I tell Wolfy as he cries like a baby.

Jesus, this guy isn't even a *shadow* of the little jerk I remember. Nights ago, he snuck into the home of Niccolò Romano and killed a handful of Italian men all by himself. And now he's crying uncontrollably and clinging to his older brother like I'm all he's got in this world.

I *am* all he's got.

And maybe it's because he's finally realized how hard we've all been fighting—how close to death we've all been for months now—that everything is finally sinking in. All at once.

This life is not a game. The mafia is not some silly show to binge on weekends. It's real. And it isn't pretty.

"Bruder!" Wolfgang gasps. He pulls away and clutches at my shirt, and I realize he's checking me for wounds.

I lean back and watch him. He was like this when we were boys, always acting tough—until everything finally clicked. Until he realized just how serious the mission was, and then he'd get spooked, and I'd have to clean up his mess. But we aren't boys anymore. And the consequence of our failure isn't a scolding from Vater. It's death.

Wolf is still grabbing at my shirt, panic in his eyes as he wipes at splotches of blood, trying to figure out if it's mine or someone else's. *God*, he's such a kid right now.

I catch his shaking hands. "I'm fine," I say softly. When he keeps staring at the stains on my clothes, I grab his face and make him look at me. "I'm fine, Wolfy. *You're* fine. It's over."

He hugs me, muffling his words against my chest. "I'm sorry, Amy."

It's a name only Rosa has ever used. But it sounds fine coming from him too, especially after everything that's happened. We should have died today. And no one knows that better than Wolfgang. He knows all of this is his fault, all the death, all the fighting. And now that's he's finally out of Stonehall, facing this reality on his own, he's finally learned his lesson. He's finally sorry for what he's caused.

I hug him tighter. "It's over, Wolfy. Finally."

"No, it's not," Conrad says across the room.

I make sure my little brother can stand on his own before I pull away and join my cousin at the sofa; my jaw falls open at the sight before me.

Eliana Moreno is slumped over on the couch, leaning against Gio's body as she cradles a bullet wound in her stomach. She blinks at me wearily as I slowly sit beside her, gentle eyes fluttering behind dark lashes. This is the calmest I've ever seen her, and it breaks my heart.

There is no anger in her visage, no hatred, no jealousy, no lust or childish frustration. This is Eliana Moreno, a woman in pain. And there is nothing I can do to help her.

"Liana," I whisper, taking her into my arms. I rest her over my lap, supporting her head so she can look up at me.

181

Her hand goes to my cheek, smearing blood across it. I take it and plant a crimson kiss on her palm. "You saved my life. And my brother's. And my cousin's." We would be dead if it weren't for her. I'll never forget that.

"I lied to you," she exhales painfully.

"For the first time," I whisper. "But you saved us in the end."

She laughs. "And look what it did for me."

"Liana..."

Slowly, almost tiredly, she drags her hand from my cheek to her neck, tugging feebly at her collar. "Don't let me die wearing this. I don't want to die belonging to him."

I shift her in my arms so I can unbuckle the leather strap.

"I'm not a slave," she whispers, and I can't tell if she's talking to me or herself. I suppose it doesn't matter.

When the collar falls to the floor, she sighs. I can see the faint impression of the strap against her olive skin. I wonder how long Volkov had her wearing it. If he removed it on days he knew we'd be seeing each other, so it wouldn't cause suspicion. He didn't bother removing it today. Because I wasn't supposed to make it out of this room alive.

The war was going to end today. But now it can't because Emilio Moreno will want vengeance for his daughter's death. Even though I didn't kill her. Even though she's dying in my arms and it hurts so much I feel like I'm dying with her.

He will blame me.

I can't say I don't blame myself. Eliana wouldn't be here if it weren't for me. If I had married her like I was supposed to.

"I'm so sorry…" the words are strangled, clawing their way from my throat as tears blur my vision.

I'm alive. But what was the cost of saving my life?

Maximilian, Klaus, possibly Morgen and Eike. And now Eliana.

She pats my cheek again. "Was it true, my love?"

I blink at her, my tears landing on her cheeks and sliding down, streaking through the blood.

"Am I a woman worth loving? If things were different?"

It's what I'd said to her in the field of lilies. As we'd made love for the last time. I hate the reminder of what I've done, how I cheated on my wife, but I'm glad that's the last thing Eliana will remember before she dies. Instead of the collar around her neck. Instead of the things Volkov did to her—in private and public.

I nod slowly. "I meant every word."

She laughs, though it almost sounds like a sob. "Will you say it? Just once. Tell me you love me, Amory."

I stare down at her. My lips part, but no words come forth.

I've made a lot of mistakes in my marriage. I've done things I regret, things I could never make up for. But I won't do this. Not now. Not even for a dying woman.

Eliana gives me the saddest smile I've ever seen. "You truly love her, don't you?"

"Liana…"

She brushes away a tear that slips down my cheek. "I'm so … jealous."

I take her hand, gasping as her grip weakens. The light begins to fade from her eyes, sending me into a panic.

"Eliana?" I say quietly.

She doesn't answer.

I grab her by the shoulders and stare down at her. She stares back, but her gaze is lifeless and dull.

"Eliana!"

I don't realize I'm screaming until Conrad grabs me by the shoulder. It takes him and Wolfgang both to drag me from the sofa and pry Eliana's dead body from my arms.

"She's gone!" Conrad shouts in my face.

I blink at him, dazed and confused.

"Look around," Conny growls. "*Everyone* is gone."

"Not everyone," says a raspy voice from the doorway.

I look over to find Hans leaning against the doorframe, Morgen is under his arm, helping him stay on his feet. Eike is beside him, along with two men from the Stronghold.

"Bruder…" Conrad stumbles over and pulls Morgen into a hug. I know how he feels.

Jared steps into the room. "Sorry we were late. The Wolves held us up in Brooklyn."

"In *Brooklyn?*" Conrad clarifies. "They attacked our turf?"

Jared looks grim. "We managed to chase them away."

"For how long?" Morgen asks, staring at Eliana's body.

"The Morenos will want blood," Conrad agrees. "This war isn't over yet."

No, it isn't. But things are better than they were before. One of our enemies is dead. One more to go.

I walk to the middle of the room. "We did a good job today, all things considered."

Wolfgang nods.

"Giovanni De Luca is dead. Mikhail Volkov is dead."

Jared smiles.

"But Maximilian and Klaus are also dead, and probably dozens of other Hunters." I glance back at the couch. "And Eliana Moreno."

The room shifts, smiles melt away.

"The Morenos will want blood for her death. We've survived this long. Let's finish this."

Fourteen

The air is cool as it flows between my fingers, my hand hanging out the window with Douglass driving down the highway. We're going back to New York, even though I vowed I wouldn't return until I was sure Amory had learned his lesson for what he'd done. But with everything that's happened *outside* our marriage, I'm willing to put the sins between us aside. I'm ready to forgive him and move on. Or at least try to move on.

No one ever said it would be easy to overlook his mistake—or that it had to be overlooked at all. We need to address his infidelity. We need to address the trust he's broken and the faith he's destroyed. But that can wait for now.

If there was ever a time for me to grow up, to kill the girl inside, it's now. Amory needs me to be strong—stronger than him. I feel like that's all I can offer right now.

Things went well in Norman. Better than I imagined they would—in fact, Melissa was sad to see me go so soon, but after getting a confirmed date for my meeting with Arthur, I had to go home to tell Amory about everything. I could call him. I could text him. I could even send a message through Douglass if I felt he might ignore my attempts to communicate with him, but I want to discuss this in person. If this meeting goes well, everything will change. That's not a conversation I want to have over the phone.

It takes Douglass and I an extra hour to get home since we stop for lunch at a small diner along the highway. I have a stack of pancakes and he enjoys an omelet stuffed with cheese and spicy peppers. It's breakfast for dinner and it leaves me tired and groggy, I can't help but nod off as we finish the last hour of the trip.

When Douglass gently shakes me awake, I groan and blink at the evening sky.

"We're here," he says, and the caution in his voice makes me sit upright and stare at him.

"What's wrong?"

He glances out the window, drawing my attention to my surroundings. We're not at the Jäger estate, this is a safehouse.

"Why are we here?" I frown.

"I got an alert from Hunter security guards. Something's wrong. Something's happening in the city. I didn't trust the estate."

I don't blame him, considering what happened to Stonehall. I'm a little wary of going to the estate too, but there is no guarantee of safety here either. If the Wolves could get to Stonehall, then they could get anywhere they wanted.

"Let's go inside," I say, opening my door.

Douglass becomes my shadow, following me through the parking lot of the hotel/safehouse up to the front doors. The guards immediately recognize us and step aside without question, though I do catch the bewildered look on their faces, as if to say—*what are you doing here?* Truth be told, I don't know. I feel like I have less of a chance at seeing Amory here than if I'd gone home, but there's no point being there if it'll get us both killed.

When I enter the hotel lobby, it's clear Douglass's concerns were warranted. Everyone in the safehouse has gathered in the open lounge, just like we used to when Christina would summon us all for meetings late at night. Except now, Christina isn't the Mistress anymore—and she's not even living in the city. Amory told me she moved in with his aunt after Oberon's death. He hinted at having them both move into the estate, which I didn't mind, but we both felt they were safer outside NYC. Tonight may prove we were right about that.

Gisela is standing in the center of the room with Petra and Adella by her side. Being the underboss's wife makes her next in line as Mistress, I'm not surprised she's taken control in my absence. But now that I'm here, there'll be an expectation for me to take my place—even though I'm fine with Glizzy running things.

She sees me as I make my way through the crowd of women and worried children, Douglass close behind. Nothing but joy captures her features, and I can't help but smile back. Even Adella and Petra turn and grin when they spot me, welcoming me back with warm hugs.

"What are you doing here, flower?" Glizzy asks, brushing a curl from my face.

I squeeze her hand. "I was actually trying to figure out what's going on. I didn't realize we'd all moved back into the safehouses." Last I knew, most of the men had moved their women and kids back home after Morgen's funeral—I won't even mention how shocked I was at his miraculous revival. The things my husband and his men do to keep the Hunting Grounds alive and prosperous... Sometimes I don't want to know all the details. Sometimes I don't need the whole truth.

Gisela looks worried. "I don't know much, just that we were woken up by the fire alarms an hour ago. Information is trickling in, and it doesn't contain anything particularly useful."

Adella steps beside Gisela. "I finally got a message through to Jared."

"Did he reply?" Petra asks, her voice is wobbly, and her eyes are wet with unshed tears.

The sight of her threatens to send me into a panic. I pull out my own phone and check for messages from Amory—there aren't any.

Adella reads from her phone, "Mission took a turn. Stay alert tonight."

"Stay alert..." Petra repeats shakily. When no one says anything, she blinks at us and gasps. "What does that mean?"

"It could mean anything," I say. "But whatever it is, it isn't good."

As if on cue, the lights all turn out, draping us in a veil of black. Screams go off throughout the room, but they don't

189

sound like the calls of people being assaulted, just shrilly cries of frightened women and children.

I feel someone latch onto my arm and I yelp as I'm jerked to the side. Panic jolts through me, but when the lights flicker on and off again, I catch a glimpse of Douglass and my nerves settle somewhat.

"We've got to get you to safety, Mistress," he says in a shockingly calm voice.

"I'm not leaving Gisela and the others," I tell him, trying to twist my arm away.

The lights flicker again, but this time, the sudden flash is accompanied by the popping of bullets. Now the screams turn to horror and the fear is tainted black. I hear the windows shatter, sending a ripple of chaos throughout the hotel.

People begin to run in every direction. With the lights out, all we can see are flashes of each other here and there between the sporadic sprays of gunfire. I'm being dragged through the room by Douglass, my arm burns from his tight grip, getting worse as I twist and writhe to get free. I'm not leaving my cousin and underlady behind. I'd be the worst Mistress in the history of the Hunting Grounds, abandoning both family and friend.

Douglass isn't having any of it. I see his face as gunfire lights up the room, it's twisted in both fear and anger, but I won't back down on this.

"I'm not leaving them!" I shout as someone rams into me from behind. We tumble to the floor as bullets spray around us, and I realize it's a guard.

190

He's large and dark with smooth brown skin just like Douglass—someone from the Stronghold. Blood from his torso stains the front of my dress. I want to scream, but I don't have the air in my lungs. He took me to the ground when he fell into me, landing on top like a dead lover. I shove at him with all my might and as screams fill the lobby, I realize this encounter may be a blessing in disguise.

The bodies of women drop around me, gunned down in cold blood. Someone sets off a flare, lighting up the room in red. I'm thankful for the faint glow, though it sends a chill up my spine as I get the full scope of the carnage around me.

The walls are sprayed with blood. Women and children are still running, screaming, and trying to get away. In the crowd, there are men in uniforms walking slowly, holding assault rifles and making their way through the open lounge. I can't make out their faces in the hazy red glow of the flare, but I know they're not Hunters or soldiers from the Stronghold.

Suddenly, a weight is lifted from my chest as Douglass heaves the massive guard off me. I suck for precious air and hold on to him as he lifts me from the ground, but I don't let him carry me away.

"Adella—" I pant, gripping his arm as he stables me.

Douglass doesn't get to answer. A uniformed gunman fires at him, but he catches the glint of the weapon before the shot goes off and dodges the bullet. In a split second, he lifts his own gun and fires back, shoving me down so I'm out of the line of fire.

There are two more men approaching. We're sitting ducks in the middle of the room. But the woman of the hour arrives just in time.

Adella lets out a roar of anger as she whacks one of the gunmen over the head with what looks like a lounge chair. He crumples to the floor with a cry of pain, but Della makes sure he stays there, snatching up his dropped weapon and putting two holes in his head. Douglass takes out the other man with ease, but he doesn't see the Russian who jumps onto his back, tackling him to the floor.

In a sudden flash of panic, I scream and react without thinking, kicking the man hard right in the top of his head—but I'm only wearing ballet flats, so I hurt my foot more than I hurt him. Fortunately, none of that matters. My feeble attack is enough to distract him for the half-second Douglass needs to flip himself over and regain control of their little scuffle. He gets the man in a headlock and begins to choke him out, but there are more men moving in.

Someone over Douglass's shoulder raises his weapon, I see it happen almost in slow motion and I dive for his discarded gun before fear takes over.

I get the gun up in time, and I squeeze the trigger. But I do it with my eyes closed and end up missing by a mile. Fortunately, seeing me lift the weapon is enough to scare the guard, he ducks before I fire—and then curses as he realizes how bad of a shot I am. He just missed his only chance to kill Douglass. I won't give him another.

At least that's what I hope as I lift the gun again. This time, it misfires and jams, sending burning pain jolting through my wrist and forearm. I screech in both pain and absolute shock—but I don't have time to sort out the gun. The Russian guard is back on his feet, aiming his weapon again.

Douglass is still fighting for his life. Adella is taking down a Spanish gunman across the room. I'm all alone with a jammed weapon and a sprained wrist.

"God, help me!" I shout, throwing the stupid gun across the room.

That's the best aim I've ever had. It hits the man right in the face, his head whipping back with a snap, and then he hits the floor and doesn't get back up.

I won't allow myself to wonder if he's dead or alive. Instead, I turn to Douglass who's still on the floor with the man from before. He's managed to twist out of the chokehold, but Douglass is still holding him from behind, arms hooked under his pits to keep him in place.

I glare at the man, filled with rage and fear—plenty of fear. But the anger creates a storm. I raise my foot again—*not the head this time, that'll hurt too much*—and bring it down on his soft groin.

The man screams, jerking forward, and Douglass uses the momentum to flip him and snap his neck. He stands and pulls out another gun from a holster in his boot. Grabs me roughly by the arm.

"I've got to get you to safety."

I let him guide me away, slowly coming down from my rage-filled adrenaline high. But I'm not dazed enough to forget about Adella and the others.

When I spot Gisela and Petra huddled behind a sofa, I yank away from Douglass and dart toward them. He shoots a Spanish soldier who tries to go for me—I never miss a beat, sprinting through the mad chaos to get to my friends.

Petra crushes me in a hug, sobbing as she says, "This can't be happening!"

"We've got to go!" I say, dragging her back toward Douglass. Him and Adella hold point, fearlessly leading the three of us through the lobby.

The exits are all blocked by clusters of Russian and Spanish guards, forcing us to move toward the backdoors instead. When we stumble into the outside corridor, the silence that follows is almost deafening. There are bodies in the hallway, women, children, and a few of the Stronghold soldiers who'd been guarding them. I keep my vision forward as we run.

Douglass kicks in a random door and ushers us inside. The only light in the room comes from the little nightlight plug-ins that line the wall, but it's enough for me to recognize the room as a bathroom. The urinal on the wall tells me it's the men's room.

"Stay quiet," Douglass orders, panting for breath.

When I step closer to him, I realize he's been shot.

"You're hurt!" I gasp.

He waves me away, sliding down the wall so he's sitting on the floor. "I'll be fine."

"Let me have a look."

"Don't waste your energy on me."

"Douglass—"

He points behind me. "You have bigger issues, Mistress."

When I turn around, I almost faint.

Gisela is sitting on the floor beside Petra, holding her bloody hand. "She's hurt," Glizzy whispers. Her voice trembles and her chin quivers as she tries to hold back her tears.

I fall to my knees beside Petra, hands shaking as I peel her shirt from her abdomen to find the bullet hole in her side. She winces in pain and then laughs to herself.

"How bad is it?"

"We can help you," I say with a sniffle. "Della! Help me!"

Adella is by my side in an instant, but she sucks air through her teeth and shakes her head. "She needs a doctor."

"There must be a first aid somewhere," I say quickly. I press my hands to her wound, trying to stop the bleeding. "We just need to apply pressure."

Petra groans in pain.

Gisela grabs at my arm, trying to pull me away. "You're hurting her!" she cries.

"We have to stop the bleeding!" I tell her.

Petra touches my arm. "It's all right, Mistress."

"No, it's not!" I sob. I can't even see past my tears, but I can make out enough to know that Petra is somehow smiling, despite the pain she must feel. Despite knowing she's going to die on a bathroom floor, shot down by the Wolves.

It must have happened when we ran through the lounge. She'd been fine when I'd first found her and Gisela. She had even crushed me in a hug. And now she's bleeding out. She would have been fine if she'd stayed in her hiding spot.

I've done this. I've killed her.

I choke on a sob. "Petra…"

She shakes her head. "Don't cry for me. I'm going home, Mistress."

The truth is so sad.

"I used to hate it when you tried to get us all to pray." Petra laughs. "But now I'm grateful. I'm not afraid to die."

"We can save you!" I scream, then I start going through the 23rd Psalms. I shout every scripture I can think of. I ask God to heal her. I plead the Blood of Jesus. I rebuke the injury. I speak in Tongues.

But Petra slowly dies.

Not because God won't heal her, it's because she's ready to go.

"Let me die," Petra whispers. "The only way out of this life is death. Let me go, Rosa."

I shake my head. "Think of Eike!"

"Pray for him," she says. "Like you did for me."

"Petra…"

She lets go of my arm, head lolling as she stares at the ceiling. Her throat sounds dry as she begins to hum, but she finds the strength to turn her humming to singing. Her lyrics pierce my soul.

The Gates of Heaven open, and I am free

I will sing loud and true
As the angels wave me through
I will sing a song of praise
As I am held in His embrace
Welcome home, Child of God
Welcome home...

The room is dead silent after she finishes her song. I can't keep it together anymore. Something inside me breaks, shattering the silence as my sobs fill the room.

After a moment, Gisela grabs my hand and Adella kneels beside me, placing her gun on the floor as she rubs circles on my back. We sit there like that for what seems like hours, staring at Petra's lifeless body, her song echoing through the room, our tears wetting our cheeks. It's the saddest day of my life—and it only gets worse as I hear the sound of thunderous footsteps marching down hall.

Douglass shifts, but he's too weak to even lift his weapon now. "Adella," he rasps.

She's the only one here tough enough to take point, but what can she do with one stolen weapon against a team of Russian and Spanish mafiosi?

Before my cousin can respond, the bathroom door flies open. A Russian guard steps inside, weapon aimed and ready.

A gunshot goes off before he can hit the trigger—but it's not Adella who fires.

I blink as gun smoke drifts into the air. Tears blur my vision. I have a history of terrible aim—so I'm shocked when the man clutches his chest and topples face first to the floor. I don't even remember grabbing my cousin's gun. But it's in my hands and the man is dead now.

I just killed someone.

Adella gently touches my shoulder. She's whispering something about giving her the gun now, but I can't make out the words. I can't hear anything over the rushing in my ears, the pounding in my chest.

Another figure steps into the room.

I fire again—this time, I miss my shot and I'm thankful to God because when I blink away my tears, I see Amory standing in the doorway.

Fifteen

We almost got the call too late. Just as we'd celebrated our brief victory over Mikhail Volkov, Jared gave us the news that we'd been attacked by the Wolves on our own turf. The Stronghold managed to push back the Russian teams but when word got out about the death of Mikhail and Eliana, the Morenos and the Volkovs rallied their forces.

I remember when Wolfgang burst into my bedroom, the day after we stormed into Gio's penthouse. I moved him into the estate since his release from Stonehall—I would've waited to talk to Rosa about it first but after his breakdown in Gio's penthouse, he hasn't left my side. His eyes were wild and filled with panic when he flung my door open, not even caring that I was dead asleep in my boxers. When he passed me his phone and explained the situation, I was thankful he didn't care enough to wait for me to rise on my own.

The Morenos and the Volkovs had come together, determined to take us out once and for all. Even though we'd taken out their mole, the damage Gio had done still left us vulnerable. They knew the location of our safehouses—of even our personal homes. After losing the Alpha Wolf and the Moreno princess, our enemies wanted blood. Innocent blood.

The only thing that kept my hands from shaking as I'd slipped into my clothes was the fact that Rosa wasn't in New York. I didn't have to worry about her dying in one of the safehouses, a bullet to the head, her body being paraded around by vengeful Wolves.

And then I'd made it to the safehouse. And I got word from one of my men that they'd spotted Douglass inside—Douglass, my personal guard. The man I'd assigned to keep my wife safe. If he was in the safehouse, then so was Rosa. And that changed everything.

The only thought in my head was of my wife. I didn't care that there were people dying all around me, blood spraying the walls, bullets flying in every direction. I didn't care when my own men went down as I stormed through the hotel, screaming mad. There was no room in my head for me to care—I had been completely taken over by panic and fear. Fear that I wouldn't be able to find her, that I wouldn't get to her in time, that the only thing left of her would be an empty shell.

The thought threatened to send me to my knees as I rushed into the hall, following the trail of bodies left by people who'd tried to escape. I heard the voices coming from the bathroom and moved without thinking, my body acting on its own. But a Russian soldier beat me there, only to fall flat on his face as he was shot upon entry.

Seeing him dead on the floor gave me the courage I needed—whoever had shot him must have been one of ours. I was only hoping it was Rosa; truly, what were the odds?

And then I'd stepped inside.

Rosa screams as she fires the gun. I jerk backwards and duck, almost squeezing the trigger of my own gun on pure instinct. But I catch the wild fear in her eyes, and I lower my weapon, completely shocked that she's the one holding the gun. She just shot a Wolf in cold blood, no questions asked. My little rose.

There's no time to be proud of her. She's still holding the gun, tears streaming down both her cheeks as she gasps and sucks for breath. She's having a panic attack, but Adella does her best to calm her down, rubbing her back and whispering gently as she tries to get her to lower the gun.

With my hands in the air, I slowly walk across the room and kneel in front of Rosa. I don't allow myself to react to Petra's body lying before me. If I acknowledge the stab of pain I feel in my heart—even for a second—I won't be able to recover. I need to keep it together right now more than ever. If not for myself or the Hunting Grounds or the three scared women in front of me, then at least for my wife. The only woman who matters.

"Rosie," I whisper, gently reaching for her. I slowly wrap my fingers around the gun, and I feel it trembling in her grip. "Give me the gun, love."

She heaves a sob and blubbers my name, like she can't believe I'm here right now. I could say the same about her, but I'm just thankful she's alive despite all that's happened. "Amy…" she gasps again, blinking wildly. "Amy…"

"I'm right here," I say softly, tugging on the weapon. "Let me have the gun."

"I—I killed him."

"I know."

"I shot at you."

"It's okay." I lean toward her, still holding the cool metal. "It's over now. You can let go."

It finally clicks. With a teary-eyed blink, she lets go of the gun and falls forward into my arms, sobbing against my chest. I tuck the gun into my waistband and nod at Adella who grabs Gisela and ushers her outside where I know Conrad and the others have cleared out the rest of our enemies.

Rosa screams, literally *screams,* as she cries. It's the most heartbreaking thing I've ever witnessed, and I feel totally clueless as to how I can help her right now. The only comfort I've got is a gentle kiss to her temple as I hold her.

"You're okay," I tell her, even though I don't feel sure about it at all. I think she might have reached her limit. Might have finally broken beyond repair. And who wouldn't, after living through that? She had survived a vicious attack, fought for her life, watched her friend die on the floor, and then killed someone. She'd stayed strong for as long as she could.

"I'm sorry," she whispers.

"Don't be," I say. "I should have been here." I pull away and grab her hands, kiss each one. "These weren't meant for killing."

Rosa blinks at me, then she gasps like she just remembered something. "Douglass! He's been shot!"

For the first time, I look over her shoulder and spot him leaning against a stall. There's a red stain on his shirt and his eyes are weak and half-lidded, but he's still alive.

I stand, carefully pulling Rosa to her feet. "I'll get one of the men to help me take him out of here."

Rosa squeezes my hand, but it isn't a comforting gesture, it feels more like she doesn't want to let me go. I'm flattered—honestly, the little boy in me is blushing like a girl—but I have to take care of this. I've got to take care of everything.

How many people have we lost in these last few days alone? How many more will follow?

I don't allow myself to think about the loss as we clear out the hotel. I refuse to let in the grief as we collect our dead and notify families. It isn't until we start the long lineup of funerals that it all hits me.

Exactly four days after the attack on the safehouse, we finally lay our loved ones to rest. I have to attend each and every memorial service. As the Jägermeister of the Hunting Grounds, it's my duty to pay my respects. To kiss the hands of the wives left behind, to promise vengeance to the brothers who must say goodbye, to hug the children who are now fatherless, motherless, or missing siblings.

We lost 52 people between Gio's penthouse and the ravaged safehouse. I blame myself. I blame my obsessive desire to catch the mole. I blame my stupidity in ever trusting Giovanni De Luca. I blame the mistake of not taking out Volkov when I had him sitting across from me at the dinner table.

I had tried so hard. Had fought with everything inside me. Had set aside my morals, marriage, and beliefs to chase a peace that only feels empty and bitter. Emilio Moreno is still alive and still seeking vengeance. We aren't safe yet, but we don't feel threatened anymore. His forces are done. That safehouse storm was his last attempt at getting the payback he thinks he deserves. But I don't feel victorious.

I don't feel anything.

There is a blackness growing inside me. A void that threatens to swallow me whole. I can feel it's gaping mouth drawing near, its sharp fangs piercing into my heart as it devours me. I try to fight it, but my efforts are weak. There's only so much I can do when I'm staring down at 52 coffins.

We don't even hold the funeral in a church—there isn't a sanctuary in the city large enough for all the caskets and family members who've come to give their respects. We're in one of our warehouses, gutted and dressed up like a nice little popup church. There's a raised platform for the Jäger family and high-ranking members of respective gangs, a pulpit, and even a giant gold cross that hangs on the wall behind us. Father Serrano from the Garden is here, as well as Father Leonhart from the Hunting Grounds, and Pastor Sandra Davidson from the

Stronghold. All three church leaders whisper a prayer and deliver a nugget sermon.

I don't listen. All I can focus on are the coffins and the people gathered around them. We lost Maximilian. We lost Klaus—even lost his wife in the safehouse, and Petra too. Eike is burying his father, mother, and wife all in the same day. My heart crumbles for him as I glance down the raised platform and spot him wiping at his eyes. But right beside him is Morgen and his new bride, Silke. We're burying one of her sisters, Aloisia Bieker, who died in the safehouse.

On my other side is Jameson Willis, he's strong and stern as he stands beside me, but I can hear the pain in his voice as he grumbles through the speech he delivers in honor of his lost daughter-in-law, Diamond Willis—mother of Adella and Nona.

The girls stand behind us with my wife whose red eyes tell me everything I need to know when I look back and reach for her hand. It tears her up that she was right there in the safehouse with her own aunt and hadn't been able to save her. But at least she'd gotten to Adella in time, and I'm thankful to God that Nona had been away during the attack, sneaking off with friends.

The procession begins when Pastor Sandra finishes her closing remarks. Rosa's hand trembles in mine as we step off the dais and follow the crowd out. We're the last ones in line, walking behind a chorus of sniffles and sobs. The coffins remain where they are, men will come in to take them to the burial site once everyone is gone.

As we walk toward the door, I feel Rosa lean into me and I wrap an arm around her shoulders. She hasn't been the same since the safehouse attack. None of us have. But I think it's impacted her on a new level. She lost both her parents and her own brother, but she's never experienced anything like this. Despite being the daughter of a don, Rosa has never lived the true mafia life. Gio Sr. kept her sheltered, made sure she grew up with a fanciful view of the world that's only served to cripple her now.

She tugs on my sleeve as she slows to a stop in front of a casket I'm sure half my men believe shouldn't be here now. It belongs to Giovanni De Luca Jr.

I feel bad as Rosa wipes at her eyes. She's totally alone now, and part of that is because of me. We haven't talked about it yet, and I'm not sure we ever will. Her older brother is dead because he betrayed me. I wasn't the one who pulled the trigger, but still. I'm sure it's all the same to her. He's gone.

There's a pang in my chest as I watch my wife cry. She reaches up and touches the coffin, leaving a warm palmprint on the cool, glossy exterior. Then she pulls away and tucks her face into my chest.

"I'm sorry," I whisper.

She only sobs in response.

I have to hold her up as we walk down the aisle, coffins on either side of us. Our shoes hit the cement floor and echo throughout the warehouse, it sounds like an alarm going off—no, like the toll of a bell. The ones they ring at the church when someone dies. How fitting.

I wonder, as we near the exit, how many times would the bell ring for a gangster? They rang them all day at St. Peter's Cathedral when I was a kid and the mayor of New York City died. No one cared about the guy, but I guess being mayor gets you brownie points with God—if not at least the clergy.

There aren't any bells ringing now. No one cares about these men and women. To the rest of the city—the world— we are nothing but trouble. Even though they idolize us, even though they treat us as celebrities, there are plenty who still see us as nothing but a black stain on a once cleaner society. To them, we are scum they can't wait to get rid of. Well, the mission's almost been accomplished. I'm not sure how much longer we can last like this, how much longer we can go on. But duty calls.

There is no club to meet at anymore, but I know the men want to meet regardless. Conrad will call for blood—to finish off the Morenos while they're licking their wounds. Morgen will want vengeance too, on behalf of his dead sister-in-law. I have no idea what King James will say, but he won't be opposed to getting justice for Diamond.

I don't blame the men for their cry for blood, but as I look at the coffins around me, I can't find any of that black anger inside myself. There is no hateful rage, no thirsty plea for blood. There's nothing but darkness, a shadow looming over me—and that's what scares me the most. That I've begun to feel numb. That I've lost myself to the mafia.

I take a slow breath as something churns inside me, disgust, desperation, I don't know. Something that entirely rejects who I am. Something that knows I can't go on like this.

Even though I'm the one holding Rosa up, it's me who stumbles as we walk that dark aisle. I clutch at my chest as I drop to my knees right in the middle of this makeshift church. Unbidden tears fill my eyes, a croaking sob tears from my lips. I drop my head and rest there on my hands and knees, trembling and scared out of my mind.

What's happening to me?

"Amy?" Rosa sounds afraid. "Amy!" She drops to her knees beside me, shaking my shoulder. I can hear footsteps rushing back inside, and then Wolfgang's panicky voice, but Rosa steers him away and tells him to keep the others out. Then she's beside me again and I feel her warm hand rubbing circles on my back.

"Talk to me," she whispers. "Amy, please."

I lift my head, blinking away the loose strands of hair that've fallen into my face. Her eyes are red, her cheeks are puffy, there's a stream of tears flowing from her eyes, but she manages a smile, and it breaks my heart.

"You're okay," she says, the same way I'd said it to her in the safehouse. Oh, how the tables have turned.

I reach for her hand, shaking my head. "I'm not okay."

"We've won," she says. "We won the war."

"Did we?"

Together, we glance around the room, taking in the cost of our victory.

"We didn't win anything. We're falling apart, right before our own eyes."

Rosa takes a slow breath, like she doesn't want to speak her next words. "Maybe this is fate."

"What?"

"God wants to get the mafia out of New York—"

I shake my head, anger snapping through me like a whip. "No, Rosa."

"Amy—"

"I said *no*. Not now."

I don't want to hear about God or His Voice or His plans. I love Rosa, and I respect her faith, but … Not now.

We sit in silence for a while, until I can stable my breathing and relax. I sit on the floor, leaning against a casket, and stare at Rosa. She's sitting on the floor too, her black dress pooling around her as she gazes at me.

Neither of us speaks.

She looks beautiful, despite her makeup being washed off by her tears. Despite the strange anger I see taking over her features. I know she has more to say, I know she isn't done with this God talk, so I nod slowly and release a sigh.

"Go ahead," I say calmly, "tell me what's storming through that head of yours."

"God has a plan, Amory."

I harrumph. "Was it His plan to let all these people die?"

"He didn't let them die."

"Then who did?"

"You."

209

I blink at her, completely shocked by her response. "*I* let them die?"

She nods.

"Think again, sweetheart. I was trying to save them. I did everything I could—"

"And it wasn't enough." She glares at me, but her features soften into a look of pity after a moment. "You've been doing everything you can, I believe you when you say that. But you'll just keep falling short until you step back and allow God to do it. Let Him fight your battles."

"Rosa…"

"Think about it!" she nearly shouts. "Tell me it doesn't make sense to you!"

It does. I just don't want to admit it. Because then all this death around me will truly be my fault. I tried to rescue Morgen in my own strength and ended up making the war worse than before. I tried to catch the mole my own way and got Amana killed. Then I tried again and ended up breaking my wedding vows. I sought vengeance on my own and lost Klaus and Maximilian and so many more.

I'd had a choice that day—and so many others—and I consistently chose wrong.

The only time I did step back and try to let God handle things, I ignored his Voice and Vater and Onkel ended up dying. Every choice I've made—everything I've done—has ended in some sort of failure.

"How many more have to die?" Rosa whispers. "How much worse does it have to get before you understand?"

210

I lean forward, elbows on my knees, and bury my face in my hands. This all seems so surreal to me. So unbelievable. Rosa's been trying to get me saved since Gio forced her to marry me. I've thought about it at times, but never too seriously. Part of me is honestly unsure if God would actually accept me.

Look at all the things I've done. Lied, killed, cheated, fornicated—the list goes on. How could a truly fair and just God forgive all of that? Just wipe it away and never hold it against me.

Rosa's sweet smile appears in my mind's eye. *She's* forgiven me. For everything I've just listed. I've lied to her, killed people because I thought it would protect her, cheated on her with Eliana—and she still forgave me. She still loves me.

How much more would God?

I shake my head. Even if He does accept me. How could I accept Him? How could I, a mafia boss, truly live as a Christian?

"I can't do it, Rosa," I say quietly. "I'm the *Jägermeister*. That's who the mafia needs me to be."

"What about what God needs you to be?"

"Do you really expect me to believe God wants me to be *successful* as a mafia boss?" I question.

She doesn't flinch at the sarcasm in my voice. "Not at all. In fact, He wants you to become the worst Jägermeister in the history of the German mafia."

I blink at her.

"God wants to destroy the mafia. Not just the Hunting Grounds. He wants all five boroughs cleansed—He wants anarchy gone. And He wants to use you to do that."

I don't realize I'm shaking my head until Rosa is beside me, reaching for my hands. "You said it yourself, the mafia is crumbling. You don't have to fall with it."

I stare at her. "What are you saying?"

"If you let God in, He'll get you out."

Out of the mafia. I can't even imagine a life outside the one I've been living. What would it be like? What would I even do? The thought scares me, but not as much as it did before. After all the fighting and the death and the horrible friction in my marriage, I welcome the idea. At the end of the day, Rosa is right. What have I got to lose?

"Okay," I whisper, squeezing Rosa's hand. "I'll do it."

She smiles shyly. "Do what?"

"I'll ..." *Jesus, it sounds so corny.* "I'll let God in."

Rosa kisses my cheek. "This is called the Sinner's Prayer. Just repeat after me."

Sixteen

The last two days have been a whirlwind for me. Making home visits to all the families who lost people in the attack we suffered and the failed one we initiated. Death is part of this life, I'm no stranger to it by any means, but this side of it is difficult. I can handle myself when I'm in the thick of things, when I've got a gun in my hand and an enemy to point it at. But once the dust has settled and I'm faced with my dead—with the reality of this dark life—that's when it all hits me.

My father used to make these visits when he was alive. I'd gone on his behalf once or twice, but he preferred to do it himself. Said the Hunting Grounds was his responsibility; if he wasn't going to be on the frontlines of the action then he could at least be at the forefront of the aftermath. I don't know how he did it. I don't know how he found the strength to keep a straight face while a woman wept on her own sofa because you just told her that her husband's dead or her father's gone or she'll never see her son again. But he did it. And now it's my turn.

I hate every second of it, and the thought of quitting works its way into my head more than a few times, but I find a way to keep going. It isn't a sense of duty to the German mafia, it's the woman standing by my side.

Rosa is the calm to my storm. She handles herself perfectly with each and every visit we make. At first, I thought she would be the one sniffling and breaking down, but she holds her head high and keeps herself composed, even when some of the family members get angry at the news. Wolfgang is there to stop any drama from happening, but he's never really needed.

Rosa finds a way to diffuse every situation that rises, she even calms Maximilian's father and shocks everyone by reading him a scripture from the Bible and then finishing with a prayer. He lets her and then breaks down in tears once she's finished.

It's a humbling sight. Max was a big man, his father is even larger. Seeing a 6'8 German bear bawl his eyes out like a child makes my stomach clench with emotion. But my wife keeps her head on. I've never been prouder. And I've never been more embarrassed.

I should be the one taking charge and keeping things in order. I'm the Jägermeister, but instead of leading the last of the Hunters to their bloody vengeance, I'm hiding behind my wife's chiffon skirt as she reads the Bible like its group study.

I know… I should be happy about reading the Word of God, I'm a Christian now—might as well start all that soon, right? But I'm still in the mafia. I've still got responsibilities and expectations to meet. That hasn't changed. But it *can* change.

While the last few days have been busy and emotionally draining, I've found time to put together a plan with my wife. One that will end things once and for all. To absolutely no one's surprise, Rosa is the one who really brought everything together. It seems her trip back to Norman was more successful than I thought it'd be. Not only did she return with a heart full of forgiveness toward me and my crimes against our marriage, but she came back with an idea that's managed to take over almost every thought in my head.

"We're getting out of the mafia," is what she'd told me when I'd finally settled down to hear her out about God's plans for the city—as she'd called it. Admittedly, the whole thing sounded like cockamamie nonsense, but it wasn't any wilder than our day-to-day routine as a mafia power couple.

In a one-hour conversation, I was convinced that Rosa was right, or that she was at least headed down the right path. And I knew that if I joined her, things would definitely start going in the right direction. But it wouldn't be enough for me to jump into this—her plans would require the cooperation of the entire German mafia and the Stronghold and the Garden combined. That is what gave me pause.

When I went over the plan with Douglass, sitting by his hospital bed as his nurse changed the bandages of his bullet wound, he nodded slowly and gave me a tired smile. Said it sounded decent and that he was with me no matter what I decided; I wasn't surprised. Not only is Douglass fiercely loyal,

215

but he's also recovering from yet another bullet he took for me—this one was for my wife, but it's all the same. He's in no condition to fight, brokering for peace is all he can hope for.

Unfortunately, Douglass isn't a high enough rank within the Hunting Grounds for his opinion to hold much weight. I'll have to convince the other generals in my mafia to go along with our plan and so far, things aren't looking great.

After leaving the hospital, I immediately brought the plan before Conrad, my underboss. I wasn't expecting him to start singing praises over the whole idea, but I was absolutely floored when he laughed in my face and told me I was crazy.

"You want to bring down the organization that raised you?" he'd asked, hands on his hips. When I didn't answer, he realized I was serious. "Oh God, you're not kidding."

I shrugged. It wasn't easy for me to say it. It wasn't easy for me to even fully accept it. I was helping my wife tear down the empire my forefathers had built—but I wasn't alone. Rosa was raised in the mafia too. She'd be taking down her family's legacy as well, both the Garden and the Stronghold. Conrad made some incredible points with all his yelling as he exploded on me about how crazy I was being, but I couldn't side with him.

My cousin didn't see this the way I did. He wasn't tired. He wasn't fed up. He didn't know just how badly we were already crumbling. He didn't realize how close we were to breaking beyond repair. All he saw was Emilio Moreno and the vengeance he wanted to exact on him. But I was tired. I was fed up with vengeance and bloodshed and pointless pride. If it didn't end here, then it wouldn't end at all.

Thankfully, Conrad isn't the only general I've got to convince—I doubt they'll be as welcoming as Douglass was, but I'm willing to take my chances. I've *got* to take my chances, without everyone on deck helping out, the plan won't work. The saddest part is that the Hunting Grounds will fall no matter what, we're too far gone to come back from the damage we've suffered. Our only choice now is to decide if we'll fall with it.

I've chosen to try to get out before it gets too ugly. Conrad has decided he wants to fight. But his other half isn't ready to pick up a gun and join the fray again.

Gisela may be a mafia wife with little power in this world ruled by men and weapons, but she is the underlady, and she does get a say at my table. At my meeting with Conrad, she watches him leave in silence. When he stops at the door and turns back around, her eyes meet his with an unwavering strength I've never seen before.

"Let's go," he says in German.

She doesn't move. "I'm staying."

"Excuse me?"

Rosa, who's been sitting beside me at the dinner table, grips her napkin nervously, but her voice comes out very calmly. "Maybe Gisela sees things the way we do."

"I didn't ask how she sees things," Conrad growls in English now. He marches back over to the table and grabs his wife roughly by the elbow. "I said *let's go*." The words are hissed through his teeth, but Gisela seems immune to his venom today. Any other time, she would cower and obey like a good little Christian wife. Submit and all that.

But today she straightens her spine and looks Conrad in the eye as she replies in German, "I'm staying. You can't make me go."

"How dare you defy me." Conny raises his hand. "In front of the *Jägermeister.*" When he swings, Glizzy doesn't flinch.

She catches his wrist, shocking everyone in the room. "I said I'm staying!" she practically yells. Then she shoves him backwards three steps and snatches up her steak knife from the table. "You can't make me go!"

I fly to my feet before someone ends up dead. "That's enough! Both of you!"

Gisela grips the knife, but I grab her wrist from behind and twist just enough to make her drop it. Conrad starts yelling in German, Gisela screams right back. Rosa starts crying.

God, *now* she breaks down? After staying so strong for all this time? Maybe it's just now getting to her. Or maybe it hurts to see how far Conny's pushed Gisela. She's never been this loud, this wild, or this dramatic. By anyone's standards, she's always been a good wife—a good *mafia* wife. She obeys Conrad, doesn't ask questions about the gang, and keeps her nose out of his affairs.

It's no secret that Conny's had a few women here and there, he's the former owner of The Club. Being around naked women all day long isn't easy, not even when you've got a wife as hot as Glizzy waiting at home. But even when Gisela knew that her husband was cheating, she never spoke up about it. Never caused him any trouble. Never brought shame to his name.

Gisela was a good wife. And now she's reached her limit.

It's not surprising that it wasn't the infidelity that pushed her over the edge. It wasn't Conrad's lack of faith or commitment to God. It was his own hand that literally pushed his wife away.

I've seen the bruises here and there. I've heard him call his own wife a whore in front of other people. This wouldn't even be the first time Gisela's been dragged out of a room by Conrad—when they first got married, he took the strap to her right in front of me. At the time, I hadn't thought anything of it, really. That was the same way Vater had treated Christina, and the same way I'd intended to treat my future wife if she ever mouthed off or embarrassed me. That's how life in the mafia goes.

Obviously, I've changed over the years. Rosa and I have had our fair share of arguments. I've carried her over my shoulder, threatened her, yelled at her—I'm no Prince Charming by any means. But I have never hit her. Not a single time.

Okay... There was this one time, but it was more for pleasure than pain. My pleasure, her pain. But it was *that* kind of night, and she'd actually liked it—*loved* it. But the point is ... I've never hit her without permission. And I'm not going to let Conrad hit Gisela right in front of me, in my own home.

I pull Glizzy toward me and she finally collapses into a fit of tears. She's almost hysterical, but her emotions cool Conny's rage. He stares at her as she heaves into my chest, and maybe it's the sight of his wife taking comfort in another man's arms, or maybe it's the fact that she's taking comfort in another man's arms because of him—but he sags his shoulders and cracks too.

"*Perle...*" he says in German. It means 'pearl' and it's the perfect name for Gisela. She's a gift in this dark world, a true treasure if I've ever seen one. And Conrad doesn't deserve her in the least.

Nevertheless, she pulls from me and sniffles as she faces him. When Conrad opens his arms, she slowly goes to him. He whispers something in German that I can't quite hear, and Gisela starts crying again. It's only when I see tears streaming down Conny's face that I feel sure he isn't going to hurt her again.

He glances up at me, petting Glizzy's head like she's a poodle. "I'm sorry, Jägermeister."

"Say that to her," I tell him. "And don't you ever touch her again."

He nods at me, then looks down at Gisela and whispers something only she can hear.

When Gisela pulls away, she's immediately yanked into a hug by Rosa who's come over from across the dining room. I almost roll my eyes; women are always hugging.

"I'm going home," Conrad says. He clears his throat and causally wipes at his eyes like he wasn't just crying in front of me.

I fold my hands into my pockets. "Still leaving."

"You're the one who's leaving."

I sigh. "The Hunting Grounds will fall, that's a fact."

He shakes his head. "We can stop it if you cared enough to try."

"Think about your future, Conny. Do you want us to end up like our fathers? Both dead together?"

He winces. "If we crush the Morenos, no one will be left to harm or threaten us."

"Volkov has a son. And the Morenos are a big family."

"Then we'll kill them all."

"I'm not killing kids," I hiss.

"Volkov's boy is seventeen. He's not a kid—not in this life."

He's telling the truth. I became a man at 15—physically, mentally, and sexually. I heard it's 12 for the Russians.

I sigh. "Let's talk about this later, how's that?"

Conrad nods, strokes his beard as he watches the women smile and kiss each other. My eyes are on Rosa, my thoughts focusing on her future, on what sort of life we'll be able to live once this is over.

"I want to live longer than Uwe did. I want to leave my son a business he can be proud of."

Conrad grunts. "So do I."

Seventeen

We spend the day driving to Norman. With Douglass in the hospital, we end up driving alone. Wolfgang offered to play bodyguard for the day, but Amy insisted it was better for just the two of us to go.

So far, he's been right.

We have eight hours to ourselves; locked in a car to talk and laugh and behave the way a normal couple would. For just eight hours, I forget that we're in the mafia. I forget that we're both victims who've lost almost everything but each other. I forget the death that plagued us days ago and I even find the strength to forget my husband's sins.

I laugh when he tells me a joke, my head falling back against the headrest. I listen closely when Amory sings along with the radio, totally shocked by how good he is. He blushes when I compliment him, but my cheeks turn pink when he reaches over and takes my hand, keeping his other on the steering wheel. It's a simple gesture, one that should only swoon shy teenagers, but my heart races as Amy intertwines his fingers with mine and squeezes.

How long has it been since we've had a moment like this? When was the last time we experienced pure passion? Simple love?

This drive feels like an eight-hour date. Amory and I hold hands until he pulls into a burger shack and he's forced to pull away so he can back into a parking spot. But his hand finds mine again as soon as we finish our food. We sit in the lot, staring out at the traffic passing by. If you asked me where we're going, I wouldn't want to answer. It would just remind me of all the chaos waiting for us back in New York and the possible chaos we're riding into in Norman.

"Everything will change after this," I whisper.

Amy squeezes my hand. "You sure we've got a meeting?"

I nod. Arthur had promised and assured me that everything was set up; I know Amory won't be happy to see him, but he hasn't mentioned it yet, so I decide not to bring him up. Instead, I say, "I'm happy you're with me on this."

"So am I." He pauses. "I'm surprised you want me here with you, after everything I've done."

"Don't," I say, gently squeezing his hand. "I've forgiven you. Don't go back and open old wounds." The wounds are hardly old. I still feel the sharp sting of pain whenever I think of my husband and Eliana—but then I remember that she's passed on, and the pain subsides. I refuse to be jealous or angry over a woman who isn't even here anymore. And while I am

223

grateful that Amy is sensitive to my pain, the only way for me to move on from it is to let it go.

I can't let it go if he keeps bringing it up.

"I'm still sorry," he whispers beside me. "I wanted you to hear me say that."

I nod, still staring straight ahead.

"And not just for Eliana. I'm sorry about Gio."

My heart flutters.

"I wasn't the one who killed him. I had every intention to, I won't deny that, but in the end, it was someone else who pulled the trigger."

I'm grateful for that. I'm grateful that it wasn't my husband who murdered my brother. Giovanni was a horrible person who had been marked for death by more than just my husband, I knew he was going to die—if not then, then maybe weeks later at someone else's hand. But I'm so happy Amory hadn't pulled the trigger. I'm happy God intervened; only He could've stepped in and saved our marriage from the black stain of death it would have suffered.

I shift in my seat and look up at Amory's face, studying his perfect square jaw and his molten grey eyes. Every feature, every plane of his face is absolutely beautiful. I lean toward him without thinking, and he welcomes me with a surprising vigor.

We haven't touched each other in weeks. Things were complicated, if not strained. First the mess with Eliana, then the frightening violence at the safehouse. We needed space, but now we've finally found our way back to each other.

What unfolds is both hesitant and desperate. Amory kisses me until I can't breathe, and then he nuzzles my neck until I catch my breath and his mouth covers mine once more. When I climb into his lap, he groans and picks me up, jerks his car door open, and shamelessly carries me around the car to the backseats. I don't have the courage or the time to glance around and see if any of the customers in the parking lot are watching. My only comfort is that the windows are tinted and rolled up, that way no one sees us tearing at each other's clothes, no one hears me cry out Amory's name—again and again. We make love like it's our last time together, and when it's over, we do it again.

I feel exhausted as I slowly sit up in the seats. I want a shower, or one of Amy's hot baths. But we're in the parking lot of a greasy burger shack on the side of the highway— shamefully, all I've got is a small pack of travel wet wipes in the overnight bag I packed. I use them to clean myself as best I can, Amory watches the entire time, saying absolutely nothing. When I'm dressed again, he reaches for the pack and wipes himself down.

"That was amazing," he says softly. "You were amazing."

I feel a shiver dance down my spine. "I missed you. Even when I was angry, all I wanted was to be near you again."

"Everything I've done is for you, Rosa. Even the things that broke your heart the most."

"I know." I sniffle.

He pulls me in for a hug and kisses my forehead. "I love you."

"I love you too."

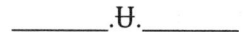

Due to our pitstop, it takes us an extra two hours to make it to Norman. By the time we check in to our hotel, we're too exhausted to do anything but fall into bed and go straight to sleep. When I wake in the middle of the night, I smell food and realize Amy ordered room service. There's beef on weck with a thick gravy and roasted potatoes and carrots. I vow to only eat half, but my hunger overtakes me, and I stuff the whole sandwich down my throat, not even caring that it's lukewarm.

With my strength renewed, I finally get to have a hot shower, but it's interrupted when Amy pulls the curtain aside and steps in to join me. Of course, we don't shower at all. The only thing that pulls us apart is a sudden, violent spray of ice-cold water as the showerhead sputters. We both yelp and jerk away, trying to escape the stream, then we erupt in a fit of cackles. It's the most ridiculous thing I've ever experienced, but I'm happy, nonetheless.

Amory gives me a massage when I dry off, rubbing baby oil over my tense muscles. I'd love to say we made love again, but the truth is that both of us are too tired.

"I'm getting old," Amory groans jokingly. He rolls onto his side and pulls me against his chest. We're both still naked and I stick to his flesh, slick from the baby oil, but we fall asleep with smiles on our faces, ready to take on whatever lies ahead.

To my surprise, Melissa and Pastor Marcia are both waiting with Arthur when we walk into the coffee shop the next morning. I pause, wondering if something's gone wrong, but their smiles reassure me, and I take Amy's hand as we approach. He squeezes it, but it isn't to comfort me; when I glance up at my husband, I trace his gaze across the room to Arthur. They're both glaring at each other.

Oh boy.

I clear my throat, reaching up to pat Amy's shoulder with my free hand. He barely notices. The two men are both so rigid, they're like planks of wood standing face to face. Even Melissa glances back and forth, but Pastor Marcia hardly seems to notice.

She boldly steps forward and extends her hand to Amory. "Would you believe me if I said this isn't my first time meeting a mafioso?" She grins.

Amory's frozen grimace cracks as a smile etches onto his face. "Yes." He laughs and takes her hand, but it's a gentle gesture filled with respect for her as a woman and as a Pastor. "Even thugs need a little guidance."

Pastor Marcia seems pleased with his response. "Looks like you've got yourself a good one, Rose," she says with a wink.

Melissa agrees with a nod. "We've heard a lot about you, Mr. Jäger. It's nice to finally meet."

"It is," he says, taking her hand now.

When it's Arthur's turn to speak, he hesitates for a fraction of a second and Amy catches it. The corner of his mouth turns up the slightest bit as pride seeps into his conscience. He's won whatever silent spat they were having; Arthur's hesitation may have been insignificant to others, but to Amory it's clear defeat—admission of Arthur's fear, if not outright inferiority.

Amy extends his hand. "Nice to see you again."

"And you," Arthur says in a gruff tone.

There is no surprise on Melissa's face at their exchange; I guess Arthur honored his word and told her everything, otherwise, she'd be shocked to learn they'd seen each other before.

"Now that we've all met," Arthur says, "let's get this over with."

We take a seat in the back corner, all five of us squeezed into a booth, huddled over our mugs of hot brown liquid. Pastor Marcia gets a vanilla cappuccino, Melissa takes a decaf with hazelnut cream, I have hot chocolate, both Amory and Arthur order black coffee.

While we wait for the officer to arrive, Arthur explains our options. It's obvious that he's thought about this with how many details he goes into. I appreciate everything he tells us, except when he says that Amory will be meeting with the officer alone.

"Why'd we all bother meeting here then?" I say quickly.

Amy places his arm over my shoulders to calm me.

Arthur just blinks at me. "We don't want anyone following us. There are a lot of eyes in Norman, a lot of cops working for criminals."

"Just like you," I mutter.

He shifts uncomfortably but doesn't say anything back, not to me at least. "When I get the call, Amory and I will leave—"

"And go where?" my voice cracks. Arthur could be setting him up, he could be waiting with a squad of cops to arrest him or shoot him down like he's just another gangster. It's not like they wouldn't recognize him, even out here in Norman. Amory's the head of the German mafia, his face is on the news at least twice a week. I've even seen him on the cover of a magazine before—listed in the top 100 'Hottest Mafia Bad Boys.' I won't tell you what number he was, but it was high enough to have his face on the front of that issue.

Amory shifts in his chair, his hand finding mine on the table. The touch draws my gaze to his. I'm shocked to find him smiling warmly at me. "I'll be fine, love. Arthur can't hurt me."

I blink at him. "But—"

Arthur's phone rings and cuts me off. My eyes widen, but before I can try to convince him not to go, Amory stands and buttons his suit jacket. He's ready before Arthur even finishes the call.

"Ladies," Amy nods at Pastor Marcia and Melissa. He looks down at me, cups my chin and then kisses me like my own Pastor isn't right in front of us. I know it's just a show for Arthur, but I can't stop myself from blushing like a little girl when he pulls away. The scowl on Arthur's face doesn't faze me at all. Or Amory who winks at me before leaving. I grip the table to keep from fainting.

Melissa laughs and catches my attention. "Young love."

Pastor Marcia grins. "How does love like that last in the mafia?"

"Well ..." I honestly have no clue. It isn't as if the mafia is short on love—Gisela and Conrad love each other, but he also cheats on her and hits her. Petra and Eike loved each other, right up until she was shot and killed. Morgen and Silke are in love, but they had to get married in secret and on a whim because we weren't sure how much longer he would live. The mafia is full of love, it's commitment and longevity that's threatened.

"It's God," I whisper, more to myself than to the women before me.

What else could it be? In a world shrouded in darkness, only the Light of Christ could help us keep it together. We've had plenty of difficult moments between us, but it's our faith that's kept us from drowning completely. And now that we both finally share that faith, I truly believe nothing can tear us apart.

Look at how much we've survived. Far more than what most other couples could ever live through—lying, cheating, living apart for weeks. It's a miracle we can still look at each without feeling disgusted. Our marriage reminds me of a scripture I absolutely love.

Therefore what God has joined together, let no one separate. **Mark 10:9**

230

It is divine proof that Amory and I are made for each other. That we'll always be together. Our fate is etched in stone, the threads of our soul tied together by God Almighty. Suddenly, I'm not afraid for Amory anymore. I still don't trust Arthur, but I have no worries that he'll do anything that could separate us. So instead of worrying myself to death, I order another hot chocolate and spend the afternoon chatting with my adoptive mother and my wonderful Pastor.

When we get tired of coffee, Melissa takes us to her home and fries catfish for us. She serves it with hushpuppies and simmered green beans that threaten to raise my cholesterol, but it's delicious, nonetheless. I haven't had soul food in what feels like forever—I haven't even cooked in what feels like forever, so I'm excited when Mel asks for help with dessert.

By then, Minnie is home from school, so she joins us in the kitchen, along with Pastor Marcia. We make the most amazing poundcake I've ever tasted. It takes us until evening, but once it's ready we enjoy two slices each and then nearly pass out on the sofa. I'm half asleep when the doorbell rings and Arthur walks in with Amory right behind.

"Smells good in here," Arthur's deep timbre fills the room, snapping me to attention. Even though he's the one who spoke, my eyes immediately find my husband and the look on his face makes me worry.

"What happened?" I say, getting straight to the point.

Minnie cuts off his answer as she lets out a squeal. "It's really you! The Jägermeister!"

I'd forgotten about her obsession with the mafia; a true teenage fangirl.

Minnie runs toward him, eyes glittering with stars. "I've seen you so many times! You're so much more handsome in person!" She squeals again, dancing around in a little circle before snatching out her phone. "Can I please get a picture?"

"Minnie," Melissa warns. "Put that phone away and go upstairs."

"*Mom*," she whines.

Amory chuckles and takes Minnie's phone from her hands, he kneels so they're eye to eye, and then raises the camera and smiles. Minnie can hardly contain herself; she latches her arms around his neck and beams, grinning wide for one more photo.

"I saw an article about you in Teen Four-Five-Oh," she says when he passes her the phone.

I roll my eyes. *Teen450h* is a trashy magazine that publishes nothing but mafia gossip—all written in PG-13 language so not to offend concerned parents. They did a small write-up about Amory when he became the Jägermeister, I actually saw it in passing while scrolling social media once.

Minnie's obsession, and the fact that an entire magazine is dedicated to feeding mafia news to vulnerable teens, makes me excited to finally take down the gangs of New York. By the way … Today, in NYC, 450 is the police code when calling in a disturbance involving gang related activity. Now it's the name of a mob magazine published across the nation. Awesome.

Melissa clears her throat. "Time to do your homework, Minnie."

Reluctantly, Minnie nods and scampers off without argument.

Pastor Marcia stands, but waits for Minnie's footsteps to fade before she says, "Did it go well?"

Amory nods. "As well as can be expected."

"What does that mean?" I twiddle my fingers, though I really want to rip my hair out.

"We'll talk about it later," he says plainly.

I want to tell him that isn't fair. That I'm not some meek little wife who's just going to nod and bow and 'talk later'— when he's ready to talk. But I can tell from the look on his face that the decision doesn't come from a sense of control or domination, it's from necessity.

I force a smile and nod, smoothing the wrinkles in my skirt. "Let's go back to the hotel, then."

"Take some cake with you," Melissa says. Her voice is chipper enough to cut the tension in the room, suddenly it feels like we can all breathe again.

Amory actually cracks a smile. "I'd love a slice to go. Sorry I missed lunch, Ms. Hart."

She waves him off and heads to the kitchen while Pastor Marcia delivers her goodbye. "It was nice meeting you, Mr. Jäger. I'll be praying for the best."

"I appreciate it, Pastor."

I nod agreement. "We'll need your prayers."

"Don't forget to pray on your own as well," she advises.

We both mumble goodbyes to Arthur and then head for the exit, poundcake in tow. Barely two blocks later, I can't take the anxiety anymore.

"Talk to me," I say firmly—it sounds almost like an order.

Amory glances at me. "The officer seems legit. She's a detective from Norman FBI. Says she can work things out and start an investigation."

"That's good," I say.

"Yeah." He grips the steering wheel.

"What else?"

"The investigation will have to be big if we want it to cause the fall of five different mafia organizations. That means it'll require participation from people on the inside."

A moment of silence unrolls in the car. "People like you."

"Yes," he mutters.

We knew we would have to make sacrifices. We knew it wouldn't be easy to take down the mafia, but neither of us guessed it would mean joining the investigation ourselves.

"I'll have to provide evidence against other mafioso. Records, documents, video surveillance."

Basically, he'll become the biggest snitch in mafia history.

"You'll put a target on your back," I say shakily. He's had one on his back for months with the war going on, but this will be different. He'll be sending his own brothers to prison. That's the lowest form of betrayal in the mafia—right next to murdering your own kin. Giovanni committed the latter and look what happened to him in the end.

"Is there no other way?"

He sighs. "If I don't help with the investigation, I'll be the one getting investigated."

"They'll arrest you." My hands begin to shake as I realize what's going on. They've backed us into a corner with a dangerous threat. Testify against the gangsters you lead or join them behind bars. "This can't be happening," I whisper.

Amory pulls into the parking lot of our hotel. "I'm going to do it," he says as he cuts the engine.

I snap my vision toward him. "Amy, no."

"*Yes*," he says sternly.

"They'll kill you if you talk."

"Not if they talk too."

I blink at him.

"The detective told me the deal is open for anyone who'll cooperate. Turn in incriminating evidence and you'll receive immunity."

"Just like that?" I ask incredulously.

He nods. "There's fine print. The evidence has to be good, and you've got to cooperate with police one hundred percent. Right now, their investigation surrounds Volkov and Giovanni since they were directly involved in your kidnapping and the sex trafficking."

"Even though they're both dead?"

"Being dead doesn't absolve you of your crimes."

"I guess not," I mutter.

"Any evidence turned in will have to help them pin the current suspects. That will keep my men from turning on each other."

"For now," I say. "Once the investigation expands, everyone will start scrambling. Like crabs in a pot."

"But they have the chance to secure immunity now."

"Do you think they'll take that chance while there's still time?"

"I don't know," he says so quietly it almost sounds like a whisper.

Most likely, the Hunters won't take the deal. Not until the investigation gets too big and it's too late. Then they'll start turning on each other just to stay out of prison or to snag deals with the prosecution for shorter prison terms. It'll be utter chaos. No one will be safe. Unless we convince them to take the deal.

"We've got to talk to them." I grab the handle to my car door. "We're leaving tonight."

"Tonight?" Amory repeats.

I look over at him. "The faster we get back to New York, the more time we'll have to convince the Hunters that this is the right thing to do."

"They'll never agree to work with cops, Rosa."

"They will if it means avoiding a life term in prison."

He sighs. "I don't want to go back to New York tonight."

"Amory—"

"We'll be working nonstop once we get home. Give us one more night. Just you and me."

I fumble for words. "Uh—I guess … Well—"

He chuckles and leans over to kiss my neck, murmuring against the sensitive skin, "Forget about business for a few hours."

I am starstruck by his sultry smirk, unable to do anything more than sigh and roll my eyes to the back of my head as he kisses me sweetly. My words are nothing more than a breathy sigh, "Okay, one more night."

Eighteen

My men think I'm insane. I knew it would be difficult for them to swallow my grand plans, but I didn't think they would outright speak out against me. Then again, I am asking them to hand over incriminating evidence and cooperate with police—something we have never done before.

As kids, we loved to say *snitches get stitches*. Now, I'm asking my men to do the very thing we've grown up recognizing as an act of sin. It goes against everything we believe in. It turns us into the very sort of man I've executed before.

When I finish my speech about the walls crumbling around us and facing our defeat like men, I am met with silence. I feel a single drop of sweat run down the side of my face as I stare at everyone. We're standing in one of our warehouses, all three gangs are present. The soldiers of the Willis Stronghold stand behind King James, the Garden huddles behind Niccolò—all twelve members. It's a sad sight, but I'm glad they're here despite everything that's happened, especially because they're the only ones who speak up in a somewhat positive manner.

Aldo actually raises his hand like a child and waits for me to call on him. I don't give him slack for it since he's only got one now. I just nod and wait for him to go on.

"If we work with the Norman detectives, they'll keep us from going to jail?"

I nod again. "That's the deal they've offered."

"You want us to turn on each other?" Hans asks. He's off to my left, standing with the rest of the Hunters, arm in a sling and his shirt buttoned only halfway to reveal his bandaged torso. He'd been shot during the storm on Gio's penthouse, but he's strong enough to stand here today. Right now, I kind of wish he was still in the hospital, then he wouldn't be here to hiss insults at me like I'm the enemy.

I clench my jaw and then unscrew it to answer, "We won't have to turn against each other if we all take the deal."

"What if we don't need the deal?" Hans shoots back. "What if this investigation goes nowhere?"

"They're not going to let it go," I say.

"Why not?"

"Because the rest of the country hates us." My voice comes out like a whip, snapping each word at a rapid speed. "They might idolize us on television but in reality, we're still thugs to them—a bunch of gangsters making money by slinging dope and killing each other right out in the open." I step toward him. "They've been itching for a chance to slap the cuffs on our wrists."

239

"And now you're giving it to them." The voice doesn't surprise me, just the malice in it.

I turn around to stare at Conrad, taking in his hands balled into fists at his sides, his thick brows flattened into one angry line. His mouth twists beneath his beard as he grates out his words, "You're handing the Hunting Grounds over to the police."

"Conny—"

"I'm willing to do it," Niccolò says.

Every eye snaps over to him but he doesn't let it faze him.

"Whether we want to admit it or not," he says in his smooth Italian accent, "we are crumbling. All three mafias lost soldiers and loved ones in that last attack."

"So we're just giving up? What about avenging our lost brothers?" Conrad jabs a finger at the air. "The Morenos are on the run!"

"Look at us!" Niccolò snaps, his tone is so sharp, it immediately silences my cousin. If he weren't don of the Italian mafia, I'd have his tongue for disrespecting my underboss so boldly, but I'm the one who helped Niccolò take over the Garden—and he's making a good point right now, so I keep my mouth shut.

Niccolò sweeps his arm out toward the Italians behind him. "This is what a destroyed mafia looks like. But you have a chance to save yourselves before it reaches this point."

"Working with police won't be saving anything. It'll *guarantee* our downfall," Conrad hisses.

Niccolò shakes his head. "Do you really want to live the rest of your life like this? Bow out, Conrad, while you still can."

"Men like us don't bow out. We don't turn on each other."

"You don't have to turn on anyone," Niccolò says, his tone much gentler now. "Pin everything on the Garden."

Silence storms through the warehouse. Behind me, I can hear Wolfgang clear his throat—he does that when he's nervous.

"What do you mean, pin everything on the Garden?" I say.

Niccolò takes a breath. "The Garden is wilted, it has been since before you got married, Jägermeister. We have nothing to preserve—"

"Which is why handing over evidence will work in your favor," I interrupt, but he shakes his head.

"It's why we won't lose anything if we take the fall." Niccolò slides his hands into his pockets. "Our former don is dead, his sister is safe in another mafia, the rest of us owe nothing to the Garden."

"Except generations of culture and tradition!" Conrad growls like he's Italian and offended. At this point, he'll snap at anyone, but Niccolò remains calm.

"My son is crippled for life. He is useless to the Garden, as his father, it is my responsibility to help him now."

Conrad laughs, the sound is dark and haunting as it echoes through the warehouse. "Basically, you want out and this is your pathetic excuse."

"It's not an excuse," I say calmly, glaring at Conrad for his disrespect. I don't like that Niccolò seems ready to abandon ship either, it makes me wonder if he would have been a strong ally had I decided to continue the war instead of work with the police. But Conrad doesn't get to insult him to his face when he's defending his son.

I went to war with the Wolves over my little brother. I understand the importance of family better than anyone in this room right now. A part of me sympathizes with the old don.

"Niccolò is giving us a chance to lay the blame at his feet," I explain.

"Not at mine," he corrects. "Lay it at Giovanni's feet."

"Gio is dead." Conrad squints.

"Exactly." Niccolò smiles and I immediately understand.

"He isn't here to defend himself." Not that he would be able to. Aldo and his father already have all the records and documents to show how much money he stole from his businesses, and Arthur has documentation of his involvement in the sex trafficking ring he was running with Volkov.

"Blaming Gio means no one else will have to go to prison," I say.

The room hushes as the gears begin to turn in everyone's head. I can see them contemplating my every word, putting the pieces together.

"That only clears the crimes of the Garden," Conrad says. He's no longer simmering in anger, but his shoulders are still tense, like he wants to punch something—or someone. "What about the Hunting Grounds? Or the Stronghold?"

"Blame me." Morgen steps beside his brother, gasping as Conrad whirls and grabs him by the collar.

He presses his forehead to his brother's and seethes at him, "Don't you dare."

"Bruder—"

"Don't you *dare!*" Conrad shouts, shoving Morgen back a step. He stumbles and almost falls to the concrete but catches himself and straightens his shirt like he's not embarrassed at all.

"I'm dead, Conny," he says in a small voice. "I won't go to jail for anything."

Conrad blinks dumbly, but his silence tells me he understands what his brother is saying.

"Volkov killed Morgen Jäger weeks ago," I say into the silence. "We buried him."

Conrad nods slowly. "So the cops won't have anyone to arrest."

"Even though he's been out of hiding?" Hans asks.

I nod. "The Norman cops don't know that."

"You'll have to change your name and leave town for good," Conrad says to Morgen. His gaze is glued to him like they're the only two people in the room. His concern for his brother rivals mine; I let them have this moment.

Morgen nods meekly, scratching the stubble on his jaw. "I know. But leaving will remove Silke from the city. I want her safe more than anything."

Every man in this room can relate to that. Rosa is the reason I'm doing all of this, and I know I'm the reason she's working hard too. As the German Mistress, she's meeting with the women right now, explaining things to them just like I'm doing with the men. We thought it'd be easier to separate everyone and talk alone. Mafia guys aren't used to handling business or making decisions with a woman's input, they won't be happy that we've let their wives in on what's going down. But I wasn't willing to leave this decision to them alone.

We all need to be prepared—especially the women. Mafia wives aren't like other wives; they're all pampered princesses who've never had to work a day in their lives. And why would they when their husbands and fathers make more money than they could ever spend in five lifetimes?

Working with the cops will change everything. We won't be gangsters making millions by the day from selling drugs and weapons and illegally mined jewels. We'll be everyday men who'll have to hold a nine-to-five job and pay taxes for once. That won't be easy for our ladies. Which is why Rosa is with them now, trying to get them prepped for what's to come. I can only hope she's having more success than I am.

Conrad runs a hand through his hair. "While Morgen is running off, and the Garden is cowering, who'll be left to take down the Morenos?"

I sigh. "We're not fighting anymore—"

"We aren't, but *they* are," Conny interjects.

He has a point. Even though the Morenos are down, they're not completely out. There is a chance they could try something again—it's a small chance, but still.

"You'll fight," I say without thinking.

Conrad's eyes widen.

"It's clear you disagree with my plan to cooperate with the investigation," I say, "so stay here and defend our territory while we handle things with the cops."

My cousin blinks at me, unsure if I'm insulting him or rewarding him. To make things clear, and to keep down hostility toward me for being a 'turncoat,' I step forward and hold up my hand, showing everyone my Jägermeister ring. "I'm still the Master of the Hunting Grounds. But anyone who doesn't want to work with the cops will follow Conrad. He'll be in total control of our defenses."

Murmurs ripple through the room, and someone raises a hand—it's Eike this time.

"Go on," I say.

"What do we do once this is over? The ones who cooperate, I mean."

I swallow. This is the hard part ... convincing a warehouse full of gangsters to get regular jobs and actually work for a living.

"Chances are, once the investigation is over, police will have control over New York City again."

The room grumbles, but I keep going.

"All five mafias are already weak or destroyed anyway. After the investigation, we'll be pretty much left with nothing." I take a good look at the men before me, hoping they can sense how serious this is. "By working with police, you'll have your records cleared and you won't have to serve time in prison. But you'll be expected to stay out of trouble after that."

"What does that mean?" Hans asks.

"It means you won't be mafioso anymore."

Conrad frowns, but I speak before he does.

"Most of you should already have jobs you can fall back on." Conny used to have The Club, a completely legal bar and lounge, right until it went up in flames. The place was insured, so he only lost the building. When the dust settles, he can rebuild and go right back to business if he wants. Or he can sell the joint and get out of New York. The choice is his and Gisela's.

"The Jägers own a dozen jewelry stores," I say. "They're all legal and they're all in my name." They used to be in my father's with just one under my name, but I inherited everything when he passed. "I'd be willing to hire as many of you as I can."

"That's not enough." Hans shakes his head. "And I don't want to spend the rest of my life selling rings."

"You can work for us." King James's deep voice rumbles around us as it fills the warehouse. He smiles wide enough for us all to see his gold tooth, I swear it shines in the fluorescent lights. "My granddaughter owns a legal gym; she plans to open another soon. Not to mention her husband owns a private security business. Something I'm sure will interest men with our *expertise*."

I almost laugh, but manage to hold it in. "The point is, we have options," I say loudly. "No one has to make any permanent decisions right now, but you do have to decide." I give them a slow, thoughtful nod. "Go home. Make love to your wives. And think about everything we discussed today."

Nineteen

I'm sitting at a small but impressive dining table for two. There's a wonderful display of food before me, grilled meats and fresh vegetables, rice pilaf, buttered bread. I feel like a king, but that's no surprise—I am in a palace, after all.

King James takes a sip of his ice water and then leans back in his chair. He hasn't touched his food, the water seems to be the only thing he's interested in, that and his cigar. The entire room is filled with smoke from his puffing and huffing, it billows from his mouth like he's a great dragon, voice rumbling across the room when he says, "Hungry, Jägermeister?"

"Yes," I say truthfully, and then I grab a slice of bread and top it with grilled chicken breast. "I'm thankful for your invitation to lunch."

He nods, puffs his cigar once again. "I wanted to speak to you one on one. Man to man."

I glance at him, my eyes narrowing. "What's going on?"

"I like the courage you showed in our meeting the other day."

I almost laugh. Two days ago, my men wanted my head on a skewer for trying to keep them from falling with the gang. Now, King James is telling me he's pleased with my courage. I'm honored by the compliment, but his kind words can't help me much with the situation.

"Thank you," I say politely.

Jameson taps the ash off his cigar. "Giovanni will take the fall for the Garden."

I nod. It might sound cruel to pin everything on a dead man, but the truth is that all the evidence we have truly points to him. Gio was dirty, even for a mafioso. We aren't ruining his name, we're shining light on who he really was.

"And Morgen will take the fall for the Hunting Grounds," Jameson adds.

I nod again. "Along with my father." Another dead man taking the fall, but, like Gio, the records and documents point back to Vater more than anyone else. He was our Jägermeister for nearly four decades, his signature is on every receipt and his seal on every envelope. I may have taken over after his death, but most of the contracts are still in my father's name.

Morgen will be taking the fall for more recent events, things like the attack on Niccolò's home—the men Wolfgang killed will be pinned on him. We'll have to rearrange the paper trail, considering we buried Morgen weeks before Wolf killed Niccolò's security but that won't be difficult to manage.

"Smart man," King James says, then he takes another sip of water and sighs heavily, like a great grizzly settling in for a rest.

I blink at him. "Seems like you've got more on your mind."

"Who will take the fall for the Stronghold." The way he speaks doesn't sound like a question at all. It seems more like he's already got things figured out.

"Who?" I ask cautiously.

"I will."

I'm so shocked, I actually jerk forward in my chair. "King James..."

He waves a hand. "I've already thought about it. My mind is made up."

"You'll be going to prison—"

"As I should."

"You can't be serious!" I rise to my feet. "Giovanni is taking the fall because he's dead. Morgen is taking the fall because he's been ruled as dead and wants a fresh start with his wife."

"And I'm taking the fall because it's the right thing to do."

"You'll spend the rest of your life in prison."

He shrugs one large shoulder. "I'm old, Jäger. Haven't got many years left, to be honest."

"Do you want your people to see their king in handcuffs?"

"I want them to see me take responsibility."

"You built this kingdom from nothing—"

"Do not presume to tell me of my accomplishments. I'm the one who achieved them." He glares daggers at me for a

250

single heartbeat of silence, but just as quickly as the anger rose in his voice, it's replaced by a quiet sadness as he says, "This borough—this city—was much different when I was young."

I nod and return to my seat, unsure what to say.

"I was just another Black kid from the ghetto. Nobody cared about me. And I didn't care about nobody." He chuckles, puffs his cigar. Smoke rolls from his lips when he speaks again. "Look at me now. A King."

"That's why you shouldn't take the fall, King James."

He keeps speaking like I'm not even there. "I grew up without a father. Never even knew his name." He shrugs. "Single mothers are a dime a dozen for people who look like me, who come from neighborhoods like me. I'm part of a culture that stopped training its men to take responsibility for their actions *generations* ago." His free hand curls into a fist on the table. "That's why I'm taking the fall. To demonstrate what it means to be a man. To be held accountable for your decisions."

"It doesn't have to be this way..." I get what he's saying— maybe not on a personal level, but I do understand. My wife is half-Black, neither of us would ever dare to ignore the culture she comes from and the struggles—or the *joys*—that come with it. But what King James is saying, the struggles he's describing, they're not his responsibility to bear alone. He can't change the mindset of an entire culture. And he shouldn't have to. But I know just by looking at him that nothing I say will change his mind. He's a stubborn old bear.

251

He taps his cigar on the ashtray. "I'm doing this because I am the King. I built this borough up from nothing. Turned a bunch of ghettos into a flourishing kingdom. But I did it illegally, and its time I pay for it." He sighs. "My family is important to me, Jäger. They're the reason I found the strength and the will to accomplish all that you see. And they're the reason I'm pinning everything on me."

"You're protecting them."

"Ultimately, that is a King's duty. Is it not?"

I nod slowly. When I think about it, Gio and Vater are both taking the fall for their respective gangs. Both are bosses, both are leaders. I'm not doing anything.

"I'm leaving behind a great legacy. When they slap those cuffs on my wrists, I want to make sure that legacy won't be shackled with me." King James stares at me, his eyes calm but serious. "My boys, Trenton and Tyrese. They've been trained to take over the Stronghold since they were born. Trenton is the oldest, even though he's lost his wife recently, I know he'll bounce back. He's responsible for taking care of all our businesses, acquiring proper licenses and certificates so we can operate at one hundred percent legality."

I nod, thinking of the gyms, training facilities, and gun ranges owned by the Willis family. As gangsters, they'd specialized in dealing arms and other unmarked weapons, but if Trenton truly manages to get everything legalized, they'll be able to stay afloat without a problem. They might not rake in hundreds of millions of untaxed dollars like they do today, but they'll still be able to take a pretty penny to the bank on payday.

252

"Meanwhile," King James continues, "Tyrese will handle the rest. My legacy."

"Which is?" I ask—because I thought his organization and his businesses were his legacy.

He senses my confusion and smiles. "I built up this kingdom to protect my family and my people. When you look like me, you've got the same chance of being gunned down by the cops as you do the thugs hiding in the dark alley. I've given my people a sense of safety they've never felt anywhere else in this country. That cannot die with my arrest."

"How will Tyrese keep it alive?"

"He will take on a role that will guarantee my legacy not only lives but goes beyond the Bronx. His duty is not to simply protect our family or our people, but to look after all of New York City once I'm gone."

My eyes widen as understanding filters in. "You want him to run for mayor."

King James's face hardens. "I want him to *become* the mayor."

"How is that even possible?"

"It will be part of my deal with the police. I'll take the fall for everything within the Stronghold. I'll even let their little news cameras film it all—the arrest of Jameson Willis. The fall of a King." He frowns. "I'll do it. But a prince must rise from the ashes."

"The next election isn't for a while," I say.

"Whenever it is, Tyrese's name *will* be on the ballot."

"How do you expect Norman or New York police to pick the next mayor?" I shake my head. "They don't have that kind of influence."

"That's for them to figure out." He laughs. "I've got enough evidence to motivate them."

"Do you think they'll take the deal?"

"I'm not talking about evidence on *my* crimes," he says coolly. "I have half the police force on my payroll—that includes cops and detectives from Norman and New York City. Dirty officers."

My mouth hangs open. "You want to blackmail the police?"

"Have you seen the news?" he asks sharply. "They've been painting a picture I haven't seen."

I know what he's talking about. The media has been having a field day since Norman detectives officially launched their investigation into the rumored sex trafficking ring Rosa reported. She gave a statement to a detective the same day we told our men and women about our plans. Quotes from her statement have made headlines across the nation—details on how she was kidnapped, and how her own brother might have been responsible.

The most shocking part, however, is how the cops have all been hailed as heroes gearing up to rid the city of mafia filth. It's like the country's forgotten how they used to worship us as celebrities overnight. Now, we're just a bunch of thugs who've been using our power to hold the city hostage. Funny that no one's bothered to mention how a bunch of dirty cops helped us stay in power all this time, even helped keep up the very trafficking ring they're investigating.

Ahem ... Arthur Hart.

But no. The only thing the news has been reporting is stories that make us look like exactly what we've always been. Criminals. All at once, the excitement and thrill of the mafia is gone. Justice is rolling on like a river, and the nation is eating it up.

"You think they'll let a former gangster become mayor?" I ask in a serious tone.

"If they do anything to block his success, I'll start singing like a bird from my prison cell," King James threatens. "I'll name every dirty cop I know, and Tyrese will release the records to the public. For now, I'm holding on to my evidence against them. I'll only use it if I must."

Wise decision.

"So, Trenton legalizes the family businesses. Tyrese becomes the mayor. And you take the fall to make sure it all happens." My shoulders rise and fall. "What does any of this have to do with me?"

King James smiles again, his gold tooth winks in the light. "My sons will be busy doing all they can to make sure our plans play out smoothly. But I still have a wife and two precious granddaughters."

Adella and Nona.

"Adella has Jared. He's a good kid. And I know he'll take care of her—even if he doesn't, Della is strong enough to handle herself. But Nona…" his voice trails off for a moment. "She's more like Rosa."

Which basically means she's fragile and can't take care of herself.

"Rosa has gotten stronger," King James nods, "I will acknowledge that. But she's not like her older cousin."

"Not quite," I admit.

"I am sure Adella and Jared and both my sons will look after Nona and Monique," Jameson says, "but I have watched you take care of Rosa. I have watched you do everything in your power to love her and protect her as a husband should." He leans forward, pointing his cigar at me. I stare at the glowing red tip as he speaks. "I want you to promise me you'll be there if my family ever needs you. Promise me you'll look after my girls with the same fervor you've looked after yours."

It's an honor I don't deserve.

I answer without hesitation. "I promise."

Satisfied, King James sits back in his chair and stubs out his cigar. He lets go of a long, heavy breath. "One more thing."

"Yes?"

"Don't tell anyone what we discussed here today."

"Your family doesn't know you're taking the fall," I say quietly.

He nods. "The arrests will happen in a few days. Police let me know when I first approached them about cooperating with the investigation. I'm going to speak with a detective and my lawyer tomorrow to finalize things."

"And then everything will go down."

He smiles solemnly. "And then the dominoes will fall."

"Are you ready?"

The table quakes with the deep laugh he lets out. "Absolutely."

Twenty

Amory and I stand side by side as police officers, clad in uniform, march through our home. They've been in and out all morning, clearing out the boxes and boxes of documents we piled up last night. That's everything ever planned, signed, and sealed by the leaders of the Hunting Grounds for the last ten years. Contracts, receipts, reports, files—even photos that should have been turned in as crime scene evidence years ago.

We went through everything by hand; me, Amory, Gisela, Wolfgang, and Douglass. Took us all night, but we got it done. We didn't want to hand over anything that would incriminate anyone else except Uwe Jäger, and if we couldn't entirely pin it on him, then Morgen altered whatever he could and had his own name added to the paperwork.

Part of me feels bad about the whole thing. Altering the documentation is wrong. We're technically lying to police. I told Amory I couldn't help with any of that. I wasn't trying to

258

keep my hands clean; I was trying to do what's right before God.

Lying is wrong, no matter who you're lying to or what for.

When I told this to my husband, he was torn. I'm not the only Christian in the house anymore; he's got to answer to God too. But—to my shock—he reminded me of the story of Rahab the prostitute and how she hid the men of God and lied to authorities to keep them safe. Rahab was doubly rewarded for her actions—not because she had lied, but because she had done whatever she could to protect the righteous men of God.

She was already a sinner, so she was judged by a sinner's standard. If she had been righteous and had used dishonesty to achieve her goals, I doubt she would have been rewarded for anything. But as the story goes, she received great recognition for her bravery. Not only was Rahab's household saved from destruction, but she was also included in the lineage of Christ Jesus, the greatest honor anyone could ever hope for.

I wouldn't dare compare our actions to Rahab's—unlike Amory—especially because we're not doing this to protect righteous men of God. But I am proud of my husband for reading his Bible enough to recall the story so well, even if his personal comparison is a little skewed.

I did my best to explain the differences to him; that Rahab was helping Believers who desperately needed it, we're just keeping thugs out of prison. But Amory countered with a reminder that the fall of the mafia is part of God's will for the city.

"We're carrying it out the best way we can," he'd told me last night.

His tone had been stern, and I knew that was the end of the conversation no matter what points I brought up. I could have spoken up more. I *should* have spoken up more. But I know my husband; when his mind is made up, there isn't anything I can do. The best I got out of him was a haphazard agreement that he wouldn't do the alterations himself. I hope that counts for something.

Amy places his arm over my shoulders and pulls me closer to him as the officers clear out the last boxes. "They'll be making arrests all afternoon once they start looking at the evidence."

"Hopefully not," I say quietly.

He tilts his head as he glances down at me.

"Uwe is dead, and Morgen is supposedly dead. They shouldn't be arresting anyone at all."

He nods. "Others are turning in evidence of their own. I'm sure the Italians have plenty of records that incriminate a few high-ranking Russians."

"Probably," I agree, thinking of Gio and all his dealings with Volkov—even his involvement in the sex ring running through Staten Island. I silently wonder if Arthur turned in any evidence. I hadn't mentioned his name when I gave a statement of my kidnapping to Norman and NYC police, but I'm sure he approached detectives on his own. Arthur is a snake, despite taking my word and my money, he would have wanted to make sure his name wouldn't be mixed up in any of this. I'm almost positive he struck a deal with detectives.

I blow away my frustrations with a sigh. It doesn't matter if Arthur made a deal. Any evidence he has would only be damning against himself, Gio, and Volkov. The Hunting Grounds and the Stronghold were genuinely uninvolved in whatever crimes they'd been committing altogether. So I'm certain anything he's done behind my back won't impact our operation at all. In fact, it should only serve to strengthen our plans. Anything that makes Volkov and Gio look like the monsters they truly were will be better for us.

"We're all done here," says Detective Bennett. She walks over to Amory and I and stands before us with a tight smile on her face.

I smile back, though its reserved and cautious. I've only met with Det. Bennett three times before today, and although she's never been rude or conniving—at least not to my face— I can't say I fully trust her. But Amory seems at ease, shifting his weight from one foot to the other as he extends his free hand to her.

"Nice to see you again."

She shakes his hand. "Likewise. Thanks for all your cooperation."

Det. Bennett is tall for a woman, with broad shoulders and full eyebrows that always seem to find each other in the middle of her forehead. I know she's wearing a smile, but I can't help but interpret the flat-brow expression as a grimace.

No matter her appearance, Arthur was right to go to her with the investigation. She's been chasing our leads like a stubborn bulldog, never letting up—not even for a second. But as relentless as she's been at pursuing the case, she's also been fair and just in her judgment. The deals with the prosecution were all her idea. It's because of Det. Bennett that Amory isn't in cuffs right now, that his arm is still over my shoulders instead of behind his back, getting patted down by officers.

My wary smile slowly warms as I glance up at my husband. *We did it*, I beam. *It's finally over.*

"Arrests should begin soon," Amory says to the detective.

She glances at me. "Actually, Mr. Jäger, they're beginning right now."

Panic arrows through my heart at the sound of her words, but before I can even register the sudden jolt of anxiety, a thunderclap of raw fear storms through me as two officers step beside Det. Bennett and start toward Amory.

"No," I whisper.

"We had a deal," Amory snarls as they near us. One of them unclasps the cuffs from his utility belt and Amory responds by stepping forward and simultaneously shoving me back behind him. "I handed over evidence. I'm supposed to be granted immunity."

"You have been," Det. Bennett says, her eyes locked on me.

The officers pass by my husband and appear at my side. My knees buckle, but one of the officers keeps me steady by grabbing hold of my arm—and promptly twisting it behind my back.

"Amory!" I scream, realizing what's happening.

He turns and his face curdles in a mixture of fear, panic, and pure outrage.

"Rosa…" his voice betrays his expression, whispering so calmly, I'm not sure he understands what's happening, but when the officer grabs my other arm, he screams, "Rosa!"

We both lose it.

I twist free of the officer's hold and run toward Amy, but I don't get more than a step before I'm dragged back. Amory starts toward me, but the other cop quickly intervenes, grabbing him from behind. There's a scuffle; I can hear Amory shouting and cursing—spit flying as he screams at Det. Bennett.

"We have a deal! We have a deal!"

He's right. He does have a deal with law enforcement. But I don't. I never made one because I haven't committed any crimes. The entire investigation began with my kidnapping—somehow, I'm the one in cuffs now.

I feel the coolness of the metal as the officer slides the restraints over my wrists. The distinct *click* of the cuffs snaps everything into place.

I start to panic all over again; my heart is racing, my eyes are wild with fear. I can still hear Amory shouting—I'm screaming too, jerking against the cuffs as I try to reach for him, to no avail.

"Please!" I cry.

Det. Bennett speaks calmly, "Rosa Jäger, due to evidence turned in to police this morning, you are under arrest for the murder of Boris Ivanov."

Boris Ivanov?

"*Who* is that?" Amory shouts at the detective. "She didn't murder anyone!"

But I did. I shot that Russian in the safehouse—he'd died instantly.

I gasp as I realize how trapped I am. "Amory..." my voice is nothing but a trembling whisper, but Amy hears me loud and clear. He instantly whips his head in my direction, grey eyes like two storms in his angry face.

I can't find any more words. There's nothing else to say except that I'm going to jail. As the thought thunders through me, I let out a sob of fear and sorrow.

"Rosa," he says so gently it shatters me. "I'll get us a lawyer."

I start shaking my head. "No, no, no..."

"I'll take care of this!" he shouts as I panic.

"I can't—" I can't *breathe*. "I can't go to jail!" I cry.

"I'll take care of this!" Amory's clothes are all disheveled from him trying to wrestle away from the shockingly strong officer who's still holding him. His hair is falling into his face, there's a tear on one of his sleeves, but he doesn't care. All of his attention is focused entirely on me, trying his best to keep me calm, to reassure me.

His words fall on deaf ears.

I can't hear anything but my hysterical screaming. I'm so scared, I can't think straight.

"Amy!" I cry as the officer begins to tug me away. I slip, but not because of his firm grasp—as I glance down, I realize I've wet myself. Urine pools at my bare feet as my panic ratchets up even more. At the sight of it, I double over and lose my bladder completely.

My knees tremble as I lock them together, skirt bunching between my legs. I gasp and try hard to stop the flow, but I can't. I pee myself right in front of my husband and a handful of cops.

To their honor, no one says a word. They just let me finish in shameful silence, looking away as the warmth trickles down my exposed thighs.

Amory doesn't look away. He stares at my legs, eyes formed into perfectly round circles in his head—the image of utter shock. And then, to my own surprise, he hiccups and begins to cry.

"I'm so sorry…" his voice trembles. And that's the last thing I hear from him before the officer pulls me along.

Twenty-One

I can't believe this. Rosa was arrested. They put cuffs on her wrists. They dragged her away. They took her from me. My wife. My woman.

I haven't slept since that day. I don't even remember the last time I consumed anything other than a mug of black coffee. There isn't time for any sleep or food; since I watched Rosa climb into the back of a police car, I've been on the phone with every connection I think will make a difference. I've called seven lawyers, met with four of them, spoken to two journalists, and rallied half of my generals.

King James was livid, but his anger only lasted a moment—he was arrested three hours after Rosa. His family went nuts, but I managed to calm them after revealing that was part of his grand plan. In a sad way, I was happy about his arrest, it took some of the attention off of Rosa. The media has been eating up her story, tearing her apart on the news and ripping into her online.

The country wants blood. They're excited about the cops swooping in to deliver justice for the city, but once word got out about all our immunity deals, the excitement burned into hateful anger. They don't want to hear about gangsters breaking deals with prosecution, they want someone to go to prison. They want someone to pay for all the crimes that have been committed under the mafia's hold over New York.

Ten years of anarchy. Ten years of unfiltered violence.

Rosa is our sacrifice. And what an offering she makes. A spoiled mafia princess finally getting what she deserves. The media is painting a picture of an evil, little demon meeting a worthy end. They're calling the day of her arrest 'Judgment Day' and they're cheering in the streets about it.

At least, they *were* cheering until the cops took down someone bigger. King James. Unlike Rosa, his arrest was filmed live by news cameras and TV show hosts. The internet has been on fire since that day, offering nonstop coverage of all the arrests and updates on the convictions that aren't happening.

I've even been on the news. My face appears right beside my wife's, detailing all the horrible crimes I've committed, reporting things I've done even before the defunding. They went so far into my past it's shameful. My mugshot from my early twenties is on some pathetic crime investigation show right now, the television in my bedroom goes over the time I was arrested and served six months in prison. After they're done going through my rap sheet, a psychologist comes out and analyzes each one of my tattoos—32 total. They can't get enough of the bullseye on my chest, it's only overshadowed by all the scars they can see beneath the ink.

No one asks where the scars come from, they assume I got them committing crimes and killing people. If only they knew how much darker the truth really is. But I don't care that they're smearing my name and reputation. I was born and raised in the mafia, I had a rap sheet and a horrible reputation before the defunding. We didn't celebrate the defunding because it'd finally given us a chance to become respectable citizens, we were happy about it because it finally gave us the chance to be who we've always been out in the open.

I'm the boss of the German American mafia. I'm a murderer, a thief, a liar, a con—a monster. But I've never fooled myself into thinking I was anything else or could ever be anything else. But Rosa...

Rosa was born into the mafia just like me, but she never took on the role the way I did. In fact, she ran away from it every chance she got. The only reason she managed to warm up to me is because God Himself pretty much ordered her to stay in New York and work things out so we could carry out His will.

But where has that gotten us?

I trusted my wife and agreed to do God's will because I thought it was the right thing to do. Rosa told me that letting God in would make a difference—that God would work everything out in the end.

Look at us.

What's the point in handing things over to God if you end up in jail after it's all said and done?

The worst part is that it's Rosa and not me. I'm the one who's lived a life of crime and lawlessness. I'm the one who doesn't even know how many women I've bedded. I'm the one who just handed my life over to God—I've got less than 30 days of living a *sort of* Christian life under my belt. Meanwhile, Rosa has been saved all her life. She grew up with a Christian mother who read her Bible stories before bed and taught her how to pray over her meals. She lived with Melissa and attended a beautiful church with a wonderful Pastor who cares enough about her to have our backs in this dilemma right now.

After Rosa was arrested, she called me and offered her support—said she was going to speak to officers and lawyers on our behalf. As a strong activist in the community, she's confident her word will have some sway, if not on law enforcement, then at least with the public who's been having a ball at trashing my wife.

Even so, none of that changes anything. Rosa's kindness, her gentleness, her relationship with Pastor Marcia, her life as a Believer hasn't made a difference. In the end, she got left out to dry. She's the one who fought for God and she's the one who's getting punished for it.

I turn off the television and throw my remote across the room. "Where are You..." I mutter. It's the first prayer I've whispered since I got saved. I doubt it makes a difference, but I don't let the resentment sink in. Rosa wouldn't want me simmering in anger, especially not toward God. She would want me to stand up and be strong, even though all I feel is weak.

I've been defeated at every turn. Losing men in the war, losing my wife to the cops, losing my faith to my sorrows. The only sense of peace I have comes from Rosa's extended family. Since Jameson's arrest, his sons have jumped into action, just like he'd hoped they would. Tyrese has met with several detectives and has been on the news nonstop, trying to do damage control as journalists tear us apart. He's fighting hard, but not as hard as Jared and Trenton who've been locked in legal battles trying to get their businesses certified.

Despite being focused on other tasks, the Stronghold has been kind enough to send spare men to reinforce our ranks with Conrad. My cousin has been giving his all to maintain defenses against the Morenos and whatever remains of the Volkovs. Apparently, there was a shootout two days after the arrests, we lost thirteen more men, but we took twenty from them. I'm proud of Conrad, especially since he's away from Gisela and had to say goodbye to Morgen a few days ago. He left with Silke the day before Rosa was taken into custody. I don't know where they're at, but they promised to contact us once they got their new identities and settled down.

That's all good news. *Great* news. But I don't have time to dwell on anything besides my wife. Rosa is my one and only concern right now.

I have a meeting with our lawyer today, we're going downtown to see her for the first time since she was dragged away from me. I'm nervous for so many reasons; we're putting together her defensive strategy, but besides that—I'm nervous because I haven't seen Rosa in what seems like forever. I don't know how much of the news she's had access to, if she's seen how much crap they've been giving her online and in the papers. But I'm also concerned with how she's been handling herself regardless of the media.

Rosa wasn't made for prison—she wasn't even made for the mafia. She wet herself right in front of me and a room full of cops, I don't want to think about how she's coping behind bars.

I've been to prison. I know what it's like. I know what prisoners go through—and I was only there for six months. It was more than ten years ago, a job gone horribly wrong. I was sentenced to four years, but the defunding happened and Vater made sure the first thing he did was get rid of politicians and officials who couldn't be bought or intimidated. Then he ushered in lawmakers, lawyers, judges, and cops who would follow his orders.

Not only was my case overturned, but Vater took the liberty of having legislature revised to his liking. Since the defunding, no one convicted of a crime in New York City has been sentenced to more than 10 years behind bars. At the time of my early release, I was just happy to be getting out of prison, but now I see just how wise my father truly was. He wasn't looking at the here-and-now—just getting his son out of prison and moving on—he was looking at the future. At what would happen if the mafia ever fell and we faced prison sentences again.

That gives me hope for Rosa's future. If she faces a conviction of murder, it won't matter if it's first degree or manslaughter, she won't be sentenced to any more than a decade. Courtesy of my dear old dad.

Still, ten years is a long time. I could barely handle six months of prison; I won't even allow myself to entertain thoughts of what it'll be like for my sweet rose to spend an entire decade behind bars.

There's a knock on my bedroom door. I sigh and push to my feet. I already know who it is before I answer—because I don't *get* to answer the door, it swings open on its own to reveal my little brother. He remains in the doorway, leaning against the frame with his hands stuffed into his pockets, sharp eyes watching me closely.

I meet Wolfgang at the door; for a moment, neither of us speaks. Wolf moved in after the incident at Gio's penthouse, to my surprise, he got along well with Rosa. They made breakfast together almost every morning, speaking in Italian and trading spices like they were chefs who'd worked together for years. I was surprised by how well both of them could cook, and by how well they seemed to enjoy each other's company.

To no one's surprise, Rosa had an impact on my brother. He didn't turn into an overnight Bible thumper, but he was respectful whenever Rosa read the Word to him, and he even reminded her to pray over their meals together.

I have a distinct memory of them sitting on the floor in the living room, all the files, documents, and boxes of evidence spread out around them. Wolf had been smiling, sorting through papers, and he'd asked Rosa to sing him something to pass the time. She'd chosen a hymn I'd never heard before, and she sang it in Italian. By the end, he'd joined in, and they'd finished with smiles on their faces.

I'm not at all surprised to see the mixture of anger and worry on my brother's face when I stand before him. He's wearing a large t-shirt and a pair of oversized sweatpants I'm sure belong to me, but I don't scold him for going through my closet. His facial hair is growing in, just a few days of scruff— probably hasn't shaved since the arrests—and his head is covered in a layer of bright red fuzz. When he turns his head, I can see the dark shadow of the bullseye tattooed onto the back of his thick skull.

"You're leaving," he finally says.

I nod. "My meeting is at noon."

"Downtown."

"Yes."

He nods and then pushes from the wall. "I'll be here with Douglass, Della, and Nona."

"They'll look after you."

"I'll be fine."

He's been following me like a lost puppy since Gio died, and with Rosa gone, he's practically a mess, but I appreciate the brave front he's putting up. It would have fooled me if he hadn't taken an awkward step forward and blinked up at me like a ten-year-old kid.

I give him a sloppy smile when I realize he wants a hug. "Come here," I say, pulling him toward me.

His arms wrap around my middle, and he speaks into my shirt, "Don't go."

"I have to."

"They could arrest you."

"I have a deal with prosecution."

"They took Rosa even though they weren't supposed to."

I pull away and hold him at arm's length so I can look him in the eye—my worried kid-brother. "I'm coming back, Wolfy. Understand?"

He glances away but nods, one small jerk of the head like he's the petulant little brat I remember from our childhood. I don't blame him for his worry; the cops betrayed us by arresting my wife, and now that I'm going in alone things could take a turn for the worst.

"What am I supposed to do if you don't come back?" he mutters, still not meeting my gaze.

My heart breaks for him. We lost Vater. We lost almost half our men. We lost King James. We lost Rosa. Morgen is gone and Conrad is fighting. Wolfgang has no one but me and now he's scared he'll lose me too.

I pull him toward me again and sigh as he hugs me back, hands balling fists into my jacket. "I'm coming back, Wolfy."

"You don't know that for sure."

"If I don't come back," I say, "Mutti and Tante live just outside the city—"

He jerks back and scowls up at me. "I am *not* running away to Mom and Aunt Vikky."

I chuckle. "What about the Stronghold?" They're technically not Wolf's family, but King James is an honorable man, even though he's in prison, I don't think his family would shut their doors to my brother if I sent him to live in the Bronx for a while.

Wolf contemplates the suggestion, pressing his lips together and nodding like he's seriously weighing his options. When he's made up his mind, he says, "Nona will be there, right?"

I won't even question why on earth he cares if Nona will be there—I feel like I already know the answer. Both of my wife's cousins have been here since she was arrested, offering me emotional support and apparently offering Wolfgang something else. I've seen him and Nona on the patio together, but I haven't had the time to pay them any attention. Now, I'm wondering if maybe I should have paid attention.

It doesn't matter, I tell myself. Wolfgang will be safe in the Stronghold, if Nona will help convince him to take up shelter there, then I'll accept whatever's blooming between them.

"Yeah," I say slowly. "Nona will be there."

He tries to hide his smirk. "Then yeah, I'll go to the Stronghold if you don't come back."

"But I *will* come back." I punch his shoulder.

He rolls his eyes.

"If you're so worried, why don't you come with me?"

He scowls again, crosses his arms. "I don't like cops."

Of course he doesn't. Most men in our lifestyle can't stand them, but Wolfy takes it personally. He had a horrible encounter before the defunding, much like me, except he was arrested without injury and was released with a broken wrist, a black eye, and two fractured ribs. He never told us exactly what happened, and we couldn't prove anything or do anything before the defunding. We were just thugs to the cops and to the public; no one cared if the son of a troublesome mafia boss got what he deserved behind bars.

Whatever happened has left him screwed up and cautious of cops ever since that incident. I don't blame him for his wariness, and I don't push the issue any further.

I punch his shoulder once more. "I'll be back, Wolfy."

He mutters a quiet goodbye and then steps aside, watching me leave in silence.

Twenty-Two

I thought the worst day of my life was when I lost my mother. That was overshadowed the day Gio's men dragged me back to New York. But all of that paled in comparison to the day I was arrested. They put me in cuffs, sealing my fate and future with the clink of the metal. I was so scared I was shaking—so scared that I peed myself in a room full of people.

And now I'm sitting in a cell.

They took me in, patted me down, and locked me up like a criminal. In a way, I suppose I am a criminal. I killed a man, shot him dead right in front of my cousin and my friends, but it wasn't coldblooded murder like they've been saying on the news. It was self-defense.

They have a video recording of it. Security camera footage from the hotel we used as a safehouse—but the video is so obviously edited that it's sad. You can't see any of the carnage the Russians and Morenos left through the halls and lobbies of the building, you can't see us running for our lives and taking up shelter in the bathroom together. The video starts with an innocent-looking man walking into the room and me shooting him point-blank, no questions.

There's no footage of me freaking out afterward, no footage of Petra dying on the bathroom floor, or Douglass slowly bleeding out. There hasn't even been any question as to why there are cameras in the bathroom in the first place. It's just a six-second clip of me murdering someone—and that's all the media needs.

They've been ripping me apart since I was arrested and the video surfaced. I don't know how police got their hands on the so-called 'evidence,' but I doubt it matters. The country hates me. My case is pretty much open and shut. I've been judged as guilty by the public before my trial date has even been set.

I roll over on my thin mattress, facing the concrete wall. There's very little light in my cell, just the afternoon rays filtering in through the window high above my bed. It's how I keep track of the time, counting off the hours as the day drifts by and the sunlight begins to fade. I have nothing else to do inside my cell except wait for my horrible meals three times a day.

Every second that I'm here, I feel myself slipping away, feel my will and strength petering out. I don't belong here—not because I'm too good for prison, but because I'm not the murderous mafia gangster the news has made me out to be. This isn't fair. This isn't right.

I swipe at a tear and squeeze my eyes shut. "God… I did everything You wanted. I completed the job. I carried out Your will." I sigh. "Is this my reward?"

Despair works its way into my heart, but I force it away as I recite one of my favorite scriptures. "So do not fear, for I am with you; do not be dismayed, for I am your God. I will strengthen you and help you; I will uphold you with my righteous right hand."

That's Isaiah 41:10, a verse I used to pray quite often when I first ran away from home. I felt like the world had crashed around me—my mother was dead, and I was alone in a strange new city with strange new people. I needed the reminder that my Father was with me. I needed the comfort of knowing that God was still the One on the throne, even though I had messed up and tried to handle things on my own. But now I'm doing things His way, and everything is still falling apart.

"Is this part of Your plan?" I whisper as more tears slip down my cheeks. "Is this how it ends?"

It can't be. As Gisela told me so long ago, God is a *kind* Father. He's good to His children. He would never leave me nor forsake me. But right now, I can't see past the concrete walls around me or the darkness that's slithering into my heart.

"I need to hear from You," I say aloud. "Jesus, I need a reminder that You're still here with me."

I don't expect the walls to quake or crumble around me. I don't expect the heavens to part and angels to tear down the prison that holds me. But I do hope for an answer of some sort. A Still Voice to whisper comfort, a flood of peace to keep my head on straight.

Instead, I hear the squeak of the metal door that cages me, and footsteps enter my cell. I turn over and squint at the invading stream of light that pours into the tiny room. There are two guards, one is a woman who looks at me with reserved sympathy in her hazel eyes, the other is a man who simply leans against the wall, holding a pair of shackles in his large hands.

"You've got a visitor," the woman guard says.

"Who is it?"

"Lawyer and husband."

My heartrate triples. I haven't seen or heard from anyone since they threw me in this cell days ago. Sometimes, I can hear voices from the radio as my guard listens to the trashy news reports about me and my family. But this is the first time I'm being allowed to leave this little room. The first time I'll get to see Amory.

I want to run down the hall and into his arms, but as I stand and wait for the woman to pat me down and search for weapons, I feel a familiar wave of shame roll over me. The same anxious embarrassment that'd caused me to lose my bladder in front of my own husband. The same fear that'd told me my life was over.

I wonder how Amory has been handling himself. I wonder what he thinks of me, wearing this bright orange jumpsuit, shuffling down the hall with my ankles and wrists shackled together. I don't want him to see me like this. I can barely look at myself as I pass by the reflective glass of the visiting rooms.

I'm a mess. My hair is wild, the curls have lost all definition, puffing into an angry afro that makes me look like the deranged killer everyone keeps calling me. My eyes are wide and unblinking, my skin is slick with nervous sweat. I have absolutely no makeup on, there are dark circles under my eyes, and my lips are so dry they ache when I try to practice my smile.

I feel my bottom lip split and try to suck the blood away. It stings.

When the guards open the door to my visiting room, tears spring to my eyes. So much for practicing my smile—my face immediately crumples into a distorted frown as I begin to sob.

Amory is sitting at a small table, his suit jacket slung over the back of his chair, the sleeves of his shirt rolled up to his elbows. I can see the tattoos on his arms poking from beneath the material of his white shirt, the fact that he's got them out on display tells me just how much he doesn't care about the people around him. His hair is disheveled, like he's been running his hand through it, his eyes bear dark circles underneath and I can tell it's been a few days since he last shaved.

I'm so happy to see him, even in this state he is the most beautiful man I've ever laid eyes on. I almost shy away when he stands and crosses the room to take me into his arms, lifting me from the floor. The shackles on my hands and feet clank against each other as he whispers into my hair, "You're okay. I'm right here."

I hadn't realized I'd begun to cry, but now that I've noticed, I can't get myself to stop. I sob into his chest, my body shaking with each breath; Amory just holds me, strong and unyielding, exactly what I need.

The woman guard clears her throat. "That's enough."

"Give them a moment," a man across the room speaks.

I blink at him as Amory sets me back on my feet, a thin man with grey hair and an impressive salt and pepper mustache. He's wearing an expensive suit and leather shoes polished so well, the light reflects off them. I can only guess he's the lawyer my guard mentioned.

"You have one hour," the woman guard says. She turns and unlocks my shackles, then passes them to the male guard. "We'll be just outside."

I rub at my wrists. "I'm so glad you're here."

Amory bends to kiss my cheek, reminding me of just how tall he is. "I came as soon as I could." He guides me to the table and even pulls out my chair for me like we're having dinner at a fancy restaurant.

I blush as I take my seat, nervously tucking a puffy lock of hair behind my ear. It fights back and springs out again three seconds later. I look like a disco dancer from the 70s with my unruly coils, but Amory takes my hand and stares at me like I'm the most beautiful woman in the world right now. I suppose there's nothing wrong with afro hair from the 70s. Not with my husband gazing at me like this.

I squeeze his hand. "Please tell me you have good news."

The lawyer speaks up. "Pretty good news."

"I didn't kill that man on purpose," I say.

He nods. "I know you didn't. Mr. Jäger has explained everything to me."

"There should be footage showing how everything went down. Recordings of me running for my life—the whole thing was self-defense."

The lawyer nods and takes a breath. "Let me introduce myself first."

I don't care about his name, but I shake his hand and smile. "Rosa Jäger."

"John Krämer."

That's a German last name, which somehow makes me relax a little.

"Now," I say slowly. "The rest of the footage...?"

Amory shifts in his seat but doesn't speak. John presses his lips together.

"Someone say something," I order.

John clears his throat. "There is no other footage."

"What?"

"That clip was turned in to police the morning of your arrest. There were no other recordings with it."

"Did you check the security tapes of the hotel?" I turn to Amory. "There's got to be more."

He shakes his head, forcing himself to look me in the eye. I'm shocked to find so much sorrow on his face. I'm the one who's suffering right now. I'll be the one behind bars if this doesn't work out in my favor.

God, please... I pray internally, but I don't even know what else to say. It feels like everything is stacked against me right now.

"How is there no other footage? Who got ahold of the tapes?" I ask in a shaky voice.

"The evidence was turned in by a fellow officer," John says.

All the air storms out of the room as realization settles in. I feel like I can't breathe, leaning over and clutching my chest. I don't even need John to finish his sentence—I know who the officer is.

Arthur Hart.

It wasn't enough to simply keep his nose out of things. It wasn't possible for him to ever take my word that I wouldn't mention his name and get him tied up in the case. Arthur had to make sure he was safe beyond a shadow of doubt. He wasn't taking his chances, and to guarantee his safety—his immunity—he turned me in. Gave police the perfect evidence to convict the 'Murderous Mafia Princess.'

The question isn't why as much as it is *how*, but I'm sure I've got that figured out too. Arthur was working with Gio, the mole. They had access to our security systems. It wouldn't have been difficult for him to take the footage, clip what he needed, and delete the rest. Amory and his men were too busy with the war to pay attention to the recordings at the time. Gio had already been dead, they weren't worried about another possible rat. Then again, no one knew Arthur had been so close to Gio. Not until now.

I look at Amory with tears in my eyes, but they are not tears of grief or sorrow—I'm angry, absolutely outraged by this betrayal. Yet, this must be only a sliver of the raging emotion that Amy felt when he realized my brother had turned against him. Gio had cost people their lives. I might be behind bars right now, but at least I'm not dead.

Amory squeezes my hand, but I shake my head. "Where is Arthur? I want to speak to him."

John sighs. "You can't."

"Why not?"

"He's gone."

I blink between him and Amory, noting the tightness in my husband's jaw.

"Gone? Did he go into witness protection?"

John almost laughs but catches himself. "Gone as in dead."

My jaw falls open.

"They found his body in his apartment this morning."

"How?" I whisper. My emotions are all over the place now. I know he betrayed me, but I can't say I wanted him dead for it.

"There aren't many details," John says, then he leans forward and speaks quietly. "He was supposed to join witness protection, but when he didn't show up for his meeting this morning, cops were sent to his place to check on him. Found him in his living room, throat slit and tongue cut out."

"A snitch's death," Amory says calmly.

Seems fitting, but I find no joy in the news. All I can think of is Melissa and Minnie and how much this will hurt them.

They have no idea that Arthur betrayed me and was only looking out for himself. They don't know he got double crossed by the gangsters he was once working for—he'd probably been killed by dirty cops still on Volkov's or Moreno's payroll.

To my Norman family, Arthur's death is a tragedy they may not be able to overcome. This might even turn them against me.

I gulp, realizing what Arthur's death truly means for me.

"He's a martyr," I say almost to myself.

John takes a deep breath, neither agreeing nor disagreeing.

Amory squeezes my hand even tighter. "The news is hailing him as a hero. The cop who brought down the mafia princess gets killed for his bravery days later."

"No one's even questioned how he got the footage, have they?"

He shakes his head. "No one cares. They just want to see you burn." He pauses. "And…"

"And what?"

"And your grandfather too."

I blink. "Papa Jamie?"

Amory turns toward me, speaking quickly as if he's racing against my pounding heart. He loses that race, and I start shaking my head as his words fill my ears. "He was arrested, but it was his plan—he's going to accept a deal with the prosecution."

The room starts to spin. My vision gets blurry.

"Ten years at most—" Amory is saying, but I'm not listening. My grandfather is in prison, locked in a cell like my own. This can't be happening.

I stand and sway, tripping sideways, but I feel Amory's hands on my shoulders, stabling me. His voice is in my ear. "It'll be okay," he says. And then he starts speaking in German as he hugs me from behind. I have no idea what he's saying, but just the soothing sound of his deep, masculine voice anchors me.

I lean into his embrace. "This isn't real," I whisper.

Amory kisses the back of my head. "Everything will be okay."

"How can you be so sure?"

He pauses, and when he speaks, his voice is quiet. "There's nothing left to hope for."

John clears his throat across the room. "We have a little hope."

"Tell me," I say as Amy and I return to our seats. "Is my grandfather getting out?"

"I can't answer for him. He's got his own lawyer." John shrugs one shoulder. "But I've been speaking with prosecution on your behalf, and you may be getting out soon."

"How soon?"

He starts emptying his briefcase, setting papers all over the little table between us. "After the defunding, there was a huge shift in legislature which prevented criminals from being sentenced to more than ten years behind bars."

Amory nods like he knows exactly what John is talking about.

"This was obviously done to benefit the mafia," John continues. "And it will take years to reverse, considering lawmakers will have to go about it the legal way once they retake New York. That works in your favor, Mrs. Jäger."

"It does," I agree. It means even if I'm found guilty of first-degree murder, I won't be serving more than ten years. "But ten years is still a long time."

Both John and Amory nod.

"To the public, it's not enough time," John says. "They want blood, Mrs. Jäger. The people are angry about so many mobsters getting immunity. They want you to go to jail. They want you to pay for what you did."

"It was self-defense," I almost whine.

"But they don't see it that way," John argues. "And they never will. To them, this isn't even about the man you killed. It's about all the gangsters getting away with their crimes. You're paying for their sins."

I bury my face in my hands. "It sounds like you're saying I'm going to stay here no matter what."

John sighs. "It doesn't have to be long."

It's only been a few days and it feels too long already.

"What are you saying?" I ask. "Give it to me straight, Mr. Krämer."

"The prosecution is offering a deal. Plead guilty to second-degree murder and you can get six years with the chance of parole after four."

288

I stare at him. "You want me to agree to spend six years in prison for a murder I didn't commit?"

"You did kill him," John says flatly.

"I didn't *murder* him!" I nearly yell.

Amory touches my arm, but I flinch away and glare at him. "Six years?" I snap. "You're okay with that?"

He takes a deep breath. "You could get paroled after four."

"Amy..."

"It's better than ten, Rosa."

"I didn't murder him," I say slowly. "I'm not taking a deal that requires me to admit to something I didn't do. It was self-defense. He would have killed *me* if I hadn't fired that gun!"

"We can't prove that!" Amory shouts. "There is no evidence! There's nothing on your side, Rosa. Can't you see?" He grabs me by both my shoulders, tilting his head down to look me in the eye. "This is a good deal."

"I can't do it."

"I need you," he mutters. "I need you back, Rosie."

In the silence that follows, I lift my hand and press it to his chest. His heart is racing, I can feel each pump against my flattened palm. This is ruining him as much as it's ruining me.

"I get what you're saying," he whispers, dropping his head and his shoulders in defeat. "But if the choice is between ten and possibly four, then please... Take the deal, Rosa."

"There's one more choice," I say calmly.

Amory lifts his gaze to mine, a question in his eyes.

"I get a 'not guilty' verdict and serve no time at all."

Amy sighs. "Rosa—"

"If we go to trial—"

"They'll crucify you," John interrupts. "Have you seen the news lately?"

"I've heard snippets on the radio," I admit. "I know what they're saying about me. I know the trial won't be easy."

"It'll be impossible."

"Just give me the chance to plead my case!" I say loudly, angrily.

Both men fall silent, shaking their heads together. They're both against me, but I don't take it personally. Amory cares from the bottom of his heart; he just wants me back home—to the point that he's willing to have me take a deal he knows is bogus if it means I'll spend less tine in jail. John, on the other hand, he's got a German name, a subtle German accent, and when his hair gets messy, I catch a glimpse of his bullseye tattoo. It's just behind his ear, peeking out as he tucks a grey lock behind it.

Despite the fact that I'm his client, it's obvious John is following Amy's lead. I can't fault the guy because it's clear who his real boss is, but that doesn't mean I have to let them overrule me. This is my fate. My future.

I stand and splay my hands on the table, glancing back and forth between my husband and lawyer. "I'm not taking the deal. I want to stand trial."

John starts to speak but I cut him off. "Tell the prosecution, 'No deal.' That's my decision and it's final."

Amory's hand covers my own. "Baby…"

I squeeze his hand and then lean down to kiss him; he seems hesitant, letting go of a little whimper against my lips. I nearly break as I pull away and catch the desperation on his face, but I steel myself at the sound of the metal door cranking open. "It'll be alright," I whisper.

On cue, the pair of guards from before march into the room and order me to step away from the table. I do as I'm told, lifting my arms so they can search me, and then holding my wrists together for them to shackle. Amory and John watch in silence. I don't want to look at my husband, but I force myself to meet his gaze and I'm glad that I do.

Somehow, in the last few moments of his visit, we have switched places. I'm no longer the one who needs comfort and support and strength, it's the other way around now. Amory needs me—more than I have ever needed him.

I remember his last words to me, that he would work all this out. That everything would be okay. I can't say his words have settled into my heart just yet, but I think I have more faith than he does as he clears his throat and nonchalantly swipes at his eye. He's trying not to let anyone see him cry for me, but the sight is humbling and feeds courage right into my bones— my marrow.

I've got to keep it together for both of us.

"It'll be okay," I say softly, as the woman guard turns me around. I crane my neck to peek over my shoulder before she tugs me out the room, the last thing I see is Amory burying his face in his hands.

Twenty-Three

My mind is as numb as my body. I sit in my car, staring up at the large brick building before me; there are camera crews waiting on the sidewalk, they've been there since the arrests hit the news. I thank God my windows are tinted, it leaves them in a state of confusion, unsure if they should stay ready for whoever will emerge from the vehicle or remain focused on the brick building.

I sigh and switch the heat to the A/C even though we're well into a chilly autumn now. Rosa's been in jail for over a month. On good days, she lets John and I in to speak with her about the case, on bad days, she refuses to see us and stays locked up in her cell. Alone and miserable.

Today is another bad day.

I tried to get in, even convinced the guards to let me bring her photos that Wolfgang gave me. They're just pictures of him with his new hair, he's letting it grow out—at her recommendation—and he thought it would be nice for Rosa to see his progress. But she doesn't want to see the pictures, she doesn't even want to see me.

I can't let it get to me. I know it isn't personal, she's just trying to cope and sometimes that's easier to do alone. But I need to cope as well, and I can't do it alone. I need Rosa more than she will ever know or understand. I'm crumbling just as much as she is, but I don't have a cell to cry in. I don't have four concrete walls to hide me from the world. There are camera crews everywhere, journalists camped outside my home, people following me wherever I go.

I've tried my hardest to avoid the news and the media, passing off my social accounts to Wolfgang so he can post on my behalf. He's gotten quite good at pretending to be me online, even started up a Facebook page in support of Rosa which has over 13,000 followers already. Most of the people just want updates on the case, but there are a good number who seem to genuinely support her and believe in her innocence.

Still ... none of that helps me right now.

Rosa's trial is in just three weeks. She's stuck to her guns and rejected every plea deal John has brought her. I'm proud of her determination, but it breaks my heart every time she says no. We got a deal that would have had her out in three years— to her credit, she did pause and swipe at a tear—but she rejected that one too. That's when I couldn't take it anymore.

I nearly flipped over the table in my anger, shouting that she was being stupid and stubborn and would end up losing a decade of her life for her pointless pride. She had speared me with her gaze, declaring, "This isn't pride, it's faith in God."

It'd taken everything in me not to laugh in her face.

Where is your God now? is what I'd wanted to say to her, but that would've only rubbed salt in the wound. Instead, I'd gathered my things and left. She's only accepted three of my visits since then.

A tired sigh blows from my lips as I lean my head against the window and stare at the holding center. I can't get in because Rosa didn't accept my visit, but I don't want to go home and tell everyone waiting that I failed yet again. Wolf is there, along with Adella, Nona, my mother and aunt, and even Gisela. Everyone has kind of moved in since the arrests rolled out.

Conrad isn't there because he's still fighting with the Morenos, I saw him on the news two nights ago—there's now a warrant out for his arrest. Glizzy took the news with a smile; she swears she's not bothered by it, but I can see the worry in her eyes.

At this point, the best thing for Conny to do is turn himself in. He's not wanted for murder, so he won't be facing much time, but I know my cousin. He's stubbornly committed to the Hunting Grounds. He'll go down screaming before he walks through the courthouse doors of his own freewill. That leaves Gisela hanging in limbo, unsure if he'll come home in cuffs or in a box. My heart goes out to her, she's family and she's one of Rosa's closest friends in the German mafia. She's also the underlady, and she's going to be the first of us to bring a little Hunter into this world.

Gisela is pregnant.

I'm the only one who knows, she told me after we both saw the news together which featured a clip of Conrad storming a warehouse owned by the Morenos. Glizzy had nearly fainted, which I thought had been a dramatic reaction, but when she confessed to being lightheaded for a completely different reason, I was left speechless.

Conrad has no idea, and Gisela isn't sure she's ready to tell him—or how to tell him. But we've both agreed that he needs to know. It may be the information to bring him home, convince him to put his stubborn loyalty to the gang aside and turn himself in. For his child's sake.

I can hardly believe the news myself. Gisela will make such a perfect mother, but Conrad... My best friend and closest cousin. My underboss. The man who once owned The Club and took dancers home from his own strip joint. The man who was sleeping with Amana behind my back and had once abused his own wife. He's going to be a father.

This is the humble awakening that he needs, the realization that there is more to life than honoring the mafia. That there is more to live for.

I learned that from my love for Rosa, but Gisela wasn't enough for Conny. I can only hope his future child will make the difference.

The journalists outside begin to stir as someone steps out of the holding center. I adjust in my seat to get a look and my eyes nearly pop from their sockets. It's Father Serrano.

Without thinking, I open my car door and step out. Initially, my intentions are just to see what's going on, but when I catch how rough the paparazzi are being with him, I get angry. At 6'2, my feet easily carry me through the crowd, shoving aside journalists and news reporters with ease. They squeal as they trip and topple over, but their anger is quickly replaced by a shock of excitement and curiosity.

"Mr. Jäger!" they begin to shout, shoving microphones and cameras into my face.

I ignore them and march toward the old Father still cowering at the door. "Come on," I say gruffly, reaching for his hand.

He nods and takes it, letting me lead him to my car. The doors shut with a thud, locking out the noise of all the vultures gathered around. It takes me fifteen minutes to peel away from the sidewalk as they crowd around the car, shouting and snapping pictures. Father Serrano laughs nervously, clicking his seatbelt into place.

Once we break away, we drive three blocks in complete silence before either of us speaks. "You need to hire security whenever you go out from now on," I say firmly. "The crowd doesn't care about you being an innocent old priest."

Father Serrano sighs. "I'm not hiring security."

"They'll eat you alive," I growl. "What would you have done if I weren't here today?"

He smiles at me. "Prayed someone else came along to help."

"You can't just leave everything up to chance like that!"

"It's not up to chance. It's up to God."

"If I hadn't been there—"

"But you were there," Father says calmly. "And I thank God for your intervention."

I sigh, squeezing the steering wheel. "What were you doing there anyway?"

"Don't you know?" he asks, looking at the side of my face. "I was visiting your wife."

I nearly drive off the road. "Rosa?"

He nods. "I've been meaning to go for a while now, but the church has been flooded with new members since the arrests started."

Mafiosi running scared from the police and each other, thinking now is the best time to get right with God. When your only choices are prison or death, I can't say I blame them.

"I had some free time today and went to see Rosa. I'm glad I did."

I swallow thickly. "Is … Is she doing alright?"

"She's lost a little weight. But physically, she is fine. And spiritually."

"*Spiritually*," I scoff, which earns me a quirked eyebrow from the old priest.

"Do you have an issue with Rosa's spirituality?"

I grind my teeth together, unsure how to answer. That doesn't deter Father Serrano, I'm sure he's used to people snapping at him and throwing rude questions his way all the time. He walks around in full priestly attire, a black cassock, white gloves, a zucchetto on his head. He's a cute old man, in that salt and pepper grandpa sort of way. But in his Catholic attire, he's a walking target for hatred and discrimination. Especially in today's society.

Somehow, Father Serrano not only seems unbothered by this fact, but he openly welcomes the questions and comments people hurl at him. Like my own, as I turn in my seat and face him head-on while we stop at a red light.

"Rosa did everything her God asked of her and now she's in prison for it. Where is He? I don't understand."

Father Serrano laughs.

I blink.

"*Her* God? Amory, God is God of all. Whether you acknowledge that or not—but you did acknowledge that, didn't you?"

I face forward, waiting for the light to change. "Yeah. I did."

"Rosa told me you gave your life over to Christ. You're a Christian now. Yet, you're using such isolating language. *Her* God... Is He not yours too? Is Jesus no longer the Head of your life?"

"H—He is. I just don't understand what's the point anymore."

The light changes and I hit the gas. I wait for Father Serrano to speak, but he doesn't. We drive in silence until I realize I have nowhere to go. I don't want to go home, and I'm not exactly sure if Father Serrano wants to go back to his church. He seems content to just ride along with me, smiling out the window and waving at the clusters of school kids who wait with crossing guards at stoplights.

"Father," I say softly.

"Me? Or God?" he asks.

When I blink at him, he laughs and pats my hand on the steering wheel. "It was a joke. A bad one, apparently."

I chuckle. "Oh, sorry."

"Do you know what I discussed with Rosa for our visit?"

I shake my head. "Probably praying and stuff."

"That's correct. But we didn't pray for her trial or for Rosa. She spent that entire hour praying for you, Amory."

I'm so surprised, the car jerks forward when I slam on the gas at the change of the lights. Father Serrano sways with the momentum, holding onto the dashboard and saying, "*Whoaa*," as we speed off.

"Sorry," I mumble, slowing down a bit.

He laughs heartily. "I'm guessing you're surprised by that information."

I am.

"Why would she spend her visiting hour praying for me?"

"I think it's safe to say you need it."

I scowl at the road.

"Rosa is secure in her faith," Father Serrano says. "She has chosen to trust God no matter what happens. But you've said yourself you don't even know if serving God is worth it anymore."

I sigh. "Am I wrong to wonder? Rosa is in jail even though she's been nothing but a good person."

"God doesn't care if you're *good*," he says sharply. "Those are worldly standards that have no impact on His judgment. God cares if you're righteous. If you're obedient. When you are those things, goodness follows."

"Rosa's been righteous and obedient too, and she's still being punished. Why hasn't God protected her?"

"The Bible says *trouble will come*," he replies. "That means bad things will sometimes happen to us no matter what. But even so, God *has* protected Rosa. She could have been shot down by police, but her arrest went peacefully. She could have been abused in prison, but she's been fine so far, if not a little worried. And she could have been arrested at a time where she would have been facing much more than ten years in prison, but God has provided a way for her to return home soon even if she is handed a guilty verdict."

I shake my head, trying to keep my voice calm. "She shouldn't have been arrested in the first place."

"Perhaps. But then you wouldn't be here in this trial now."

I stare at him. "Trial...?"

"Haven't you figured it out yet, son? This case isn't about Rosa or the man she killed or the mafia at all. This is *your* trial. Your salvation is on the line." He leans toward me in the car. "You gave your life to God because Rosa encouraged you to. You turned on the mafia because the walls were crumbling around you, and you essentially had no other choice. You chose to let God have His way with the city because that was easier than fighting in the gang war." He nods, like he's thinking over everything he just said. "God wants to know if you're sincere. If you will continue to serve Him without Rosa. Without the mafia. Without everything that initially placed you on the path of righteousness."

My shoulders slump. This is my test, my trial—not Rosa's. It was never about Rosa, because she will always love God no matter what predicament she faces. She ran away because she loves God. She married me and stayed in New York because she loves God and wanted to carry out His will. She convinced me, the Jägermeister, to give my life to God because she loves the Lord enough to want to share His love with me. And now, in prison, she still loves God, choosing to leave her trial in His hands instead of taking a plea deal.

I'm the one who's wavering. I'm the weak link.

The sad part is, even though I now know this, I still can't decide. I don't know what to think or believe. *If I truly lean on God, will He get Rosa out of prison?*

Father Serrano seems to read my mind. "You've got to trust and love God for you, Amory. Not for Rosa. Not for the mafia. Your salvation must be your choice alone." He pats my shoulder. "Will you believe even if things don't work out in your favor?"

I honestly have no idea.

Twenty-Four

My dress is blush pink and stops at the knee. John says it's better for me to look as 'innocent' as possible today. My trial begins in less than an hour, so I've been allowed to shower, do my hair, put on a bit of makeup, and slip into the dress and shoes John picked out for me. I don't really like the clothes, I feel like a sad Bible study teacher as I glance in the mirror, but I trust John. He's been representing accused murderers for almost as long as I've been alive, if he says looking innocent will help, then I'll wear the ugly modest clothes and pray for the best.

My stomach turns knots as I wait for my guards to retrieve me. It's not until this very moment that I think I should have taken a plea deal, that I'm in over my head. But I swallow my nerves and whisper one of my favorite scriptures for encouragement.

For our light and momentary troubles are achieving for us an eternal glory that far outweighs them all.

302

II Corinthians 4:17 … a verse I made sure I memorized at the beginning of this whole mess. It's a reminder that the troubles we face are nothing compared to the glory God has in store for His children. The Apostle Paul wrote almost half the New Testament while in chains and he never complained a single time. Whatever I face in this trial, whatever the outcome may be, it cannot compare to the eternal glory of the Son, Christ Jesus.

My guards come in and shackle my wrists and ankles; they've been doing this for the last six weeks, so we're used to each other now. I will never be happy to see them, but I am comfortable around them. The lady guard is named Annie and the brute is called Carter, they make a great pair—except for the fact that they're being paid to keep me in chains and will shoot me down if I try anything suspicious.

Once they're done with my chains, I'm shuffled out to the hall where John is waiting patiently. He smiles and waves off the guards. "Hey there, kiddo. You ready?"

I nod and raise my heavy wrists. "As much as I'll ever be."

"You guys think you can remove the ankle shackles?" he asks my guards.

Carter doesn't respond, but Annie steps forward after hesitating a moment. "Just the ankles."

"Fine," John agrees. "I just want her to walk into the courtroom with some dignity."

I thank God for his proposal, the iron chafing my ankles is starting to bruise. When the shackles fall to the floor, I breathe a sigh of relief and hold my head a little higher—but it quickly drops in shame when we walk through the front doors and are greeted by a horrible crowd of screaming people.

Half the people are reporters, the other half are fanatic civilians. All of them are insane. They're holding signs and screaming at me; some are trying to show their support; I see signs that read **Free Rosa!** But there are also plenty more that say the exact opposite, some even use vulgar language and depict images of a rose on fire, a rose being clipped in half, or just plain old photos of my face with a gun aimed at my head.

I keep my vision forward and march to the patrol car where Annie practically shoves me into the back. John rides in front while Carter takes the wheel. Another crowd waits for us when we arrive at the courthouse; again, I tuck my chin and focus on getting inside alive.

The noise hushes when the double doors close behind us, but there isn't a moment to waste. Annie and Carter take me into the courtroom with John hot on our heels. As soon as I enter the room, I scan the waiting crowd for familiar faces. It seems like the only people inside are more reporters, then I catch a flash of vivid red hair and tears spring to my eyes.

Wolfgang is seated near the front, about five rows from the defendant's box. Gisela is on his side with Douglass, Adella, Nona, and Jared all waiting together. I crane my neck to peer down the row of seats, if Wolf is here then—

My vision lands on my husband and I gasp. Amory is right at the end, holding onto the railing as I near his row. I blink away my tears when he calls my name.

"Rosa!"

The crowd begins to murmur at his outburst, but he doesn't care—in fact, Amory hops right over the railing and runs toward me. I'm in his arms before I realize it, but the next second, I'm violently snatched away as Annie grabs me and Carter shoves Amory back a step.

"I'm right here!" he shouts as the crowd starts to panic. "I'm not leaving you, Rosa!"

"I love you!" I gasp.

Carter shoves Amory again. "Get back to your seat!" his voice booms through the room.

Wolf steps forward to calm things down before a fight breaks out. I'm thankful for his presence, he seems to snap Amy back to himself as he nods at Carter and takes his seat. Behind him, I realize the entire row is occupied by my friends and family. Christina, Mama Mo', my Uncle Trenton and Uncle Tyrese. Even Amory's Aunt Viktoria is here, holding Gisela's hand and smiling at me. Olivia is seated beside Marco Segreto and Niccolò Romano waits with his wife and Aldo in the next row.

There are certainly others who could be here, but I don't fault anyone for skipping out. The Hunting Grounds is still at war with the Morenos, the Garden is still trying to rebuild itself, the Stronghold is still reeling after losing Papa Jamie. Not to mention all the people who've left the mafia and are trying to get their lives together now. I wonder what Adella and Nona will do now that Grandpa is gone. I wonder what Wolfgang will do now that he's no longer the brother of the

Jägermeister—what will *Amory* do now that he's no longer the Jägermeister?

If I weren't in handcuffs right now, we'd probably be out of New York City, rebuilding our lives, chasing whatever dreams we used to have only at night. We're free now.

Well ... almost.

Annie and Carter escort me to my side of the courtroom where John takes a seat right next to me. While we wait for the judge to enter, he whispers to me to stay calm, even though his knee is bouncing like a jackrabbit's.

"We were really fortunate to forgo a jury for this case," he says softly.

I glance over at the section where the jury would normally be seated. It's completely empty, thanks to John's pleading with the courts. He fought his hardest to make sure I'd be given a fair trial—with all the media coverage, he convinced his officials that the prosecution and defense would have a difficult time finding jurors who wouldn't be biased. My entire case is being presented to a single judge, that works in my favor, but to keep the scales even, the chosen judge isn't from New York City. Prosecution argued they couldn't be sure that the judge wasn't on mafia payroll, so they worked with John to settle on a judge from outside the city with no ties to the five famous gangs.

I take a slow breath as the judge enters the room. We all fall silent and stand until he's seated. Once he's comfortable, he eyes the crowd and then his gaze lands flatly on me, like I'm a speck of dirt on his nice shoes. I fidget beneath his scrutiny, wondering what he's thinking of me. Normally, I would tell myself his thoughts don't matter, but my fate is in his hands right now.

No, it isn't, I remind myself. *God is still on the throne. He's still in charge.*

"Let us begin," the judge says. He's an older man—even older than John—with no hair and hard eyes. He's hefty, but I'm not sure if it's the robe or truly his size, then again, his chin wobbles as he leans forward and motions to the lawyers in the room.

"Opening statements," he orders.

The prosecution goes first, a man and woman who work together to make me look like the spawn of Satan. They point their fingers at me and call me names in their remarks, even go as far as saying I seduced Amory into marrying me so I could rule over three different gangs at once. Even if that were true, I have no idea what that has to do with me killing one random man in a hotel, but I bite my tongue and suffer the insults in silence.

When it's John's turn to speak, he does his best to bandage the wound. I'm not the child of the devil, or a power-hungry seductress, I'm just a woman who was in the wrong place at the wrong time. He brings up a picture of Gio that makes my eyes burn with tears and tells everyone that he's the real villain here.

"It all started with him," John says, walking slowly around the room. "This man kidnapped his own sister and dragged her into a life she never wanted to live. And because of that, she's here now." He points at me, and I do my best to keep from crying, even though John said that shedding tears would work in my favor.

I don't like what he's doing to my brother. I don't like that it feels like I'm throwing him under the bus, but at the end of the day, John's only telling the truth. I just wish the truth wasn't so dark.

The next hour is painful. The prosecution paints a picture of a woman I don't even recognize. They make me sound worse than Eliana; according to them, I was running the sex trafficking ring myself, taking women from Melissa's shelters and handing them over to Volkov and Gio. When they didn't pay me my share, I turned on them and seduced Amory to help me gain troops for the war I wanted to launch against the Wolves and my own brother.

I sent Wolfgang out to take down as many Russians as he could. When he failed, they responded by killing Amy's father. Gio betrayed me by selling secrets to Volkov, to which I responded by raining bullets down on the Wolves.

They prove Gio's betrayal by playing security footage he stole from us. There are tapes of Amory and I in bed, which makes me scream in shock and stun everyone in the room. The judge threatens to have me gagged if I don't keep quiet—he doesn't have to tell me twice, but I can't stop the quiet sobs that wrack me as the prosecution plays another tape.

When they turn on a third, John speaks up. "This isn't evidence, Your Honor! It's shameful. They're just trying to hurt my client."

Mercifully, the judge agrees and tells the prosecution to turn off the videos.

I wipe at my eyes, hoping my makeup isn't totally ruined. I had to sit there in silence while an entire courtroom watched videos of me making love with my husband. The shame I feel is so heavy, I don't know how my chair can stand the weight any longer.

I can't stop myself from glancing back into the crowd to find Amory. He's sitting in the same spot, but his head is in his hands. He'd also cried out when they first started the tapes. Carter had to go over and haul him out the room for trying to climb over the railing again. The only reason he wasn't arrested is because the judge agreed with John, declaring the tapes to be crude and unnecessary. Apparently, Amy was fined for his outburst. Not that he cares.

Beside him, Wolfgang rubs his back and whispers something in his ear. Amy lifts his head and immediately finds me looking at him. He forces a smile that doesn't last at all, it cracks as he hiccups and wipes at his eyes.

I love you, I mouth the words to him and he nods, struggling to find the strength to mouth it back.

I love—he manages, and then tears stream from his eyes and he buries his face in his large hands again. Wolfgang leans over and pats his own chest, wordlessly apologizing on Amy's behalf. All I can do is nod and turn back around.

The prosecution obeys the judge's orders and finally puts away the lewd tapes, but they have one more. It's the video of me shooting that Russian man.

"She did it because her brother got his hands on her disgusting sex tapes," the male lawyer says, pointing right at me. They have a life-sized poster of the man I killed on display in the middle of the courtroom. There's a ring of flowers hanging over the frame, like a little memorial has been set up for him.

I stare at his picture as the judge dismisses us for the day, trying my hardest to remember his name.

Boris Ivanov ... the name comes back to me in my prison cell at night. I whisper it over and over, wondering who he truly was and what sort of life he'd lived until I took it from him.

Yes, I did kill Boris, but I didn't *murder* him. It wasn't a death stemmed from malicious intent. I didn't pull the trigger out of hatred—I hadn't even realized I'd grabbed the gun until after it'd gone off.

Does that excuse what's happened? Does that mean I should walk free?

I have no answer... but I pray to God to have mercy and spare me, nonetheless.

The next day is the same routine. I get to wear an off-white dress this time and Annie doesn't bother shackling my ankles. John is calm and quiet, trying to stay focused. Today is his turn to take the stand and tell my side of the story. I feel nervous at his silence, but the sight of Amory and the rest of our friends and family crowded in the courtroom today puts a smile on my face.

Again, Amy hops the rail and hugs me. Annie and Carter yank us apart, but not as quickly or as roughly as the day before. I even feel Wolfgang pat my shoulder as I walk by. He says something in German that I don't understand, but I smile and nod anyway. I need all the kind words I can get. I'm tired of hearing nothing but insults and lies.

The prosecution has Boris's picture on display again. It's got a fresh ring of flowers rimming the poster and I notice a small family of Russians sitting on the other side of the courtroom as I take my seat.

"Boris's family," John tells me as he leans close. "They're here for sympathy points on behalf of the prosecution."

I nod nervously.

"Don't worry." John pinches me gently. "We've got people here for sympathy too."

I glance around the room, trying to find whoever he's talking about, but I don't see any more familiar faces. There's a striking woman with a streak of grey hair through her otherwise dark glossy bangs. She's in the far corner of the room, staring right at me, but I don't recognize her at all. Before I can point her out to John, the judge walks in and we all fall quiet and stand on cue.

"Let's begin with the defense today," the judge orders.

John stands and squeezes my shoulder before walking off.

He points at Boris's photo. "That man wasn't innocent..." Then John brings up a life-sized print out of the man's rap sheet. He's committed every crime you can think of.

"Meanwhile," John holds up *my* rap sheet. It's written on a sticky note. "My client has never been convicted of a single crime. This case is her first offense and it's absolutely bogus."

John has photos from my wedding day on display now. I look miserable in each one.

"She never wanted to marry Amory Jäger," he explains to the judge. "But she's in love with him now—not because she's a demon spawn who used the mafia to her own benefit. Rosa Jäger loves her husband because she's a sweet woman with a kind heart. She found it in her heart to love a man who would have killed her if he'd been ordered to." John points at me. "This woman is not a murderer. She's a victim."

The crowd disagrees with angry murmurs, but John keeps right on talking. He displays bank statements that detail the monetary transactions between Gio and Amory, the money Amy paid to marry me. The contract we signed as a mafia couple.

"She was bought and sold like livestock," John explains. "Does that sound like a murderer to anyone?"

The prosecution counter by saying I became bitter after being 'bought and sold.'

"She saw an opportunity to rip apart the people who enslaved her," the woman lawyer says. "She took down her enemies one by one."

They bring Emilio to the stand so he can explain how I seduced Amory back into my bed after he managed to get away from me. Emilio tells the judge that I assaulted his late daughter and used my wiles to ruin their happy engagement

312

and take Amy from her. I have to grip my seat to keep from flying out of it and attacking him. I know Emilio is hurt for what happened to Eliana, but I never thought he would sink so low.

John tries to turn the story back around, explaining that Amory and I found our way back to each other out of love, but I feel like his words are falling on deaf ears at this point. Despite how bad it looks, he surges on. We go back and forth through testimonies and evidence for the next three hours until the judge calls a lunch break.

John passes me a ham sandwich and a Coke. I drink the Coke greedily, it's the first time I've had one since before I was arrested. "This isn't as bad as I thought it would be," he says as he sits across from me. "They surprised me by bringing Emilio to the stand. But this isn't over, Rosa. Hang in there."

I nod and burp.

Back in the courtroom, I sigh as the prosecution tears into me again. They shock everyone in the room when they bring Conrad to the stand. He places his hand on a Bible and then tells so many lies, I hear Gisela break down in sobs behind me. It's a shock to everyone, but I don't let the sting of his betrayal get to me.

Conrad's wearing an orange jumpsuit and his wrists and ankles are shackled as he testifies. He's on the stand because he doesn't have a choice. I heard about his arrest last week, right before my trial began. He turned himself in, but he obviously didn't walk away the way Amory and Wolfgang and the others did. He's testifying so he won't spend the next ten years in prison. He's probably doing it for Gisela's sake, which is why she's crying so hard while my eyes are dry. He's betraying me and his own cousin for his wife. It couldn't have been an easy decision, but that doesn't make it any easier to hear his vicious lies.

Conrad never makes eye contact with me as he tells the judge how I had Amory wrapped around my finger. How I even tried to convince Gisela to join me in overthrowing the Hunting Grounds. The prosecution uses his statement as best they can, painting an even crueler image of me than the previous day, but they mess up when they try to blame me for Morgen's death.

Somehow, John manages to pin Morgen's 'murder' on Volkov. It's not a solid case, but he shows us the texts Volkov sent to Amory and the photo of him bound and gagged in his house in Staten Island. That does severe damage to the prosecution's credibility and actually puts a smile on my face. Things get even worse when they try to blame me for Ja'meek's death. He was a soldier of the Stronghold who died on a mission with Amory in Staten Island.

Not only is John able to prove I was in a safehouse at the time—using some of the stolen security footage that Gio had access to—but he also reminds the judge that King James just confessed to sending Ja'meek on that mission weeks ago when he was first arrested.

For the first time, I sigh in relief and allow hope to bloom in my heart. When I glance back through the courtroom, I catch Amory sitting up for once. His eyes are still red and bleary, but he doesn't look as defeated as before.

This is good, I tell myself. *This is the turning point.*

John hammers it home when he brings in his surprise witness. Even my jaw falls open at the sight of Melissa Hart taking the stand to testify for the defense. She tells the judge how she found me dazed and bloody when I first showed up in Norman, how she took me in and treated me as her own daughter. She explains how afraid I was of being taken back to New York, all while dabbing at the tears in her eyes.

It's a powerful testimony that draws sympathy from everyone in the room, just like John promised. On cross-examination, the prosecution tries to tear Melissa apart. They remind everyone that her women's ministries were accepting dirty money and that women from her shelters had been disappearing for months right under her nose. They try to hint that she was helping me run Volkov's sex ring and that when Arthur intervened—being the gallant and heroic officer that he was—we conspired and had him killed.

Melissa nearly faints on the stand at the accusation, but she manages to hold on and look the pair of lawyers in the eye as she says, "My son was an officer, but he was not honorable. I don't say that with pride. It horrifies me to admit the truth. But God loves the truth and I love God. I must be honest."

I almost stand up and applaud when she finishes her testimony. John makes sure to right the wrongs of the prosecution when he presents bank statements from Melissa's account, showing the judge how Arthur had been accessing her

315

accounts without her permission for months. He completely debunks the prosecution's theory of Melissa helping me kidnap women from her shelters by bringing Pastor Marcia to the stand to testify about how sweet Mel is and how she would never harm the women she cared for.

Next, Father Serrano takes the stand and I almost burst into tears of joy. He tells the judge how serious I've always been about my faith. How apprehensive I'd been about marrying Amory because he wasn't saved back then. He delivers his words with a kind smile on his face that the prosecution can't crack when they try to destroy his credibility.

They ask him to roll up his sleeves and show everyone his rose tattoo, proof that he'd once worked with the De Lucas as part of the Italian mafia. Father Serrano is unbothered and complies without complaint, ignoring the gasps from the journalists who've been allowed inside. I hear cameras flashing as they take pictures, but they stop when Father Serrano explains that he's been out of the mafia for as long as I've been alive.

"Repentance, forgiveness ... these are the fundamental elements of the Christian faith," he says, and then he launches into a ten-minute sermon that leaves some people in tears. I even catch Pastor Marcia nodding her agreement while he speaks.

Embarrassed by their distasteful attack on an innocent Priest, the prosecution ends the second day of testimony with their heads hanging low. They don't even give any remarks before the judge dismisses us for the day.

John is so pleased with the turnout; he takes my hand and beams at me before Annie slaps the cuffs on again. "We've got this," he says firmly. "One more day."

On day three, the final day of my trial, the courtroom is overflowing. The crowd outside is still as divided as the crowd inside, but I feel confident. Amory looks much better, reaching out for me as I pass by. He's fresh out of warnings from the judge and has racked up almost half a million in fines for hopping the rail so many times. Today, he stays on his side of the beam and simply takes my hand as I brush past. It's a small gesture, but it sets my heart racing.

This is it, Jesus, I pray inside.

The prosecution starts off strong, bringing Volkov's son to the stand to tell everyone how happy he'd been in his engagement to Eliana. I almost laugh because even *I* know that's a lie. Eliana was *Volkov's* mistress, she wasn't engaged to his son at all—in fact, two days ago the prosecution had Emilio testify to me seducing Amory away from Eliana. Now she was happily in love with Volkov's teenage son?? Right up until I apparently had her killed out of jealous spite because of her ongoing affair with my husband.

John fights back by bringing Belén Moreno to the stand. She testifies through her tears, sharing stories of how cruel Volkov and his son had been to her and Eliana—and even Emilio. My heart breaks for her, she's only nineteen and she's being put on the stand to testify for the defense, going directly against her own father's testimony. I wonder how difficult things must be for her at home, if Emilio is treating her kindly.

The prosecution has one last trick up their sleeves. In their final statements, they display a giant photo of Arthur in his police uniform. And right beside it is a set of photos from his crime scene; he's lying on his back in a pool of his own blood, his throat slit and his tongue cut out.

A snitch's death.

Melissa shrieks in the back of the courtroom at the sight of the photos. After a few agonizing moments of her hysterical cries, the bailiff removes her, and the judge urges the prosecution to continue. I glance back in time to see Pastor Marcia and, shockingly, Amory running out to comfort her.

The prosecution reminds everyone how valiantly Arthur tried to do the right thing. He's the one who turned me in. He's the one who started this investigation. Without him, New York City would still be ruled by the mafia.

"And look at what his kindness got him," the male lawyer says. "This is what happens when you show mercy to these monsters."

John is nervous when it's his turn to deliver his final statements. Neither of us predicted the prosecution would end with Arthur's display, especially after John showed Melissa's bank statements the previous day and proved that he wasn't a saint at all.

John doesn't waste time combating the Arthur story. There isn't really a point. Even though Arthur was dirty, he was still a cop. Sometimes it doesn't matter how scummy you are, if you've got a badge, you'll never be guilty.

Instead, John shows pictures of Petra and tells the judge that she was killed by Boris. The very man whose murder they're trying to pin on me.

"It was self-defense," he insists. "If Rosa hadn't fired first, Boris Ivanov would have killed everyone in that room." John replays the video of his killing and pauses it right before I fire my gun. "If you look closely," he says to the judge, "you'll see our victim is armed too."

I squint at the television screen.

John is right. The image is a bit blurry, but you can tell Boris is holding something in his hands. I know it's a gun, I just hope the judge recognizes it as one too.

John turns off the television. "You've heard a lot from a lot of different people. You've seen things that have probably given you a terrible idea of who Rosa truly is and a false idea of who some others may have been." I don't miss the conspicuous glance he casts at Arthur's photo. "The point here today isn't to defame Rosa or to praise others. The point is to prove this… Rosa fired first." The courtroom gasps as one. "But her actions *weren't* unwarranted," John insists. "It was kill or be killed."

My head is spinning, but John is by my side when the judge stands and announces he's going to deliberate and go over the case in private.

"When I return," he says, eyeing me in a thick moment of silence, "I'll have my verdict."

Twenty-Five

My hands shake as I pour myself a glass of juice. I'd much prefer scotch right now, but Pastor Marcia and Melissa are waiting for me in the dining room, along with Gisela who's two months pregnant. *All these women…* I sigh, my house is full of ladies all of a sudden.

Adella and Nona have been here since Rosa was arrested, going on two months now. Gisela showed up once Conny's warrant went out, with him in jail now, she doesn't want to be home alone while she's carrying a child. I don't blame her for the caution, and it's not like I don't have the room. Mutti and Tante came about a week ago to help me prepare for the trial, and also because I called Mutti and told her Wolfy needed some motherly attention. He's been moping ever since we came home and found Nona giggling and helping Douglass change his bandages. He's healed up pretty good since taking a bullet at the safehouse, but he still needs help getting dressed some days.

I told Wolf not to take it personally—Nona and Douglass are both from the Stronghold and Douglass is a little younger than Wolf, closer to Nona's age. But my bratty little brother has been walking around the estate in a daze, only Rosa's trial has managed to stir him, though he was happy to see Mutti and Tante.

Pastor Marcia and Melissa showed up on day two of the trial, they drove eight hours together after John called and asked if they wouldn't mind speaking in Rosa's defense. I had to offer them my home as gratitude, they'd offered theirs when Rosa had no place else to go, and they'd driven across state lines to show their support for her.

I can't say thank you enough… Especially knowing how much it hurt Melissa to speak against Arthur on the stand. I hated the guy, for more reasons than just the fact that he'd had a fling with my wife. I didn't like Arthur because he was a scumbag. There were plenty of dirty cops in New York and Norman, but Arthur was the only one who tried to justify himself.

I'm mafia. I've never tried to hide or sugarcoat that fact. That's who I am and probably a part of who I'll always be. Like the bullseye tattooed over my heart, it's permanent. I've spilled as much blood as I've shed, stolen as much as I've provided. But I know who I am, and I've never tried to be anyone else. Guys like Arthur… Men who do whatever they want and blame the world for their mistakes. He's exactly where he needs to be. It's only for Melissa's sake that I hope he made things right with God before they slit his throat.

Melissa is wiping at her eyes when I bring in the drinks and the charcuterie board for them to munch on. She forces a smile and reaches for a grape. "This looks yummy."

"Late night snack." I sigh and serve the ladies their drinks, then I sit and roll up the sleeves of my dress shirt.

Gisela sits beside me, crossing her legs one over the other, I grab one which makes her gasp. She kicks at me, feigning a fight, but I pull her foot into my lap and give her massage.

"How fat are my ankles?" she says sheepishly.

"Pretty thin for a pregnant lady, actually," I tell her.

She laughs and reaches for a slice of cheddar cheese. "I'm only two months along."

"Still pregnant."

She nods. "You're good at this."

"I used to give Rosa massages all the time," I say, and then I pause, staring down at her foot, trying not to think of the last time I did this with my wife.

Glizzy pats my shoulder. She's the only one here who can understand what I'm going through. Conrad got two years in prison after turning himself in, I'm sure testifying against Rosa knocked off some time, but it's clear he'll miss the birth of his child. Gisela cried for hours after his sentencing, and now she's here with me as we await Rosa's fate.

The judge left to deliberate two days ago. He's taking his dear sweet time to go over all the evidence. John says that could be a good thing, it could mean he hasn't been brainwashed by the media and isn't jumping to conclusions. I don't know what it means, I just want to hear the verdict so I can move on.

No matter what Rosa gets, I'll be right here. We'll still have a future together; I just don't know if it'll be me working things out in New York alone or us together getting the heck out of dodge.

Gisela gently pulls her foot from my grasp. I blink, realizing I'd zoned out. "She's coming home," Glizzy says. "I know she is."

"We've been praying for her," Pastor Marcia says. "All of us."

I nod. "Father Serrano told me she was praying for me when he visited her."

"I believe him," Melissa says firmly. "Rosa is stronger than you think."

I palm the back of my neck. She's survived almost two months in prison so far—that's two months longer than I thought was possible for her. But, honestly, the question isn't whether Rosa can survive this...

I sigh heavily. "I don't think *I* can survive her sentence."

"*If* she's sentenced," Gisela says.

"She won't be," Pastor Marcia assures. Then she leans forward and places her hand over my own, dark brown skin glowing against my pale color. "Rosa is a woman of God. Do you know what that means?"

Of course I do. I nod and squeeze her hand. "It means God's taking care of her."

"More than that," Pastor says. She smiles warmly when my eyebrows scrunch together. "When God first created Eve, she wasn't called 'Eve' at all. In fact, her first name wasn't 'Woman' either. Do you know what God first called her in Genesis?"

I shake my head. Admittedly, I haven't been reading my Bible as much as I should. I'd taken Father Serrano's advice and decided to just trust God, but I can't say I've started down a holy path. I'm still stumbling along with no idea how things are going to turn out. All I can do is wait and hope and pray. I suppose it's better than worrying or blaming and hating God.

Pastor Marcia pats my hand to gain my attention. "When God told Adam He was going to make him a companion, He called that person an '*Ezer*.'"

I repeat the word slowly. "Ezer..."

"In Hebrew, it means *strong ally*," Melissa inserts. "Some scholars even define it as a *rescuer* or a *hero*."

"That's what wives are to their husbands," Pastor Marcia says. "We aren't your cooks or your maids or your baby makers. We're your strong allies."

I smile, thinking of all the times Rosa has gotten down on her knees and gone to battle for me. Waging an unseen war, fighting things I didn't even believe in. She's weak in so many ways... Physically, emotionally, psychologically. But she's never been spiritually weak. She's always been my strong ally—even when I wasn't one for her.

"You know what's so significant about the word *Ezer*?" Pastor asks.

Both Gisela and I shake our heads, Glizzy even leans forward, blinking in awe.

"The Hebrew word Ezer appears in the Old Testament more than twenty times," Pastor Marcia says. "Sometimes, it's even used to describe God Almighty."

Glizzy sucks in a little gasp, even I'm surprised. Imagine God using the same word to describe you that He used to describe Himself. It's an honor I can't even imagine.

"God calls Himself the ally and rescuer of Israel throughout the Bible. He sees those same heroic qualities in women—He *created* them for that very purpose. To rescue their husbands. To stand side by side with them, as they were taken from the rib of Man, not from the bottom of his foot. He created them to be a strong ally, not a servant or a housemaid." Pastor Marcia puffs her chest. "Rosa has been your ally from the beginning. She's still your ally now, praying for you when she has every right to be on her knees for herself."

"I know," I mutter pathetically. "There's nothing I can do for her."

"Isn't there?" Pastor Marcia asks. I look up to find her extending her palm, offering it to me. "You can be a strong ally too, Amory."

"The verdict hasn't been announced just yet." Gisela hurriedly takes Pastor Marcia's other hand, and Melissa's too.

The women blink at me, waiting for me to make a move. To make a choice.

Father Serrano's words come back to me. *Will you believe even if things don't work out in your favor?*

I take a slow breath and reach for their hands, joining the circle.

"Let's pray," I say softly.

Twenty-Six

The crowd outside the courthouse is more than triple the size it was the last time I was here. That was almost a week ago, when testimony ended, and the judge went to deliberate on his own. I wasn't allowed any visitors which meant I spent every agonizing second alone except for the brief moments someone came to deliver my food. Even though the solitude nearly gave me ulcers, I felt an odd sense of peace while I was in my cell.

"God's got this," was my mantra all week and it's what I whisper to myself as Annie and Carter escort me inside.

Amory is hanging over the railing when I walk down the aisle, he already stands out in his pressed suit and tie, but the frantic waving he's doing draws my attention to him like a magnet.

Despite the weight of the situation, I find myself smiling and giving a little wave back, ignoring the clink of the shackles still hanging from my wrists. Everyone is here. Pastor Marcia, Melissa, Father Serrano, Olivia, Marco Segreto, Aldo, Niccolò

Romano, Wolfgang, Gisela, Douglass, Adella and Nona, and so many more.

This is it. I take my seat and wait quietly as John whispers reassurances. He's only making me more anxious, but as he rambles, I realize the fervent whispers are more for him than me, so I let him prattle on until the judge enters the courtroom and silences everyone.

Oddly, I am both grateful and fearful of his presence.

Since the judge heard the case alone without a jury, I'll be getting my verdict and my sentence wrapped up in one sweet little package—*if* the verdict requires a sentence. I could be walking out of here in ten minutes. But no matter what happens, this is the last time I'll be in this courtroom. It's a daunting realization.

The judge finishes his formalities and then shuffles the papers before him. His eyes seem to set my skin on fire as he gazes at me, the expression on his face is both calm and serious and it takes everything in me not to wither before him.

"Please rise," Bailiff Grace says, a young-looking man with bronze skin and dark wavy hair. A silent threat standing in front of the judge's box, Bailiff Grace has barely spoken more than five words since the trial began, the sound of his voice now is calm and soothing as he asks the prosecution to also stand and then reminds the crowd to remain seated and quiet no matter the outcome of the case. I don't miss the look he shoots at Amory.

Before the judge came out, John showed me a photo of Amy in the middle of hopping over the railing. A reporter snapped it on the first day of testimony, the caption was insulting but hilarious: **Deranged Mafioso Loses His Cool in Courtroom**.

No matter what happens, I pray my husband can *keep his cool* today. It matters now more than ever. Can't have us *both* hauled off to prison. On the same day.

The judge clears his throat and shuffles his papers again. "I've had some time to reflect on all the evidence. After everything I have seen and heard, I have come to a verdict. If this verdict requires a sentence, I will also share that with you." He looks at me. "Rosa Jäger, you entered a 'Not Guilty' plea to the charge of first-degree murder against victim, Boris Ivanov."

I hold my breath, repeating every scripture I know in my head. If I could speak, I'd start praying in Tongues and singing hymns. I'm suddenly so nervous, I fear wetting myself again. John's arm goes around my shoulders, and he gives me a slight squeeze, anchoring me.

"The prosecution has been charged with proving beyond a reasonable doubt that you are guilty of first-degree murder. That requires evidence which would demonstrate forethought and malicious intent." He takes a breath, still eyeing me the entire time. "After pondering the information brought forth in the case, it is my decision that the prosecution has failed."

I squeeze my eyes shut. *Am I hearing what I think I'm hearing?*

"I do not find you guilty of first-degree murder, Rosa Jäger."

I gasp, but I don't allow myself to celebrate just yet. The courtroom is still completely silent, a threatening hint that this isn't over.

Sure enough, the judge continues. "I find you guilty of manslaughter."

The air rushes from my lungs as I sob. John is rubbing circles on my back, leaning over to whisper in my ear. I don't hear what he's saying because my heart is pounding so loudly, and the reporters and the viewers have both gone nuts. Half the people are cheering, the other half are shouting angrily. I don't know if I should celebrate or keep crying.

"It's not first-degree murder," I hear John say beside me.

That's a good thing, but manslaughter still comes with a sentence.

The judge slams his gavel down three times to quiet the room. Bailiff Grace takes a menacing step forward, eyeing the crowd like he's ready to make an arrest—with officers Annie and Carter beside him, they look like they could take down every gangster in the audience.

"Now, for the sentence," the judge continues. His eyes are on me again … My legs almost buckle as I wait for him to send me away for the next ten years. Tears run down my cheeks, hot and salty as they streak my face. I want to look away, but I force myself to face this head-on, the same way I've faced everything else thus far.

I'm glad I keep my vision steady because the next moment, the judge shocks me by smiling.

"Rosa Jäger, I sentence you to three months in jail with six months of community service. I will count your time served and allow you to finish your sentence on house arrest."

Three months with time served... I've been in prison for two months now, and I'll be able to finish on house arrest.

"I'm going home!" I scream.

John wraps me in a hug as the courtroom once again erupts into a mix of cheers and angry shouting. I glance up to see Amy climbing over the railing, the sight of him tripping over himself to get to me makes me burst into sobs and laughter all at once. He pries me from John's embrace and lifts me clear over my chair and over the defendant's box, kissing my face the entire time.

"You're okay," he says over and over. "You're coming home."

I hold his face in my hands and kiss him hard. "I'm coming home."

The shackles are still on my wrists, so it's difficult for me to hug him, but I manage to get my arms halfway around him. Annie comes over and interrupts us long enough to remove the shackles, but she kindly reminds us that I've got to get fitted with my house arrest bracelet, so we're forced to let each other go.

Amory doesn't want to be away from me for more than a second, but Wolf and Gisela manage to keep him calm while I'm whisked away with John. Both of us are beaming when the doors shut behind us, drowning out the snapping cameras and the reporters shouting questions. It's still unclear who is happy for me and who is outraged by the outcome, but I don't care.

"Thank You, Jesus," I whisper, clasping my hands together, "Thank You, Lord."

John squeezes my shoulder again. "We did it."

I shake my head. "God did it."

He nods. "You've still got a month of house arrest, and six months of community service."

"That's nothing." I almost laugh. "After two months in jail, I'm happy to be confined to my home for thirty days." First of all, the Jäger estate is absolutely gorgeous and twice the size of a large villa. I'll have all the room I need and all the amenities I need. But more than anything, I'll have my husband. I'll have Gisela. I'll have Wolfgang. I'll have Olivia. I'll have all my friends and family.

"Thank You, Jesus," I say again.

Annie gives me a smile as she kneels and straps the belt around my ankle. She starts explaining the rules to me, how I'm not allowed to leave the assigned premises (my home) how an alarm will sound if I leave the property, authorities will be alerted, and if I don't return to the premises within 45 seconds, police will be sent to arrest me.

"You won't just spend the rest of your sentence in jail," Annie says, straightening. "You'll be sentenced to three years in prison. Minimum."

I gulp but nod.

Once I'm done getting fitted with my fancy new ankle bracelet, Annie clears her throat and goes to the door. "Mrs. Jäger, before you go, there's someone who wants to see you."

I give her a nervous smile. "Um, okay."

She glances at John who takes the hint and makes up some excuse to leave. "I'll be just outside," he says with a nod.

Annie waits until he's gone before she spears me with her serious gaze, jaw tightening. "You have two minutes. Make this quick."

I blink at her, baffled. It's not like I'm the one who asked for a visitor, but I have no choice but to agree.

"Okay," I say quietly.

Annie opens the door and in walks a woman I've never met but seems incredibly familiar. A tall, elegant creature with womanly curves and delicate features; she has a sophisticated look to her, smart glasses and dark lashes that flutter behind her chocolate bangs. Her hair is gorgeous, a short bob, disrupted only by the streak of grey through her bangs.

I gasp. I saw this woman during my trial, staring at me from across the room. That's the only time I've ever seen her before this moment.

I have no idea what to say or how to behave. For the first minute, of which we've only been given two, she just stares at me—hand on her hip and eyes narrowed. *Maybe she's an angry journalist*, I wonder internally, *maybe she's here to yell at me.*

When she steps forward, she shocks me by smiling. It feels like déjà vu.

"Rosa Jäger," her voice is silky, as smooth as her pearly white skin. "Let me introduce myself, I'm Elle Jacobs."

I squint at her, and she nods in response.

"I'm the wife of Judge Barriston Jacobs."

My eyebrows shoot up. "I'm honored," I say, extending my hand.

She takes it but shakes her head. "*I'm* honored."

"You are?"

"Of course. I wish I could have met you before all this, but I'm glad I never had the chance, otherwise, my husband wouldn't have been chosen to oversee your case."

"I don't understand," I say dumbly.

She smiles again. "My maiden name is Richter."

Richter... the name rings a bell, summoning a gasp from my lips. "Richter Associates," I whisper. The law firm that was blown up by the Volkovs and Morenos. The office Amory hired his divorce attorney from.

"Y—You're German," I say softly.

She nods, her smile stretching. "I wasn't raised in New York, my family wanted to live a clean life away from the mafia. When a talented young lawyer from the right side of the law showed interest in me, my parents practically begged him to marry me." She laughs until she snorts. "We moved away to permanently cut ties with my mafia background, even though my family was never involved. For the first time, I'm grateful my husband and I made that decision together all those years ago. It gave us the clean background we needed for him to be approved for your case."

I don't realize I'm crying until I feel a tear slide down my cheek and plop onto my hand. My mind immediately brings up my conversation with Amory months ago, before I was arrested, how he reminded me of the story of Rahab. She was a prostitute who helped men of God by giving false information to authorities. Mrs. Jacobs didn't lie for me, she never even took the stand, but I know for a fact that her place in my life, her presence here today, was orchestrated by God. If prosecution had ever made the connection between her maiden name and the law firm that once stood in Brooklyn, I'd be in prison for the next ten years of my life.

She isn't a Rahab at all, she's my ram in the bush.

"Thank You, Jesus," I whisper again.

Mrs. Jacobs reaches out and pats my shoulder. "I just wanted to meet you, Mistress." Her words shock me so badly, my head jerks up to look her in the eye. I haven't been called by that title in months. The term almost sounds foreign.

Elle gives me a small nod. "I've got to go now, but this was a great honor."

"Did you convince your husband to go light on me?" I ask as she nears the door.

She pauses, her hand hovering over the knob. "Actually, I didn't. He came to his judgment on his own."

I suck in a huge breath. "Wow," is all I can manage to say.

Mrs. Jacobs turns the knob. "What was that you said earlier?"

"Um..."

"Thank You, Jesus." She winks and then strolls out.

With my ankle bracelet on, I take Amory's hand and we walk out the courthouse together. We haven't had a moment of peace in months, and right now is anything *but* peaceful. There's a raging crowd waiting for us when we emerge from the building, cameras flashing, people screaming. But the noise seems like nothing but a murmur as Amy leans over to whisper in my ear, "This is it."

I squeeze his hand, not at all concerned with the people shouting around us. I don't care about the reporters, I don't care about the angry people with signs, I don't even care about my own supporters who throw rose petals at me as I descend the stairs. I'm happy for their cheers, but my mind is consumed by so much more.

"You're free," Amory says. His words carry more weight than he knows.

I carried out God's will. I finished the story. I'm not just free of prison, I'm free of the mafia, I'm free of the lies, I'm free of the violence, the crime, all the trouble that stood between us—it's gone now. For good.

"*We're* free," I correct him.

"God set us free."

I blink up at him, trying not to trip over my feet as we walk to our car. "Yes, He did."

Amy blushes. "I missed you."

"I missed you too. But I'm back now, and I'm never leaving again."

"You'd better not." He laughs. "This is finally over."

"I still have thirty days."

He snorts. "Thirty days locked in our home together after being separated for two months." His hand falls from mine to wrap around my waist. "Sounds like a vacation to me."

"A much-needed vacation."

Amy dips his head to look at me, and the sun splashes light across his face. His cheeks are thinner, and his eyes still have dark circles beneath them, no doubt from him not eating or sleeping much these past few months. Regardless, he's still the most beautiful man I've ever seen; smooth skin with dark stubble along his square jaw, wisps of chocolatey brown hair falling into his face. He blinks away his bangs, sharp grey eyes focusing on me.

Right there, in the middle of the moving crowd, I stop walking and take his face in my hands. "I love you, Amory Jäger."

He kisses me, lips brushing gently against my own. I feel his words murmured into my mouth, like a love song between us. "I love you too, Rosa." He sighs, smiling. "My rose."

The End.

Epilogue

One Year Later

Rosa's slender finger draws circles on my flesh. She's in bed beside me, her legs lazily draped over my own, her wild curly hair covering us both like twisted ribbons of chocolate. The air is humid, chilled by the night breeze that dances in through the open balcony door. It brings relief and the scent of sweet citrus fruit. I inhale slowly, taking a deep breath of the Portuguese air.

Goosebumps pebble my skin as Rosa giggles and looks up at me. "That was wonderful." Her eyes are dreamy and half-lidded, a look she always wears after making love.

I sigh, pleased, satisfied. "It was."

"Our 'vacation' was only supposed to be thirty days." She laughs again, this time I join her.

"I could get used to this."

The room is dark, the only light spilling in from the door and windows, curtains flowing gently in the stirring night air. Our clothes litter the stone floor, making a trail from the door to the bed. We're relaxed, tired, happy.

I pull Rosa a little closer and her mouth meets mine in a kiss, but before I can deepen the exchange, the monitor on the bedside table crackles and the sound of crying fills the room.

Rosa immediately pulls away and stares at the little device, practically crawling over me to get to it. "Oh no," she whispers, but I sit up and take the monitor from her hands.

"It's fine, I'll go check on him."

She makes a face like she doesn't trust me. I don't really blame her; I have no idea how to handle newborns.

Our son is only two months old, born exactly a week after my 32nd birthday. He wasn't planned, but he was welcomed. Like a big baby, I cried when Rosa told me the news, and then I cried even harder through all 18 hours of her labor. I thought there weren't any tears left in me until she told me the name she'd picked—Uwe Jäger.

My heart had cracked open and melted into my ribcage when she shyly made the announcement. I couldn't have been happier. My little Uwe.

Rosa brushes her hair behind her ear, eyes flicking from me to the monitor as Uwe cries. "Let me go," she says. "He's probably hungry."

"I can feed him," I insist.

She reaches up and cups her breasts. I glance away, though I don't know why. We just made love; I've seen her naked a hundred times—I've touched her breasts a hundred times—but it's different when it's about our son.

"I'm full," she says, "I should feed him."

"Rosa—"

"At least let me pump—"

"I can feed *my own* son," I say louder than I should.

She pouts.

Rosa's an attentive mother, if not a little obsessed. When she found out she was pregnant, she stopped eating red meat and only allowed organic foods into the house. She refused to let me hire a live-in nurse to help out when Uwe was first born, and she insists on breastfeeding. I'm not complaining, but I wish she would trust me a little with our son. It's not like I haven't been right here with her the entire time.

When we moved here, I took over one of the legal jewelry stores still in the Jäger name, but I hardly see the place. Wolfgang is the manager, and he does an excellent job keeping the business together. I've been here with my wife and son since we first left the airport. They're my only concern, my top priority. But Rosa still thinks I'm a bumbling idiot when it comes to Uwe.

In her defense, I did almost drop him the first time I held him. And the only time she felt comfortable leaving me alone with him, I forgot to feed him and couldn't figure out how to secure his diaper, so I let him lie around naked until she got back.

But, I've been much better since then. I promise.

Rosa crosses her arms, covering her nudity. "Fine. But make sure you warm the bottle."

"I will," I say, climbing out of bed.

"And burp him afterwards."

"I will."

"And—"

"I got it, babe." I slip into my boxers and lean over the bed to kiss her cheek. "I'll tell him goodnight for you."

She whimpers. "Sing him his favorite lullaby."

"Of course." I wink.

Uwe's room is just down the hall, it takes me all of five seconds to get there, but when I step inside, I'm not surprised to find someone's beat me to his nursery.

Christina stands by the crib with a bundle in her arms, gently bouncing Uwe up and down. She smiles when I enter the room, waving me over and motioning for me to pass her the warm bottle on the little stand beside her.

"You heard him?" I whisper as she feeds him.

She nods. "Thought I'd come check on him myself."

I stand beside her, both of us watching Uwe in silence. Mutti moved with us after everything settled down, with Wolfgang coming along, she decided it was best our family stayed together. I'm glad she did, she's been a great help with my son—and I think she gets a kick out of being able to raise little Uwe.

"He's beautiful," she says softly.

I nod. "He is."

"Nothing like his grandfather."

342

I know she doesn't mean it in a bad way, but my heart still cramps with pain. Vater wasn't a good man, father, or husband, but I still miss him. I still wish he could be here to see his grandson.

"This is our chance at starting over," Mutti says.

"We've already started over," I tell her.

After Rosa's ankle bracelet was removed, she spent six months at St. Joseph's doing her community service. She would have loved to do it at Trinity Baptist Church with Pastor Marcia or even at one of Melissa's shelters, but her sentence required her to carry out the service in the same jurisdiction the crime had been committed so she had to stay in New York. There weren't many complaints about that, Rosa loved working with Father Serrano and Mel and Pastor Marcia drove up to visit before we left the country. They even brought Minnie along to say goodbye.

With the mafia and the media behind us, we decided it was best to get out of the States. There was nothing left for us and with Rosa's pregnancy moving along, we had to make the decision quickly before she wasn't allowed to fly. Little Uwe was born one month after we arrived in Portugal, a fat baby with red cheeks and a smile to die for.

He's a fresh start for all of us. A chance to right our wrongs.

I want to raise my son in a life completely different from my own. I want him to be everything Uwe wasn't. I want him to be everything I haven't been.

"He has a family here to help him," I say softly.

Christina nods. "We'll get it right this time. With him." She looks up and holds him toward me. "Take him."

Uwe feels like he gains a pound every day, but I like having him in my arms. I hold him close as I walk back toward the crib and tuck him in. Christina starts humming his favorite lullaby behind me; as the gentle tune fills the room, I reach up to turn on the mobile hanging above him. A pale blue light glows in the small space, illuminating the bulletin board on the wall beside me.

It's filled with pictures of everyone we left behind, a timeline of the past year. Gisela smiles wide with her baby girl, a few months older than Uwe. We were there for the birth, everyone except Conrad. He may be out soon on good behavior, at least that's what Glizzy was hoping for in her last letter. Since we left, she's been managing one of the Jäger Diamonds locations in New York. There are pictures of her polishing rubies with her daughter strapped to her hip. She's honestly the hottest single mother I've ever seen—which makes Rosa jealous when I say that, then I remind her that she's not a single mother and her scowl eases away.

Hopefully, Gisela won't be a single mom for much longer. I was ticked off by Conny's betrayal, but I understand why he did it. He wrote me an apology letter from prison, begging for forgiveness not just as his cousin but as his Jägermeister. It took quite a bit of praying, but I did find it in my heart to let it all go. We're safe now. We're free. There's no need to dwell on the past.

Next to Glizzy's photo is a picture of Nona and Douglass on their wedding day. I'm proud of my boy, everyone is—except Wolfy who grimaced throughout the entire ceremony and reception. He was butthurt about the whole thing right up until he found a lady of his own, a chocolate-toned beauty named Angelena. They met here in Portugal, she was taking a semester overseas, so she had to return to the United States a few weeks ago but when she graduates, they plan to make things permanent. I'm happy for all of them, though I'm sure I'll miss Douglass more than anything.

He stayed in New York, along with Adella and Nona and Jared and pretty much everyone else. I don't blame them; King James is in prison in NYC. He was only sentenced to ten years, but with him being so old, everyone's on edge about how long he'll make it. I'm not worried at all. Jameson is a stubborn old bear; with little Uwe here and Nona two months pregnant already, I know he'll live long enough to hold his great-grandchildren in his arms one day.

Besides, if things start to look shaky, I'm sure Mayor Willis could pull some strings and get him out early. Tyrese won the election by a landslide—it was so overwhelming; I doubt King James had to threaten anyone with his evidence against the dirty cops who'd once worked for him. I think the city truly wanted Tyrese as their next leader. He had my vote, at least. And his brother's—and with all their businesses flourishing, they had the influence to sway plenty of others.

Adella opened a second gym before we left, *Finesse Fitness* works in conjunction with *Stronghold Inc.* the private security business run by Nona and Douglass. It also employs Hans and Eike who had a hard time letting go of their mafia ways. I hear they're thriving as personal guards, breaking necks and getting paid to do it. Who knew living on the right side of the law could be so exciting?

Eike isn't smiling very brightly in the photo of him with Hans standing outside of Stronghold Inc. He lost more than anyone else during the gang war, I had honestly expected him to pack up and move away from all this, but he stayed and found a new life. Olivia stayed as well, despite her father and brother leaving. Niccolò, his wife, and Aldo moved back to Italy. I haven't heard much about them, but they sent a postcard when we first arrived in Portugal; Aldo looks healthy, and his father looks like he's finally at peace.

Olivia and Marco Segreto are still married, we got an invitation to their anniversary celebration in the mail just last week. It's a party that'll double as a celebration of the opening of their third business together. After the mafia truly fell and order was restored in New York City, Olivia and Marco dipped into their savings to buy back some of the businesses Gio lost in all his bad deals. It took them a year, but they've managed to turn things around for a few of the storefronts. According to FaceTime calls with Rosa, they're no longer operating in the red. As someone who saw firsthand how screwed up the Garden had been, I must say I'm impressed.

Next to the photo of Olivia and Marco is a picture that always puts a goofy smile on my face, it's my Tante Viktoria with a blonde-haired man and his beautiful young wife. Tante moved back to Germany after everything went down. Initially, we thought she couldn't handle the media anymore but then we got this photo in the mail and realized her decision was much more pleasant than that. Morgen finally found a place to settle down with Silke. His new identity is Conrad Oberon. Yes… he named himself after his brother and father. He thinks it's funny. I think it's a dead giveaway that'll get him caught one day, but we're sure he's safe in Germany—far away from the US. Him, Silke, and Tante look happy together; according to their postcard, Morgen works for his wife's family mining diamonds for Jäger jewelry stores. I don't think he'll ever return to the States, but I'd love to see him when little Uwe is old enough to travel to Germany.

His soft snoring draws my attention from the bulletin board. "He's perfect," Christina says over my shoulder.

He is. He's everything we needed to truly leave the past behind and start our new futures. Even Wolf loves the little guy—says he can't wait to teach Uwe how to drive or give him a bullseye tattoo. Rosa and I both agreed that last part will never happen, we don't want Uwe associated with the Hunting Grounds in any way whatsoever. If I have my way, he'll never even *see* a bullseye as long as he lives.

Wolf sulked about the tattoo thing, but we agreed he could teach Uwe to speak German. I'm sure Christina would have taught him anyway, she makes sure she speaks it around him whenever possible, while Rosa speaks Italian, and I speak English—plus, he'll have to learn Portuguese when he starts school. Uwe is going to be the most culturally diverse kid I've ever seen, and he looks like it.

He's got my grey eyes and brown hair, so dark it looks black, but it's lightly curled—*just* looser than Rosa's tight coils. She passed her skin tone to him, though his complexion is a little lighter; he's a creamy oatmeal compared to her golden brown.

Uwe stirs and tries to roll over, but the effort is too much, and he starts to cry. I reach down to help him, but Christina pats my shoulder. "Go, I've got this," she says with a smile.

I tilt my head at her. "I can do it."

"I know." She gives me a onceover, raising an eyebrow at my attire. I'm suddenly aware that I'm wearing nothing but my black boxers.

Mutti chuckles at my blushing. "I'm sure Rosa's waiting. Don't leave her for too long."

With a laugh, I kiss my mother on the cheek and pad quietly down the hall back to my room. To no one's surprise, Rosa is still up and waiting for me when I open the door. She's holding the baby monitor, wide eyes filled with worry.

"Did you feed him?"

"Christina did," I tell her. "And burped him and sang to him."

She sighs and flops back onto the pillows. "Thank God. How was he?"

"Hungry." I chuckle. "And tired."

"Is he sleeping already?"

"No. Mutti is taking care of him."

Rosa tugs the blankets to cover herself. "I still should have pumped," she groans almost painfully. "Now I don't know what to do."

I give her a sly smirk as I slip off my boxers and climb into bed, pinning her to the mattress. "I can think of a thing or two."

Rosa doesn't fight me as I kiss her long and deep. It's the middle of the night, 90 degrees outside, and way too humid to be tangled in our sheets, but I make love to my giggling wife like it's our wedding night, and when I'm done, we go through our same routine. I run a bath and scrub her down—she doesn't fight me or shy away like when we first got married. In fact, I think I've spoiled her. Rosa demands a back massage after the bath and even picks out the oils herself.

Her eyes are heavy with fatigue and delight once I'm finished. I can't help myself; I kiss her again and then we make love until my legs go numb. She falls asleep across the bed, forbidding me from touching her again.

"I seriously can't take another round," are her last words.

I lie in bed staring up at the ceiling until it's too dark to make out the designs overhead. Then I slip from beneath the covers and walk naked to our balcony. The night has cooled somewhat now, and the air feels refreshing rolling over my dewy skin. I stretch out my back, feeling the scars tug and pull at my marred skin. I barely notice them anymore, crude reminders of my past. The evidence is still there, carved into my flesh; I know I can't escape that, but the pain is gone. All of it.

I take a deep breath and lean over the stone railing that keeps me from falling off the second floor. Our villa is roughly the same size as my personal home back in Brooklyn. I would have loved to buy a place equal in stature to the Jäger Estate, but we decided to downsize so I could invest in the land around us.

Fifty acres stretches out before me, almost every inch covered in seedlings. I decided to buy a vineyard. It's new land so I expect the first batch of grapes to be cruddy, but I've got the rest of my life to figure things out. The wine industry is rather healthy in Portugal, though Rosa says Christians shouldn't take part. I'm hoping one day I can convince her to let us make our very own vintage bottle. For now, I'm fine with just tending the land and learning more about my investment. When things take off, I can sell to local markets and grocers— or just make grape juice. We'll see.

The goal is to leave something to Uwe that I've done on my own, without the help or influence of the mafia. Jäger Diamonds is 100 percent legal, but Jäger Vineyards is 100 percent mine. I've been mining and selling pretty rocks all my life, I want this venture to be fresh and new. I want Uwe to have more options than I did growing up. It also helps that Wolfgang completely took over the business once we settled down anyway. I don't mind. It gives me more time with my family and more time with my land. Rosa just calls me a jumped-up farmer, but I like to think there's more ... *finesse* ... to it than that.

Regardless of all that, I'm just happy we're not dependent on one source of income. I'm happy we have more to our lives than anything that came from the mafia. I'm happy we're *happy*—even deeper than that, I'm happy we've got *joy*. Something that is everlasting. Something no man can ever take away.

I gaze out at the young grapevines before me with a smile on my face. I can picture Uwe playing in the fields around our property, sprinting barefoot through the vineyards, surrounded by thick clusters of fat grapes, so ripe they're like to burst. He'll go from creamy oatmeal to toasted honey nut in the Portuguese sun, and with his dark curls and his sharp grey eyes—I'll have to beat the girls off him with a stick. But I look forward to those days. Simple days that will be nothing like my own childhood.

All of this is mine. Not just the land or the jewelry store. The joy and the excitement and the peace are mine too.

"More than I could ever ask or imagine," I whisper, gripping the stone railing.

None of this would have been possible without God. I know that with every fiber of my being. It all started with Rosa—a Christian woman who loved God enough to run away for Him. And then loved Him enough not to fight when she was dragged back to her horrible home. She loved Him enough to stay and carry out His will—and loved me enough to share His plans with me and introduce me to His love.

Without my wife, I wouldn't be here now. I wouldn't be at peace. We lost a lot to get here, but I'm no fool, I know for a fact without the Lord we'd all be dead or doing the same thing we've always done.

Just surviving. Fighting and kicking and screaming and shooting each other; we would have lived out our days swimming through the same cesspool of darkness we were born into.

Everything I have is because of Rosa. But I only have Rosa because I have God.

I exhale a breath and shiver at the coolness of the night. The words that fill the air are a long time coming, but I mean every single one.

"Thank You, Jesus. For everything."

Enjoy my next romantic suspense novel…

Fractured Diamond

Stay in the Dark Mafia world of NYC with this story taking place ten years after the fall of the city. Meet all new characters and see what's happened with some of your favorite cast members!

Pre-Order now so you don't miss the Nov. 15th release!

More books by Valicity Elaine & TRC Publishing!

Christian Fantasy
Cross Academy
The End of the World series
The Scribe

Christian Science Fiction
I AM MAN series

Christian Romance
The Living Water
The Woof Pack

Christian Children's Fiction
Too Young

ACKNOWLEDGEMENTS

As much as I loved writing *Withered Rose*, I'm happy the trilogy is now over. It's a bittersweet ending in the sense that I am sad to see the story end but I'm happy to be moving on to my next project. Please enjoy my next book, *Fractured Diamond*. And don't forget to check out my other works too:

<u>Cross Academy</u>
<u>I AM MAN</u>

Sign up for my <u>monthly newsletter</u> to stay updated on new releases, sales, and updates! See you soon.

The Rebel Christian Publishing

We are an independent Christian publishing company focused on fantasy, science fiction, and YA reads. Visit therebelchristian.com to check out our books or click the titles below!

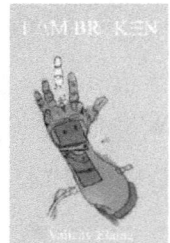